BOOKS BY HELENA N

Helena Newbury is the *New York Times* and *USA Today* bestselling author of sixteen romantic suspenses, all available where you bought this book. Find out more at helenanewbury.com.

Lying and Kissing

Punching and Kissing

Texas Kissing

Kissing My Killer

Bad For Me

Saving Liberty

Kissing the Enemy

Outlaw's Promise

Alaska Wild

Brothers

Captain Rourke

Royal Guard

Mount Mercy

The Double

Hold Me in the Dark

Deep Woods

BAD FOR ME

HELENA NEWBURY

ISBN: 978-1-914526-15-2

1

LOUISE

I'd spent my whole life being good. And then, one day, I ran smack into *bad.*

I'd been standing outside my apartment on the tenth floor, hammering the elevator call button like it was personally responsible for every crappy thing in my life. I was late, I knew I was late and it felt like the universe was moving as slow as possible just to taunt me.

I kept glancing at the stairwell: should I just run for it, pound my way down ten flights and arrive sweaty and red-faced? But each time I stepped towards the stairs, the elevator would make a promising creak and groan and I'd hang on, thinking it was about to arrive....

When the elevator doors finally shuddered open and I darted forward, I was still looking towards the stairs. That's why I didn't see the elevator was occupied until it was too late. I faced front just in time for my face to mash against the warm black cotton of his tank top. My whole body, from shoulder to ankle, was suddenly flattened against the hard, heated body of a man.

I stumbled back into the hallway. I think I knew, on some level, who it was, but my brain was rebelling against the idea. *It's probably not. It's probably some other guy—*

It wasn't. It was him.

Sean O'Harra. The scariest guy on the block.

He seemed to fill the elevator. Not just because he was well over six foot, but with sheer presence. It was as if his aura was crackling and hissing against the inside of that graffiti-coated steel box, furious at being contained.

I said, "Sorry," because that's my automatic reaction to nearly everything.

He just frowned at me. He was *good* at frowning. A combination of those heavy Irish brows and the knowledge of what he might do to you if you displeased him. He was wearing a black tank top and his bare, tanned arms were loaded with muscle, one of them wrapped entirely in a tattoo sleeve. It was difficult not to follow the dramatic *in* and *out* of those arms with my eyes: shoulders and then biceps and then forearms...God, even his forearms were the size of my legs! And he was so ruggedly, solidly *wide,* the swells of his pecs beneath the black cotton seeming to fill my whole vision like a wall.

You didn't talk to Sean O'Harra. You didn't look at him, if you could help it. You stayed the hell out of his way.

Everyone knew what he did. He destroyed things: stores and houses and cars and sometimes people. He was built for it. Those huge arms could heave men off their feet and hurl them across the room like toys. His hands, twice the size of my own, were made to punch and tear and crush, demolishing someone's business as efficiently as a wrecking ball. Even his legs looked vicious, muscled thighs stretching out the faded black denim. I imagined them kicking over tables and smashing down doors. And between those legs, outlined down the side of his thigh—

My own groin twinged as I felt the tingling, ghost impression of it. When I'd run into him, his cock had throbbed right against my thigh.

The door started to slide shut and I realized I'd been standing there like an idiot, staring at his body, for several seconds. The air hissed out of me, simultaneous frustration that now I'd be even later and relief that I wasn't going to have to share an elevator with *him.* God, imagine *that!* Being cooped up in a six-foot metal box with *Sean O'Harra.* Just the thought of it made my stomach twist and knot...and a tiny, forbidden thread of heat lash down to my groin. That would have been—

A hand slammed against the edge of the elevator door, halting it an inch from closed. Then, with a rumble that shook the floor, Sean pushed it open again and held it there.

I'd never dared to look him in the face before. On the few occasions I'd seen him around the apartment block, I'd ducked my head and scuttled past. But now, I was so surprised that I forgot to be scared. I looked up—and *up*—and found myself staring into eyes that didn't deserve to be in such a brutal body. Shockingly blue—and so *light!*—almost cobalt-blue, a color I'd only seen on postcards from tropical islands. Beautiful enough to have graced any Irish choirboy...but eyes that had forgotten what innocent was like long, long ago.

I hadn't been ready for the hard line of his jaw, or the little dimples in his cheeks. The California sun had tanned him, but his Irish roots were still obvious: that gleaming black hair, the strong brow, and cheekbones.

I hadn't been expecting him to be gorgeous.

And then he said, "Are you getting in or what?"

Which woke me up and made me realize I'd been standing there *again* and now I was even later. My eyes flicked to the stairwell door, but....

I had no choice.

I nodded dumbly and stepped inside. He'd had to take a half-step forward to grab the door, so now we were even closer. God, he was so *big*, towering over me like a colossus. And even when he'd released the door, he didn't seem to be in much hurry to move back, or to retract that big, tanned, muscled forearm. His hand was hovering just a few inches from my cheek and I swore I could feel the skin there ache and tingle in the anticipation of touch.

The floor lurched and we started to move.

I didn't know what to say—I never know what to say—so I just stood there staring at him. His voice was still echoing around inside my head. Mid-Atlantic, but with the exotic twist of Irish instead of

British, like a scalding rush of liquor in what you thought was a soft drink. And so *low*, the words throbbing through my body as much as through my ears. His mouth matched the voice: hard, stubbled jaw, all power and violence, but then that full, sexy lower lip, a lip you just wanted to feel crush against yours and—

I looked up to his eyes again and saw that he was staring straight back down at me. *Why? Why is he doing that?* And that hand, the one so many people had ducked and cowered from, was still hovering next to my face.

I dropped my eyes and looked anywhere, *anywhere* but at his face, feeling my cheeks flare. I sifted through the graffiti, trying to find something readable amongst the years of overlapping tags, but it was just a multi-colored, tangled mess. It didn't matter. As long as I wasn't looking at *him*. Anything was safer than entertaining some stupid, dangerous fantasy about Sean O'Harra taking me and pushing me up against the wall and running those big hands over my—

Stop it.

And then I saw something that made my stomach do a complete somersault. Just behind him, resting against the wall of the elevator, was his hammer.

Some men are scary because they have a gun or a knife. Sean O'Harra was terrifying because he didn't need either. They say that a lot of guys just drop their weapons and run, when they see him marching towards them.

It was a sledgehammer and it suited him. The wooden shaft—almost half my height—was worn and smoothly strong. The metal head was dull gray, chipped and scratched. Brutal...and yet strangely beautiful.

Sean O'Harra scared people. That was a fact and it was also his job: he scared people for a living. The local drug gangs hired him when they wanted a meth lab put out of business or a stolen package of coke retrieved. Sometimes, smashing the place up was the point and sometimes it was a byproduct of scaring people, but it always happened, one way or another. Everyone on our block knew someone who knew someone who'd been there when Sean smashed up the local biker bar because they'd started dealing where they shouldn't, or when he hammered a guy's Mercedes into a steel pancake because he owed money, or when he tore through a slimy politician's house like a hurricane, reducing every stick of furniture to pieces smaller than your fist, because the guy had been hiring underage prostitutes. They said he'd done that last one just for fun.

There were other stories, too, different kinds of stories. Ones told by the glamorous sort of women I'm not, with their perfect hair and make-up. The ones who were too well off to live in our apartment block, but liked to slum it and be all *daring* by hanging out at the local bars. They'd giggle and tease each other about Sean O'Harra and joke about how they were going to jiggle their perfect tits in front of him that night. I'd glimpse them coming home with him, all sass and confidence, delighted at having landed a real-life bad boy. The next morning, I'd see them stumbling out of the elevator, clothes half-on and eyes glazed, all their giggles gone.

It scared me but I'd be lying if I said it didn't excite me a little, too. Sean lived one floor below me and sometimes I'd lie awake in the early hours listening to the thumps and the groans and the breathless female cries that climbed higher and higher and always ended in wailing, frantic pleas.

But now, looking at that hammer, I was reminded of what he really was. Not just someone who worked for the drug gangs but someone they were scared of. He didn't even have that slim vestige of loyalty and honor that came from belonging to one of them: people said he was loyal to whoever was paying him, and then only for as long as the money lasted. I wasn't sure if that made him worse than the rest of them, or better because he didn't believe in all that bullshit about *respect* that the dealers thought was so important. To him, it seemed to be just a job. But what sort of man chooses to earn his living scaring people?

Someone very, very different from me. Sean's world was one utterly outside my own, a world of breaking rules and laws, of waking up to the cops banging on your door—everything I'd been raised to be terrified of. I've never even gotten a parking ticket. I might have to live surrounded by the gangs, but I keep as far away from it all as possible. Maybe that's why I could feel that thread of heat pulsing and twisting like a glowing wire inside me. I'm so *good*—I've always been so good—that the idea of a guy like Sean O'Harra taking me and—

Stripping me.

Spreading me.

Destroying me. Taking all my goodness and making me as dark and dirty as him—

I pressed my thighs together. I didn't dare look at him again. What if he was looking at me? What if he could *tell*?

I focused on the feel of the elevator clunking its way down through the floors. God, I could feel the heat of him, so close in the little metal box. Out of the corner of my eye, I glimpsed his hand finally descending...but, as it swung down, it came almost within touching range of my breast...then my hip...then my thigh. And I realized my whole body was tense, waiting for the brush of his fingers. I didn't dare look up but, when I glanced carefully sideways, I could see the hazy reflection of him in the polished steel between the graffiti. And it looked as if he was staring down at me with such intensity every inch of my skin should have been bursting into flame. Sean O'Harra was looking at *me*.

Stop it. Like I'm the sort of woman he'd be into. I couldn't be more *unlike* one of his conquests. They're always blonde and tanned. I have hair the color of copper wire and my skin refuses to tan, even after years of living in California. I can stay out of the sun or I can burn. And my boobs are on the big side, making me awkwardly top-heavy and I don't have time to wear anything but jeans and t-shirts or to spend hours on fancy make-up. I'm just a—

Well, basically I'm a mom. In every sense apart from the literal, genetic one. A sex-starved, slowly-going-insane mom who can't go out on dates or bring guys back to my apartment. *That's* why I was having crazy, fleeting fantasies about Sean O'Harra: because this brief interlude in the elevator was the closest I'd been to a man in months. That was the only reason.

At least, that's what I told myself.

The elevator stopped. I heard the doors slide open behind me and I backed out, wheeled around, and *ran* before I could do anything stupid.

And I tried to ignore the itching between my shoulder blades, the feeling that he was watching me go.

～

Ten minutes later, I was sitting at an intersection, strumming my fingers on the wheel and willing the red light to change to green. There was nothing coming in either direction but I'm the sort of person who never, *ever* runs a red. I just know there'll be a cop somewhere, hiding behind a billboard, ready to leap out and haul me off to jail.

Why was he in the elevator?

It had been niggling at me ever since I got into my car. The elevator had been on the way down and Sean lived on the ninth floor, one below me. So why had he been passing the tenth? There were only two more floors above mine...had he been visiting someone? I'd never heard of him making social calls before. Unless he'd been all the way up on the roof.

What would he be doing on the roof?

The light finally changed and I roared across the silent intersection. I was going to be late and I knew it. I shouldn't have run home to change after finishing my shift at the garden store, but I hadn't wanted to show up at the school in a dirt-covered apron.

The view didn't do anything to improve my stress levels: nothing but concrete, bleached sickly white by the sun. It was only April but the temperature was already in the seventies. I was really, *really* going to have to find the money to get the car's air conditioning fixed before summer.

I hate Los Angeles. When my folks first moved us here, they seduced us with stories of beaches and palm trees, movie stars and endless sunshine. But that was *before*. Before I had to move us from the modest but comfortable house to the crappy apartment we now inhabit, with its graffiti and cracking plaster and people like Sean O'Harra as our neighbors. Before it all went wrong.

Before it was just the two of us.

I pulled up in front of Kayley's school, swinging around manicured flower beds and slotting my wreck of a car between the gleaming SUVs the other parents drove. It's a public school but it's one of the best and the sole reason I chose our crappy apartment—it was the only place I could afford that qualified Kayley to keep going to this school. I like the place, even if I feel like a charity case next to the other parents. I like the fact it doesn't feel like a fortress and the fact it has flowers outside. It's a paltry amount of greenery, really, but it's better than the endless concrete I see everywhere else. Sometimes, when I'm picking up Kayley from school and the wind blows the scent of the flowers just right, I can kid myself that I'm back in Vermont.

I raced up the steps and straight over to the reception window. I could see Kayley through the glass, sitting swinging her legs, and tapping out messages to her classmates on her phone. "Hi," I said breathlessly. "I'm here for Kayley. Kayley Willowby."

The woman peered at me owlishly. "You're her...mom?" she asked uncertainly. Kayley is fourteen. I'm twenty-two.

"Her sister. Louise."

"Give me a minute."

I understand they have to check. I'm glad they're careful, really. And I get that it's an unusual situation. But waiting while she brought up Kayley's school record on her computer and checked I really was her legal guardian and allowed to take her out of school felt like it took a half hour.

Then Kayley was running towards me, five feet four of blonde curls and energy. Thank God she got my mom's looks and not the pale skin and red hair I got from our dad. Unlike me, she fits right in in LA. She threw herself into my arms, talking at eighty-three miles an hour about Darren, the cute boy in her math class, and the band he's formed.

And suddenly, life was bearable. It was as if I could breathe for the first time all day. I didn't care about being late, or poor, or being trapped in this concrete hell. I squeezed her close, close enough that she rolled her eyes and muttered that I was embarrassing her.

As long as I had my sister, I was okay.

"C'mon," I told her, my voice muffled by her hair. "We've got to go." And I hauled on her hand, hurrying her towards the door.

"I claim music!"

I sighed. That was our rule: whoever said it first got to choose the music. That meant a half hour of listening to British punk rock from the eighties. Why couldn't she be into boy bands like any other teenager? But I didn't care too much. Even though I didn't like pulling her out of school, even though the appointment was worrying me, it was good just to spend time together.

Minutes later, we were sitting in traffic with her babbling happily and me trying to figure out whether we'd make it on time. I don't know if it's because of the age gap, but we don't really argue. *Ever.* Even before our folks died. I've always been the serious, studious one and she's always been the fun-loving risk taker. We complement each other.

"I think I could be one of his dancers," said Kayley. She had her feet up on the dash and was touching up her toenails. "Or at least a back-up dancer. But I think I need to go more...*dark.*"

"You are *not* getting anything pierced," I said automatically.

"Maybe an eyebrow."

"No!"

"Nose?"

"No! You're perfect the way you are."

She crossed her arms and mock-scowled at me. But she *was* perfect. Smarter than me and more daring, too—not that that's difficult. And bouncing with energy.

Well...until recently.

A month ago, I'd started to have to tumble her out of bed just to wake her up. At first, I'd figured it was just teenage moodiness, but then the school started to complain about her falling asleep during lessons. Sometimes, like now, she seemed to be her old, energetic self, but sometimes she just seemed to slump. And the bruises. She would say they were from hockey at school, but lately it looked like she'd fallen down the stairs. When she'd started losing weight, I took her to the physician. *Hormones,* he'd said. *Probably a thyroid issue.* And he'd made us this appointment to have some tests run.

"Will it hurt?" asked Kayley.

"Nope," I told her confidently. My stomach tightened at the thought of anyone stabbing her with a needle, but I didn't want her to get scared.

"Liar," she said.

Dammit. She always could see straight through me. How do other moms do it? Maybe it's because we were sisters for so long before I moved into the mom role—we're too connected for me to lie convincingly.

At the hospital, I filled out about a thousand forms and Kayley chattered away happily to the male nurse taking blood from her arm. At first, I thought she was doing it to distract herself. It was only when she mentioned for the third time that I was single that I realized she was trying to match make us.

"Stop that!" I muttered when he turned away.

"He's cute!" she whispered back. "And he's totally into you!"

"Kayley!" He *was* cute, in a way. He had floppy blond hair and a nice smile—handsome in a sweet, unthreatening way. I could see why Kayley liked him. But he wasn't like—

My face went hot. Had I really just nearly thought *he's not like Sean O'Harra?*

"You need to get laid," Kayley told me innocently...

...and just loud enough for the nurse to hear. He was grinning when he turned back to us. "All done," he said, sticking a pad to the inside of Kayley's elbow. "Keep pressure on that."

"Thank you!" said Kayley, batting her eyelashes. "You're so nice. Isn't he nice, Louise?"

I towed her away, muttering my thanks to him. "You are in big trouble..."—*how would mom have done it?*—"*young lady*," I told her unconvincingly.

"He's checking out your ass," Kayley whispered, glancing behind us.

I sighed but I couldn't help smirking just a little and I squeezed her hand as I towed her along. She drove me nuts, sometimes, but I don't know what I'd do without her.

By the time we'd gotten out of the hospital and fought our way through traffic, school was over. Kayley asked if we could order pizza and I hated that even that simple request meant checking my account to see if we could afford it. She deserved so much more—back in Vermont, we'd been comfortably off. And when dad had taken the job in LA we were doing even better. But my job at the garden store paid a small fraction of what our mom and dad had earned and dropping out of college to look after Kayley meant I couldn't get anything better: I'd been a year from graduation but three quarters of a degree is worth precisely zero.

We couldn't afford the pizza but I agreed to it anyway—I'd find a way to make it work and Kayley had been through enough, these past few years. I wanted to give her any little treat I could.

The hospital called to make a follow-up appointment for the next day. That seemed weirdly fast—her blood tests must barely have been finished—but at least it meant we could get this thing fixed. I called around and reorganized my shifts so that I could take her in the next morning, then told her I was heading up to the roof for a little while.

The roof is the one part of our apartment block I like. It's not like there's anything up there, really: just air conditioning ducts and a view across a sea of concrete. But it's where I keep my plants. The apartment's too small to keep anything other than a few houseplants, some herbs in the kitchen and the flowers on the window ledges. I needed space and somewhere I could be alone, even if for just a few minutes.

Up there, I can breathe. I can feel as if I'm not in a city. For a little while, I can forget about being a mom and bills and the distinct lack of any sort of future and just...grow. Growing things has always come naturally to me, helped by a mom who used to let me help in the garden as soon as I could toddle. It calms me and it's also the only damn thing I've ever been any good at. I love both sides of it: the magical feeling of nurturing something from a seed to a plant and the hard science of it—genetics and fertilizers and crop yields. I'd been most of my way through a botany degree, with plans to do a PhD in intensive growing techniques: I was going to feed the starving in the deserts of Africa, or maybe develop fast-growing crops for NASA to take to Mars.

Up until a worn tire blew out on an eighteen wheeler. A hundred dollar chunk of rubber that made it slew across three lanes and crush our parents' car like it was made of tinfoil.

The sun was just going down, throwing out crazy, elongated shadows across the rooftop. I blinked back tears and focused on the plant I was working on, a Fuchsia that needed pruning. And that's when I saw it.

On my left forearm, there was a shadow of a leaf I didn't recognize. A very distinctive leaf.

I moved my arm around, watching the shape stroke its way across my skin. I tilted my head, squinted...

No doubt about it. It was a marijuana leaf. Which made no sense at all because I sure as hell didn't grow dope.

I stood up and turned around. The sun was setting behind me so now I was squinting into the light. Somewhere in the maze of air conditioning units and TV aerials, there must be a dope plant.

The smart thing to do would have been to leave well alone. But the lure of something growing drew me in. Maybe it was wild, a seed that had been blown by the wind and taken root in a bit of dirt. I had to find out.

In the center of the building, there was a raised section accessed by an old, rusting ladder. It took ten minutes of climbing and hunting, all the time trying to shield my eyes from the setting sun, before I found it. It wasn't wild. Three sickly-looking marijuana plants, each only a foot or so high, were lined up behind an air intake. They were well hidden—only the very top of one was poking out. If the sun hadn't hit it at just the right angle to cast the shadow, I'd never have known they were there.

Part of me wanted to break and run. What if someone saw me with them? What if someone thought they were mine? I'd never even seen a marijuana plant in real life, never smoked weed, either—not even in college. My parents had raised me with a serious respect for the law. And these days I was even more paranoid: one misstep and I might lose custody of Kayley.

But I could see the plants were sick and for me that's like hearing a sick animal howl. I crouched down and ran my fingers through the leaves. I knew what it was immediately: the pots were too small. They were watered well enough, but that would just make the roots grow faster. Hell, in this heat, their owner must come up here to water them every day—

I put it together about three seconds too late. His shadow fell across me and his hand grabbed my arm.

"What the fuck are you doing here?" snarled Sean.

2

SEAN

For some reason, I didn't really register that it was her. I mean, of course it was her. Who else in our crappy apartment block has all that long, coppery hair? But I was so mad at her for invading my one private place, I just didn't think of it.

Then I spun her around by the arm and I was staring into those same green eyes that had looked up at me in the elevator. *Lush.* That was the best way to describe them. Like deep green moss by a waterfall. And *lush* was a good word to describe her body, too. Lush and... bountiful. Natural, somehow, not like one of those Photoshopped blondes who wandered into our neighborhood looking for adventure. She looked like she'd been born in a different time. She looked like—

This is going to sound stupid. But when I was a kid, back in Ireland, my mom and dad used to take me to these stately homes: big country houses that the rich people used to charge us to mooch around on a Sunday afternoon. In the gardens, there always used to be these statues of women: pale stone, almost white, with green ivy growing up them. Sometimes the women were nude and sometimes they had a sheet or a toga or something wrapped around them, but they were always busty and they had softly curving hips and asses. Sexy as hell...yet, somehow, they always looked innocent.

That's how Louise looked: like some goddess of nature, a statue come to life. Gorgeous but innocent, completely unaware of the effect she had on me. I wanted her, even more than I had done in the elevator.

Which meant I had to scare her off.

Fortunately, I'm very good at scaring people.

I tightened my grip on her arm. God, her skin was so soft. And so pale, almost white next to my own big, tanned fingers. And she was just a little thing, the top of her head only just brushing my chin. She still hadn't spoken. "Well?" I demanded.

"Sorry!" she squeaked. "I won't tell anyone!" She said *sorry* a lot. The sort of person who'd get stuck holding the door while other people went through, too shy to step forward herself. The setting sun was lighting up her copper hair in glorious reds and yellow, turning it to fire. She was beautiful—why the fuck was she shy?

"What are you doing up here?" I grunted.

She pointed across the roof. "My plants. I grow stuff up here."

Now it made sense. I knew *someone* must be growing those plants, but I'd presumed it was some old lady—gardening's a retirement thing, in my mind. That's why I'd hidden the weed where you had to climb up to get to it. "Which ones are yours?" I asked.

She blinked at me. "All of them."

All *those?* There was a small forest of greenery there, plants I didn't even know the names of. If it was all hers, that meant we were probably the only two people who came up here—good news for me. My weed was safe, as long as she didn't blab. It wasn't the law I was worried about—I only had three plants and that's legal, these days. It was the fact they'd get stolen, if anyone knew about them.

I realized I was still holding her arm. I let it go and she slowly dropped it to her side, crossing it protectively over her chest. God, she was terrified—terrified of *me*. My stomach lurched at the thought.

Wasn't that what you wanted? To scare her away?

Yes. Damn right I did. But my eyes were drawn to her lips—so full, so soft, and the lines of her cheek and neck were so delicate. She really was like some statue carved hundreds of years before—classically beautiful. And from what I knew of her, she'd kept herself clean of all the crime around here. She really was innocent.

I wavered for a second. But she wasn't like one of the women I took home from a bar. She was so much better than that. I wasn't going to taint her, however much I wanted to. I could control myself.

Then a warm breeze blew across us and suddenly the scent of her was in my nose—flowers and warm spices and *nature,* a smell totally unfamiliar in the middle of the city. She was staring up at me with those huge green eyes and breathing just a little too fast with fear, those full breasts lifting and straining at the tight fabric of her t-shirt. I felt a sudden, overwhelming urge to just slide my hand across her cheek and kiss the fuck out of her, tell her it was all okay, that she didn't have to be scared of me. I wanted that to be true. And then I wanted to peel those tight jeans off of her, get my knee between those milky thighs and plunge my fingers into her, jerk her t-shirt up to her neck and go to work on those breasts with my lips—

"Just stay away," I grated. "Stay away from my stuff." And I jerked my head for her to leave.

Her throat worked as she swallowed. She nodded silently and hurried away—I watched her ass sway with every step, a perfect heart shape that made my palms ache with the need to get hold of it. I dug my nails into my palms.

Then she was climbing down the ladder, breasts bobbing and swaying, and running across the roof to the door that leads to the stairs. She put her hand on the handle and I knew that this was it—once she'd gone, I'd probably never see her again.

And then she did the one thing she shouldn't have done.

She turned around.

3

LOUISE

What are you doing? Louise, what the hell are you doing? But I couldn't seem to stop myself. My body was twisting, my eyes searching for him. I found him still standing on the raised section of roof, silhouetted by the sunset. "Your plants are dying," I blurted.

He just stood there. The sun behind him meant I couldn't see his expression. "They've grown too big for the pots, so the roots are being strangled. You need bigger pots, like three times as big." I nodded towards the stack of pots by my plants. "I have some spares. You're welcome to them."

He just stood there. I still couldn't see his expression but I swore he was staring at me. With hate? Anger? I was painfully aware that he could jump down the ladder and be on me before I could get down the stairs. He could grab me....

Grab me...and do what? I could feel my heart hammering in my chest but there was something else, too, a giddy, fluttery feeling that left me light-headed.

He took a step towards me. Just a single step. And suddenly I was bolting down steps two at a time, and I didn't stop until I'd reached the tenth floor and was safely back in my apartment.

"*Dirty Dancing?*" asked Kayley. "I'm fourteen, not eight."

"You need to watch more wholesome movies," I told her. "Be glad that there's kissing."

Kayley crossed her arms grumpily, but settled down to watch. Movie nights were one of our favorite traditions, even if it did mean a few compromises. I hadn't been kidding about the *wholesome* thing, though. It felt like she was growing up too fast. Fifteen would be bad. Sixteen, seventeen—*urgh*. I remembered what a pain I was when I was that age and Kayley was way more of a party animal than I ever was.

Kayley was our parents' "miracle child." Complications after me meant my mom thought she couldn't have any more children. Eight years later, out of the blue, Kayley comes along. The fact I was so much older meant that I was sort of a mom to her even before the accident.

Don't think about that.

I tried to bury myself in the movie and that kept the memories at bay until I turned in. But alone in my bedroom, with Kayley's soft snores coming through the wall, I lay awake and worried. We were close to broke. Kayley's basic medical insurance would cover the blood tests but if it *was* some hormone thing that needed regular treatments we were going to start running up some big bills.

I lay there for a full hour, staring into the darkness with my brain working overtime. I needed to sleep. We had the follow-up appointment at the hospital and I had work in the afternoon. *Think of something pleasant.*

Sean's face swum into my mind.

No! Not him! Sean was everything dark and forbidden. Dangerous, destructive, illegal...

...and hot as all hell.

What if he's out there right now? What if he was out in the hallway, standing in front of our front door?

Of course he's not. He's out at some bar with a blonde in his lap.

But what if he *was*? What if he *had* been looking at me in the elevator, and again on the rooftop? Being the object of his attention would scare the hell out of anyone...everyone knew that Sean O'Harra didn't stop until he got what he wanted. But what if he wasn't looking to beat someone up or wreck a business?

The darkness seemed to grow tighter and warmer around me as I thought of him, standing out there in the hallway in his tight jeans and tank top. Would he knock with his fist or with the tip of his hammer? Given the size of him, it would barely make a difference. I imagined it echoing through the apartment: a giant's knock, the door rattling on its hinges.

No. A man like that...he wouldn't knock at all.

I saw the door erupting inward, transformed into splinters and firewood. In my fantasy, Kayley winked out of existence and it was just me in the apartment, alone. I imagined jumping out of bed and running barefoot through the apartment, my green nightshirt flapping around my thighs. Running towards the danger, drawn to it.

He was already advancing towards me, the floor seeming to shake with each heavy footstep. He was so *big*, not just tall but wide-shouldered and broad-chested—he seemed to fill each doorway he passed through. A low coffee table was in his way and he simply crushed it underfoot, the glass shattering into a million tiny diamonds. His arms swung by his sides, the tan globes of his shoulders and biceps gleaming in the half-darkness. Part of me was pushing me towards him but another part was telling me to flee. A split-second's hesitation, standing there open-mouthed and panting, and it was too late.

He had me.

He grabbed a fistful of my nightshirt and used that to lift me off the ground. The fabric pulled tight around my struggling body as he twisted his hand. He pushed me up against the cool plaster of the wall and the solid heat of his body made me twitch and tremble like some small helpless creature pinned by a bear. With every breath, my stomach brushed against his abs and I went weak as I felt the hard ridges there—God, he didn't have an ounce of fat on him.

He still hadn't spoken a word.

"What do you want?" I panted. Somewhere far away, I was in my bed, on my side, my hand trapped between my thighs, and I whispered the same words under my breath.

He didn't answer. He just grabbed the hem of my nightshirt with his free hand and tugged it up: over my thighs, then up to my waist. Even in the room's dim light, I could see from the tilt of his head that he was gazing straight between my legs. I felt the arm holding me tense as he saw my panties. They were just simple red cotton briefs, nothing sexy, certainly not made for seduction, but I saw that powerful chest rise as he drew in a long, shuddering breath, as if he could barely contain himself. It felt as if the cotton was burning away under his gaze, leaving me naked. I felt my nipples harden under my nightshirt and, since I wasn't wearing a bra, I was painfully aware they were starting to jut out through the soft fabric, especially with it drawn tight across my breasts.

He was still holding me off the ground with one hand. The arm that extended up towards my panting body was as steady and solid as if it had been cast from iron—that was the most overwhelming thing, how *easily* he could toss me around. And with his fist twisted into my nightshirt like that, the soft mounds of my breasts brushed his knuckles each time I inhaled. Each tiny contact sent a new ripple of heat washing through me.

He tugged my nightshirt higher and the soft, pale skin of my stomach came into view. He snaked a hand over it and I gasped. His fingertips traced the line of my waist, then skimmed up, up, teasing at the nightshirt's hem just below my breasts. I was breathing in big, desperate gulps, now, panic mixed with lust, the need to escape and the need to stay.

He was still looking down at my groin, and the intensity of his stare was making me twist and melt inside, a heat like I'd never felt building fast. I realized I was unconsciously grinding my ass against the wall and tried to stop. I couldn't.

Then his eyes flicked up to meet mine. "What do *you* want, Louise?" In the half-darkness, every detail of his voice stood out. Half

Ireland, half California, rich amber liquor over sharp-edged blocks of ice. He leaned in towards me and his pecs pressed against the softness of my breasts. Even through the fabric, I knew he must be able to feel my nipples. He said it again, his accent making the words buzz through my body. "What do you want?"

I swallowed and tried to speak, but I couldn't. The heat was making my mind cloudy: a thick, spinning fog where the hard press of him against me competed with my need to be sensible, to be safe, and to be *good*. Every passing second made it spin faster, everything becoming a blur.

Something pressed between my knees: his leg, the denim rasping against my bare skin. God, he was so hard, so solid, the heat of him throbbing into me. I thought of those muscled thighs spreading mine, that long, thick cock inside me, and I made a half-hearted attempt to twist away because I knew this was wrong. But that only made my groin stroke along the taut hardness of his thigh. Bolts of pleasure shot up inside me. He groaned and I bit my lip, barely managing to stop my own throaty moan.

"What do you want?" he asked for the third time. I knew he wouldn't ask a fourth.

This is crazy. I'm up against the wall of my living room. I don't even know him. He's a criminal. I can't do this. I opened my mouth and said, "Stop. Let me go."

Except it came out as, *"You."*

My eyes went wide and my mouth fell open as I realized what I'd said. I saw those cobalt-blue eyes gleam in the darkness and narrow in lust. Then his mouth was coming towards mine and I wanted to yell, *"Stop! No! I made a mistake! I'm not like this!"*

But I barely had time to draw a breath before our lips touched. Then we were kissing and any sane thought in my head was vaporized.

I'd never been kissed like that before. It was a moving, twisting, panting epic with full orchestra that made every kiss I'd had until that night seem like a shonky rehearsal. It wasn't something we *did*; it was something we *had to do,* as if neither of us could survive unless we kissed each other right then.

I'd never felt so delicate, so insubstantial, as when I first felt Sean's kiss. I was as light as a breeze blowing between the trees of a forest and he was heavy darkness and heat, a creature born of lava and brimstone, scorching me with every touch, making the air shimmer and ripple. We whipped around each other, twisting together, good and bad, air and earth.

My head pressed back against the wall, my mouth suddenly feeling so soft next to his insistently searching lips. Every touch of him sent fresh ribbons of heat twisting down towards my groin, every breath coming faster and faster until both of us were panting, desperate for air but even more desperate to stay in contact. His tongue stroked at the join of my lips and then my mouth was flowering open under him, welcoming him in. I knew that any protest I could make would be exposed as a lie because he could *feel* how much I wanted him.

His tongue explored me, seeking me out. At first, as we twisted and panted, I just let him take the lead, going submissive, letting him invade my softness and relishing it. But every time the tip of his tongue caressed mine, it sent a jolt of heat down through me that turned to trembling, maddening need. I sought him out: tentatively at first, but every play of our tongues together felt so good I couldn't stop. I heard him growl as he felt me come alive.

Kissing him back wasn't enough, though. Not enough contact, not enough of *him.* I grabbed for him blindly, finding his muscled shoulders and going weak at the muscled bulk of them, then sliding my hands up his neck. My fingertips slid over the sandpaper fuzz at the back of his neck and buried themselves in his thick, black hair.

The kiss was still moving and changing. The only sounds in the room now were the rustle of our clothes and my soft gasps of need every time our lips parted. My mind felt like it was lifting, separating from my body, and rising up to the ceiling, leaving all my worries far below. It was hot, but it was more than that: it was floaty and magical, like that first kiss when you're a teenager, the one you've been anticipating for years. I hadn't known kissing could feel like that, as a grown up.

And then I felt the fabric of my nightshirt hauled up, my nipples catching for a second on the hem before my breasts bobbed free. The shock of air against them made me gasp and a thin thread of sanity tugged on my floating mind. *This is where you're meant to tell him to stop.*

He broke the kiss—only so that he could start kissing down my jaw and throat, but it left my mouth free. I opened my mouth to say, *"Okay, enough. Wait. This is too fast."*

But his lips felt as though they were on fire and the winding trail he was following might as well have been drawn in gunpowder. I knew exactly where it would end and the anticipation was making my whole body twitch and writhe. *Wait! What am I doing? I don't do stuff like this!*

His lips grazed the soft skin of my upper breast and I caught my breath. They glided down, ever so slowly, and I arched my back helplessly. My eyes half-opened, heavy-lidded with lust, and I watched, transfixed, as he came closer and closer to my aching nipple. A hot, moist breath from his mouth and then—

I cried out as he took me into his mouth, closing his lips around my nipple and then lashing it with his tongue. I squeezed my eyes shut as the heat rocketed up inside, thrashing my head from side to side to release the pressure. He kept up a steady, insistent stroke: left then right, back and forth. I squeezed my thighs together, locking his thigh between mine and grinding against him. The heat was like a furnace now, burning me up from the inside out, leaving no room for thought.

Just as I thought it couldn't get any better, he opened his mouth wider, taking more of me inside and enveloping me in hot, sucking wetness. He began to nibble at me with his teeth: first with his lips as padding and then, gently, without. The edge of pain was like liquid silver on top of the molten heat. I gasped and stiffened. My ankles crossed and my feet twisting against each other. I could hear the blood rushing in my ears, my orgasm swelling inside me, filling every part of me—

That's when his free hand grabbed my other breast, lifting it and squeezing it hard. He used his palm to roll it in slow circles as he squeezed and my whole body followed in response. It would have been too rough, if I hadn't been on the very edge of orgasm, but now it was perfect, brutish and hard, showing me how hungry he was for me. God, I was being held up against a wall and *mauled*—

His mouth left my breast for a second. When he spoke, each syllable was a little blast of hot air against my slickened flesh, making me dig my fingers hard into the muscles of his shoulders. *"This is what you want, isn't it?"* he growled. *"You're all innocent but you don't want innocent and fuckin' sweet. You want it hard and dirty."*

I gasped and panted for air and found myself nodding.

Suddenly, his hand dropped to my groin. Two thick fingers hooked under the front panel of my panties and, before I could even cry out, he was tugging the fabric away, stretching it clear of my body. The material held for a second and then there was a jagged ripping sound and I was naked below the waist. I saw him toss the ruined panties away and then those same two fingers were between my thighs, probing my entrance, and finding me soaking wet. They slid up inside me, stretching me, while his thumb found my aching clit and—

I came, shoulders and ass pressed hard against the wall and my back arched like a bow, thrusting my breasts out to meet him. My cry of release was so loud it shocked me, but I couldn't hold it in. And I couldn't stop: not with his hot mouth still working at my breast, not while his fingers plunged inside me, not while his thumb circled and rubbed. Not when that big, hulking body was pressed between my thighs and pinned me there so easily. And not when my eyes fluttered open and I saw that he was staring right into my eyes, those blue orbs gleaming with a lust that matched my own. I shouted all of it out in a long, keening, panting cry that rose and rose and only ended when I was utterly spent.

My eyes fluttered open and I found myself lying in my bed: no

Sean, no broken coffee table or splintered door. My panties were still in place—though I'd shoved them to the side to plunge my own fingers inside me—and my nightshirt was in place, though it was rucked up around my waist. I lay there panting and sweating, my mind slowly spinning to a halt.

Sean O'Harra?! Was I *insane*? He wasn't a guy to fantasize about! He was an actual, real-life criminal. He existed in a world I barely even came into contact with. And even if I *was* going to have some sort of crazy, bad boy fantasy about him, I didn't like it rough and up against a wall with my panties torn off...

...did I?

I closed my eyes again, reddening. Anyway, whatever I did or didn't think about Sean O'Harra, he certainly didn't think about *me* that way. That embarrassed me even more than the fantasy itself: that I could be vain enough to think some guy like him would want to jump my bones.

On the plus side, I was now very, very relaxed. My eyelids were already sliding down, my head heavy against the pillow. A bit of harmless fantasizing never hurt anyone, right? It's not like I'd ever even dare speak to him, in real life.

"We're here to see Dr. Huxler," I told the hospital receptionist.

She frowned. "I'm sorry: who?"

I dug the Post-It note out of my purse, just to make sure I'd written it down right. "Huxler."

She shook her head. "Dr. Huxler is Oncology. Next floor up."

I smiled. I actually smiled. "No, our appointment is definitely here. Endocrinology." I checked the sign. Yep, we were in the right place. "My sister has a thyroid problem. Or, you know, something like a thyroid problem."

The receptionist's gaze flicked to Kayley and then back to me. "I'm sorry," she said. "Dr. Huxler is definitely Oncology."

It was the tone of her voice that did it. She was so...apologetic.

There are some places your mind just doesn't go to, as a parent. For the first time, I went there. And suddenly, it was as if the floor had turned to nothing but spider webs, with only a midnight-black void beneath.

"What's going on?" asked Kayley in a voice I hadn't heard her use for years. The one she used to use when she woke from a nightmare and she still wasn't sure if it was real.

"Nothing," I said. "It's probably just a mistake." And I took her hand and stalked towards Oncology, pulling her away from the receptionist before she could tell her any different.

Dr. Huxler was in his late fifties with thick, fluffy curls of gray hair. There were orchids in his book-lined office: beautiful and peaceful and probably designed to make patients feel calm. They weren't helping.

"Your parents," he said, studying Kayley's records, "they're deceased?"

I always think *deceased* sounds so peaceful, as if they passed away happily in their sleep aged eighty-three instead of being snatched away from us in a heartbeat.

"Yes," I said. "They're deceased. I'm Kayley's legal guardian."

He nodded. Took a breath and held it. I was digging my nails into my knees, part of me wanting him to spit it out, and part of me wanting him to never speak again.

"Your blood tests indicate that you have leukemia," he said to Kayley.

I grabbed Kayley's hand and squeezed it harder than I ever had in my life.

"We need to do more tests to narrow down the exact type," said Doctor Huxler. "We can run those right now, if you're okay with that." He was calm, but the urgency in his voice scared the shit out of me. I nodded. Next to me, Kayley nodded too. Her jaw was firm, her hand gripped mine, and she didn't shed a single tear.

But, as we left Doctor Huxler's office, heading for the first test, she squeezed my hand in a death grip and said, "Say it's going to be okay." And I heard the crack in her voice, like a fracture in a glacier that's about to split wide open.

"It's going to be okay," I said automatically. But I could feel myself shrinking inside the parent suit I'd been wearing for the last few years. *This isn't right. I can't do this.* As we walked down the hallway, I looked around—I mean I actually, instinctively looked over my left shoulder—for my parents because I needed to hand things over to them, now, and get a hug myself.

But they weren't there.

They made Kayley strip off her clothes and I gathered them up: the artfully distressed jeans and the belt with the obscure Japanese cartoon characters on it I'd bid for on Ebay as a Christmas present; the lurid pink top we'd argued over for days before I'd let her have it. The things that made her *her*. The hospital staff gave me a bag to put them in and Kayley and I exchanged a look as I folded the top down. *This is just temporary,* we nodded to each other.

But once she was in a gown, she looked like a patient.

For the next three hours, I watched my precious, fragile sister be stabbed again and again: stabbed in her arms for more blood, stabbed in the base of her spine for spinal fluid, stabbed with a slender, howling drill to collect bone marrow. The staff were polite and caring, but in the fake, rehearsed way that airline staff swear they'll take *extra special care* of your package or your suitcase or your dog. Maybe it was because she was so stoic; maybe they just saw hundreds of patients and had gotten jaded. But I wanted to scream at them that she was a child. *My* child.

When it was all over, Dr. Huxler asked me to come into his office "for a second." He made it sound as if it was nothing important, boring paperwork that Kayley didn't have to sit through.

"I want to stay," Kayley said immediately. "I want to be in there."

Dr. Huxler caught my eye and I'll remember the look he gave me until the day I die. "Kayley," I said, fighting to keep my voice level, "go check your email. It's okay."

"I don't want to check my email," she said, her eyes huge. "I already checked it. I want to stay with you. I want to know."

A lump was swelling inside my throat. My chest hurt. I was about to break down in front of her and I couldn't let that happen. "Check it again," I said. And took a step away from her, towards the door Dr. Huxler was holding open for me.

"No," I heard Kayley say behind me. "No! I want to go in!"

Another step. *My legs are shaking.* Another. Another. I heard Kayley start forward behind me, then stop. I couldn't turn around or I'd lose it completely. Then a nurse's voice, murmuring to Kayley: *"You stay here with me, honey."*

"No!"

My heart felt like it was tearing in two. I walked into Doctor Huxler's office and he closed the door.

And then it got worse.

4

LOUISE

"This is going to be a very difficult conversation," Dr. Huxler said as soon as we sat down. "There's nothing I'm going to be able to say that's going to make this easier."

I just stared at him.

"The tests confirm that your sister has leukemia." He paused. "I'm sorry."

My whole world was exploding but, for some reason, my body just continued as if it was still there. I found myself nodding. "Um-hum. What are our, uh...what are our treatment options?" *Leukemia.* Images flashed through my head. Charity drives to take kids to Disneyland. Bald heads and bags of chemo chemicals and throwing up. I'd quit my job. I'd be with her every step of the way. We could fight this.

Dr. Huxler swallowed.

"We can hold it back," he said. "Extend things. Maybe as long as six months."

It took a while for the enormity of what he was telling me to sink in.

"No," I said. "No. You're not..."

He just looked sadly at me.

"No," I said, more determinedly, this time. "No, she's *fine*. This is bullshit, she's *fine!* She's just *tired!*"

He pressed his lips together and just waited.

"*No!* It's a mistake! I want—I want more doctors. I want a second opinion!"

"We ran every test," he said gently.

"Kids get leukemia and they get better," I said. "They have chemo and they *get better!*"

"Not this type," he said. "Nothing in medicine is certain. But in this case, the best the chemo can do is buy her time."

When we'd first been told to go to Oncology, it had felt as if I was on the verge of falling into a void. Now, though, the void was inside me. I could feel the hole growing, eating away at me. I was getting colder and colder. "Six months?" I whispered.

He nodded.

One hundred and eighty days.

Twenty-four Wednesday movie nights.

I sat there motionless as the hole inside me grew and grew, gnawing hungrily at its edges.

"There are things I can recommend," said Dr. Huxler. "There's a book—"

"A book?" I whispered.

"It can help you manage the journey."

"Journey?"

"It can help you get ready to say goodbye."

"A book?" I asked. Then the anger came, erupting out of nowhere. "A *book?!*" I yelled.

Dr. Huxler just sat there and absorbed it, which somehow scared me more than anything. I'd become just another screaming, stubborn parent and all this—all of it—was normal. We were both just playing out our roles in a drama that unfolded in this office every single day.

It was already inevitable.

"We can tell her together," said Dr. Huxler. "Or the two of you can talk first. Sometimes it's easier that way. Whichever you prefer."

I think that must have been when I started crying, at the thought of breaking it to Kayley. Dr. Huxler dissolved behind a haze of hot, wet tears but I didn't move, couldn't move. I just sat there staring at him as my face crumpled.

"You can stay here as long as you need," said Dr. Huxler. "It's okay."

The first ugly, wracking sob broke the surface, the tears spilling over and falling like hot rain onto my top. *I cannot deal with this.*

Cannot.

Deal.

I wanted my mom and dad.

My eyes screwed shut as I thought about all the things Kayley and I had shared and all the things we now never would. I thought of losing her, of being completely alone in the world, and then cursed myself for being so fucking selfish and thinking about myself when I should have been thinking about her. I tried to imagine how she'd handle it: six months of watching the hours tick away, counting down the sunsets. She'd be strong, knowing Kayley. Strong and funny, until the end. That almost made it worse.

It wasn't fair. Not after our parents. Not *her,* not after so little life. *Take me, instead!* I'd heard that, heard parents saying they'd change places with their kids when something like this happened, but I'd never really understood, not deep down. I did now. I would have changed places with her in a heartbeat.

The hole inside me had swallowed everything up, now. Every breath just brought an arctic, bone-deep cold, a nothingness where there should have been warmth and security. I cried out of loss and out of fear: this was worse than anything I'd ever imagined, but it was nothing compared to what was to come. My sister was going to be slowly ripped from me, one day at a time.

I finally moved. I leaned forward, buried my face in my hands, and sobbed my heart out. I cried and cried and I got colder and colder and colder.

And then I got mad.

It started as a tiny spark in the darkness, out in the middle of that void where nothing should have been able to survive. I snatched at it and it burned me, but that was fine. Pain was good. Pain was better than nothingness. I squeezed it between my palms and felt it grow.

It wasn't fair.

It wasn't *fucking* fair.

The spark had lit a fire. Fourteen years of memories of Kayley, of love, of affection...it all stood like a dense, tinder-dry forest that didn't catch fire so much as explode. I sat upright in one sudden move and said, "No."

"I'm sorry?" said Dr. Huxler.

"I said, *no!* This thing's going to kill her and you just *give up* and offer me a fucking book? *No!* There has to be something you can do."

There was real pain in his eyes. "I'm sorry. There isn't."

I stood up, the anger carrying me. "Well you *find something!*" I yelled. "Because I'm not going to tell a fourteen year-old girl she's not going to make fifteen!"

I had to get out of there. My anger was red hot but I knew it would run out and I didn't know what would happen when it did. I couldn't go back out into the hallway because Kayley was there. So I threw open the doors onto Dr. Huxler's little balcony.

Outside, as if to mock me, the sky was blue and the sun was pleasantly warm. Eighteen million people down there were grinning and chattering and going about their business as if this was a normal day. Kayley's passing wouldn't even leave a dent in their world.

I pressed my stomach against the railing at the edge of the balcony and leaned forward just a little. We were five floors up. How long would it take, before I hit the ground? Ten seconds, maybe? Ten seconds to think and fear, before I stopped thinking altogether. That would be a hell of lot more manageable than six months.

But then I'd be leaving Kayley on her own to deal with this. No way.

So I stood there, hands clenching and unclenching on the railing, until Dr. Huxler came to stand next to me. I already knew what he was going to say: that my anger and denial were normal, a part of the process.

"Okay," he said.

"Okay what?"

He didn't look at me, just stared out over the city. "I'm not in the business of offering false hope," he told me. "Sometimes, not every option is appropriate."

I grabbed his arm with both hands. For the first time since he'd broken the news, I felt the hole inside me flicker. A tiny, tantalizing glimpse of a future where Kayley still existed. "What?"

"There's an experimental treatment in Switzerland. They've been having good results."

"Then let's do it! Why are we even talking about this?"

Now he turned to look at me. "It costs half a million dollars. Kayley's insurance won't cover it. These people cater to the super-rich. They expect payment in advance: they won't let you run up a bill."

Money? It came down to money? *That's* what was going to determine my sister's future? I stood there staring at him for a moment. "How long do I have to find the money? You said you could give her six months. Could we start the Swiss treatment at the *end* of that time?"

He sighed. He must have thought I was crazy...but he didn't want to give up on her any more than I did. "If I really maxed out the chemo...then in theory, yes."

I nodded.

"Louise...I have to caution you on this. Six months was the *maximum*. Stretching out Kayley's time to that...it's going to make it rough on her. Treatments almost every day—she's going to be in the hospital *a lot*. It isn't what I'd normally do. Normally I'd suggest a balance between extending her time and making her comfortable."

I got what he was saying. By clinging on to this one slim chance, I was ruining Kayley's remaining time. Was I just being selfish? Wouldn't it be better to just enjoy our time together and let her slip away, three or four or five months from now?

No. I wasn't giving up on her.

"I'll find the money," I told Dr. Huxler firmly. "Give me six months."

And then I walked straight through his office and out into the hallway. Before he could try to change my mind.

We sat Kayley down and I gently explained that it was serious. "You're going to have to have some treatments," I told her. "Here in the hospital. And then, in about six months, we're going to take a trip to Europe for one last batch."

"Europe?"

"Switzerland."

I let it sink in. Kayley wasn't stupid. She could see my eyes were red from crying. "But it's going to be okay?" she asked in a small voice.

I gathered her into my arms and folded her tight against my chest. "Yes," I said. "It's going to be okay."

And I prayed to whoever was listening that I was telling the truth.

5

LOUISE

D r. Huxler insisted that Kayley should start her treatment immediately. I didn't like it. She was terrified as it was, without sleeping alone in an unfamiliar place. "Tomorrow," I said. "I'll bring her back."

He shook his head. "We need to get her started on the meds as soon as possible." He lowered his voice. "Look, you want me to give you as much time as I can: this is me doing that. It's already taken hold. I need to slow it down. We have a lot of catching up to do."

I knew he didn't mean it like that, but it still stung. I'd already been berating myself: why hadn't I brought her in sooner? A month ago, a week ago, before this creeping darkness had claimed so much of her.

I'd thought she was just *tired!*

I relented and told Kayley she'd have to stay in, then raided the hospital's store for trashy magazines and candy to cheer her up. When I got to the register, the reality of it hit me for the first time: I was having to search for loose change to pay for ten dollars' worth of stuff. Kayley's insurance would cover most of the hospital treatments, but there'd still be some bills, easily enough to eat up what meager savings we had. We were basically broke.

How the hell was I going to find *half a million dollars? What the hell am I doing?*

And then I hardened. *What choice do I have?* I wasn't going to give up. If I'd been one of the super-rich, Kayley would already be on her way to Switzerland and would be starting the treatment now. It wasn't right that her survival hinged on money.

Upstairs, Kayley had settled into her room as best she could. She was eying a nurse suspiciously as the woman prepared her first IV bag. *Her first of God knows how many.* Dr. Huxler had told me she'd be in hospital for at least the first few months: she'd need almost daily treatments and they'd leave her too weak to come home in between.

I handed over the magazines and candy and then pulled over a chair, taking Kayley's hand.

"You're staying?" Kayley asked hopefully.

"Damn right I'm staying. I'll be here until you go to sleep."

I held her hand while the needle went in and while the first dose of chemicals trickled into her system. I read to her from the magazines and got her to draw a complicated tree diagram on the back of a napkin showing which members of her favorite bands had dated which actresses. I stayed while she lay down to sleep and waited until she was breathing slow and easy.

If it had been me in the bed, I knew I wouldn't have been able to sleep. Kayley could because she still had that child's unshakeable faith: if your mom or dad tells you it's going to be okay, it's going to be okay.

I missed having that like crazy. I needed someone to tell *me* it was going to be okay. And I was absolutely terrified that Kayley had put that faith in me. I couldn't risk her waking up and seeing me crying, so I put everything I had into holding the tears back and quietly slipped out.

At home, everything felt wrong. It was the first time I could remember that I'd been in the apartment alone at night. I couldn't sleep. Whenever I went towards my bedroom, I'd pass Kayley's room with the door half open and the silence inside and I'd stumble to a stop.

Eventually, I went up on the roof. It was full-on night, now, but there was enough moonlight to see by. I picked my way carefully over to my plants and sat down amongst them. I put my arms on my knees and my head on my arms and then, only then, did I let it all out. I cried for Kayley and our parents. I cried for the friends she'd never make and the man she'd never meet, for the home they wouldn't make and the kids they'd never have. Most of all, I cried for being such a fucking bad mother, that I could allow this to happen to her. Why hadn't I gotten it diagnosed earlier? Why wasn't I some high-flying CEO with millions in the bank, instead of a college drop-out working at a garden store? *Why, why why?* And what the hell was I going to do?

And then, just as I was at my lowest low...that's when I heard the music.

6

SEAN

Some people play and they make beautiful music. I play to let shit out, and you probably wouldn't even call it playing. I'm sure as hell not very good and I don't play any songs you'd recognize. I just use the chords that feel right and I thrash the living hell out of them.

The first amplified notes crashed across the rooftop and out across the city. It was probably pretty loud, if you were above the tenth floor. But it wasn't like anyone would dare knock on my door to complain. Being the scariest fucker on the block has some advantages.

I was up on the raised part of the roof, in among all the air conditioning ducts. Playing, when I do it right, feels almost as good as swinging my hammer. Everything else stops mattering. There's no now, no future...and especially, no past. I even stop being *me* for a while and that's the biggest relief of all.

Tonight, though, it wasn't working.

Tonight, the more I escaped into the sound, the more it carried me towards copper-colored hair and pale skin, green eyes I couldn't look away from and that sweet, spicy scent.

I cursed under my breath.

Louise. I'd seen her around enough times over the years that I knew her first name. But it had taken on a whole new meaning since the elevator. There was something very clean and honest about it. A *good* name. The name of some pioneer's wife, tilling the fields, and baking bread. Not the sort of girl I was into, with their hair extensions and their giggles and their long, false nails as they wrapped their hands around my cock. The women who spent half the evening sipping multi-colored cocktails in a trashy bar, tapping their iPhones to tell their friends how fucking *daring* they were, before coming back to my place (never theirs: they wouldn't want me to know where they lived) and almost dragging me to the bed. They wanted a taste. A little adventure.

I gave it to them. Spread under me or on their knees before me, fully clothed and skirt flipped up or stripped naked, wrists tied to the bedposts. I gave it to them as hard and as long and as fast as they could handle...and then, as they started to come down again, I did it all over again. They used me and I used them. Fucking, it turned out, was as good at making me forget as playing or smashing shit up.

Louise wasn't like that. Hell, she wasn't like anything I'd seen before. How the hell had she even wound up in this crappy apartment block?

I closed my eyes and tore a few more notes from the guitar: a rising wave of sound that suddenly crashed down as I slid my hand back along the fret. I was pacing and turning, unable to stay still. The music was doing its job and taking me away from the past, but it couldn't take me away from her. Every time I closed my eyes, I could feel the warmth of her bare arm in my hand and smell the scent of her skin....

I froze and opened my eyes. The scent of her on the air was too real, too close.

I whirled around and she was there, maybe six feet away from me, watching.

Shit.

She looked amazing. With that red hair in the moonlight, she could have been some sorceress about to cast some spell on me. All she needed was a black cloak wrapped around her...and nothing on underneath. *Oh, bloody hell....*

I'd never fantasized about a girl the way I did about Louise. Every time I saw her, it sparked something new and all of those daydreams ended with those long, pale legs wrapped around me as I plunged deep inside her. Normally, if I want someone, I just make my move. I've never been into all that love-struck, watching-from-afar shit. But with her....

"What do you want?" I practically grunted it. I didn't mean to sound like such a dick, but I just had no idea what to say to her. I wasn't used to talking to women except to talk them into bed. And even though I wanted Louise in my bed more than any girl I'd ever known, I wanted to protect her from me even more.

"Nothing." She was already turning away. "I just wondered who was playing." She climbed down the ladder, heading towards the door that led inside. Another few seconds and she'd be gone.

"Thank you," I called out. The two words hung in the air between us. I honestly couldn't remember the last time I'd said it, but then I couldn't remember the last time someone had done something for me, either.

She stopped, but didn't turn around.

"I used those pots of yours. It's only been a day but...the plants don't look so sick."

She nodded. "Okay." As she said it, she glanced over her shoulder at me and—

Wait, were her eyes wet?

I put down my guitar, vaulted the railing and jumped down to where she was standing, landing right in front of her. She spun around in alarm and... yeah, her eyes were wet. Wet and red. Someone had made her cry.

Out of nowhere, I felt my chest tighten. Rage sparked and then flared inside me, growing and spreading. Its heat was familiar, but its shape wasn't.

I knew all about anger. I just wasn't used to feeling it on behalf of someone else. My hand itched for my hammer. I was going to find the guy responsible and break his skull, not stopping until I'd ground him into powder—

And then I remembered I was no white knight. I was the guy white knights are meant to save you from.

She looked deep into my eyes. Damn, when she did that, it became more than just raw lust. It became something else altogether.

I met her gaze, asking the question with a tilt of my head. But after a second, she shook her head and turned away. She didn't want to talk about it. At least, not to *me*. But she didn't head for the door to the stairs. She went over to the edge of the roof and looked out across the city.

She didn't want to be alone, either.

I followed her, suddenly aware that she'd been listening to me strangle a guitar. *She must think I'm a freak.*

Wait. Since when did I care what anyone else thought of me?

My steps got slower and slower as I approached her. What the hell was the matter with me? If this had been some woman in a bar, I'd have just gone straight over there: hell, I'd barely have acknowledged her, just got myself a beer, and let *her* throw herself at *me*. But with Louise, I felt like a kid on his first date. And the closer I got, the more I felt it—a deep, inexorable pull towards her, dragging me in. And I finally realized what it was.

I wasn't going to be able to control myself with this girl. I was like a boat next to a whirlpool, just barely holding its position. If I got any closer, I was going to spin inwards to my doom. To *both* of our dooms.

But what else could I do? Leave her like that?

"You alright?" I asked tightly.

She swallowed, and I thought she was going to start crying. That pressure in my chest again, like it was me who was in pain. Then she said, "You ever feel like the future's just...bearing down on you and there's nothing you can do to change it?"

I thought about it. It was rare enough that I spoke to anyone, let alone have someone ask me something deep. Eventually, I said, "No."

It can't have been the answer she was expecting, because she snapped her head around to look at me. *Ah, fuck.* In the moonlight, her skin was so pale it almost glowed and with those lush green eyes looking up at me...she was just the prettiest fucking thing I'd ever seen.

I turned and nodded towards where my hammer was leaning against a wall. "Most of the stuff I have to deal with gets out of the way," I told her. "Or I smash it out of the way." I paused. "I get the feeling your shit's more complicated."

She swallowed again and nodded a couple of times, then turned to the city and sniffed back a tear. She took a deep breath and what I normally would have been doing was watching that fantastic chest rise and swell under her t-shirt. Instead, all I could think was, *she's about to tell me. She's about to tell me what's going on with her.* We were connecting. I reached out to put a hand on her back to comfort her— slowly, so as not to spook her—

"I wish I was more like you," she said.

And reality slammed up to meet me. My hand froze an inch from her back.

The last thing she needed was to be around someone like me. Everything I touched turned to shit. I knew that. Why had I forgotten it?

"You don't want to be like me," I told her. And I turned and marched away. I didn't even stop to retrieve my guitar or amp before I hit the stairs. All I grabbed was my hammer. That was all I needed in my life.

Just before the stairwell door closed behind me, I heard her intake of breath—she'd turned around and realized I'd gone. She was probably amazed at what an asshole I was. She didn't realize she'd just had a lucky escape.

Whatever problems she had, they were nothing compared to the shit she'd get into if she came near my world. For her sake, I had to stay as far away from her as possible.

I had no idea that our lives were already on a collision course.

7

LOUISE

Early the next morning, I called Stacey. I didn't know what else to do.

Stacey is the anti-me. Confident. Successful. Smartly-dressed. We were at college together: she majored in business while I did botany...except she actually graduated. Even if my folks hadn't died, I don't think we would have been on remotely similar paths. I was heading for a quiet lab where I could be around plants, not people; Stacey was born to be in business.

That's why I'd called her. She was the only person in my life who I could even imagine using the phrase "half a million dollars."

I hadn't told her on the phone why I needed to see her, so she arrived all smiles, carrying two takeout coffees. I knew what she was thinking: I'd finally changed my mind and wanted to take her up on her offer of a job at the cupcake store. She was one of the franchise's star achievers: in the short time since graduating, she'd already made manager. I gave it five years before she was running the company.

Her smile faltered when she saw my face. I sat her down and laid it out for her: Kayley, the hospital, the Swiss treatment. Her tears made little dark spots on her perfect gray skirt. Hearing myself tell the story made it all real again and, when Stacey looked up at me with her face pale, I very nearly lost it myself. I was relying on her. If she didn't know what to do, who would?

After a few agonizing minutes, though, Stacey sniffed back her tears. "Right," she said, half to herself. She fixed her hair and smoothed down her blouse. "Okay," she said, still sounding shaken. She adjusted her skirt, stood up and took a deep breath. "Don't panic," she said in a steadier voice. "We're going to fight this."

And I knew I'd called the right person.

"First of all, you know that I'll give you all the money I can—you know that, right?" she asked urgently.

I nodded.

"But that's not going to be nearly enough. Let's attack this thing." And she pulled a notebook and pen from her briefcase and wrote "$500,000" at the top. "We're going to add up everything we can lay our hands on," she told me. "Let's start with the apartment." She held her pen poised.

"Rented."

"Your car?"

"Are you kidding? We'd have to pay someone to take it away."

"Savings? Stocks? Anything your parents left you?"

I let out a long, despairing sigh. There *had* been savings. But Kayley's unexpected arrival had changed everything. My parents had suddenly found themselves with a second child to care for and that had meant radically changing their outlook. They'd gone from comfortably prepared to scrambling for Kayley's college fund and that had meant taking risks they otherwise wouldn't have. Not all of them had paid off. Long-term, we probably would have been just fine. But when they died, they'd left very little behind. I still had college loans to pay off and my job barely covered the rent and bills. "We've got a few thousand. That's it."

"Could you run up debt? I mean, even if it takes the rest of your life to pay it off...."

"I'm going to have to do that anyway. Even with insurance, there'll still be hospital bills. And my credit's nowhere near good enough to borrow half a million—not even close."

"And the Swiss clinic needs the money in advance? They won't let you pay it off in installments?"

"I called them. They won't. Why would they? They're for the rich. You pay up front or they don't want to know."

We both stared at the notepad and its vast, empty white space.

Stacey flipped over the page. "Okay," she said. "You'll just have to earn the money."

"You're nuts. I mean, I love you, but you're nuts. Half a million in six months? You think someone's going to take me on at a million dollars a year?"

"You could start your own business," she said, undeterred. "You don't give yourself enough credit. You're smart."

I sighed again. I knew she was just trying to help and being an entrepreneur was what she was all about: of course she'd suggest that. But it was ridiculous. What was I going to do: jewelry making? Kids' parties?

"Let's make a list of your skills," said Stacey.

I shook my head. "The only thing I've ever been good at is growing stuff."

"Well," said Stacey, "what can you grow in six months that'll make you half a million dollars?"

Sometimes, you just have to hear the right question. I blinked at her as my brain lit up.

No, that's insane. I couldn't.

Could I?

8

LOUISE

I politely but hurriedly got rid of Stacey, telling her I'd had an idea involving *importing rare flowers from Africa, or something* and needed to think. She looked doubtful, but she had to get to her store so she hugged me and ran.

I sat down at my aging laptop and, in a testament to my naivety, typed "How to grow marijuana" into Google. It didn't occur to me until later that doing that from my own computer might not be a good idea.

For the next seven hours, I didn't move. I fumbled for my phone, dialed the garden store, and called in sick without my eyes once leaving the screen. For the first hour, I was hesitant and tentative. I was so afraid of getting my hopes up, I was like a scientist trying to disprove a theory. I tried every way to destroy the idea that I could. *Maybe I couldn't grow a crop in time. Maybe it wouldn't be worth enough. Maybe the startup costs are too high.*

One by one, I eliminated those questions. It began to look viable, in terms of money. That left the botany.

I immersed myself in science. I read up on the plant itself, on gene lines and fertilizers and pest control. There was a huge amount to research, but the internet had all the information I needed. As I read more and more, I started to get excited. Growing weed, I learned, is complicated and tricky...if you're a civilian. But for a botany student and gardener like me it was actually relatively simple. Hell, I'd actually specialized in this stuff at college. I could even see a few ways I could improve on the methods people were posting about online. *I could be good at this.* The skill I'd thought was so useless might actually be able to save us.

It was possible.

That left: could I actually go through with it?

I sat back from the screen. I *never* broke the law. I never even broke the rules. This was so far outside anything I'd normally consider, it was absurd. *Me? Grow drugs?*

I hesitantly clicked a few more Google links and read about raids on local grow houses, about the farmers being sentenced not to three months in county jail, but to 20 years in a federal penitentiary. Weed may be effectively legalized, especially in liberal California, but growing your own large-scale crop of it certainly wasn't. I saw pictures of hollow-eyed men—and even a few women—in orange jumpsuits. Some of them weren't much older than me.

It wasn't just that I'd go to jail: it was that Kayley's only chance would evaporate. Worse, I'd miss the remaining time we had together.

I can't do this.

But if I didn't, she was going to die.

I clicked more links, unable to stop. Reports of shootings and arson attacks. Paid hits. I'd been thinking of it as a business, but I'd been glossing over the fact that the business took place in that shadow world of crime most of us only see when it spills over into the headlines. If I was going to do this, I'd have to join that world.

That was the part I definitely couldn't do. I knew how to grow things; I had no idea how to be a criminal. I'd last a week.

Unless I had help.

9

LOUISE

I stood in front of his door and tried to control my racing heart.

It's because I'm excited. I'm excited by the plan.

Yeah, that's absolutely what it is.

It still stung that he'd walked away from me like that on the roof. But that was all irrelevant, now. No more time for stupid fantasies. I needed his help.

I rapped three times on the door, feeling my breathing quicken. The paint was chipped and the wood was cracked in one place. Someone had tried to break in, at some point in the past. They'd found out where he lived and come for him.

I suspected it hadn't ended well for them.

No response from inside. Was he out? I put my ear to the door. Holding my breath, I could just pick out a sound: a faint, rhythmic creaking. I knocked again, louder, and the creaking paused...then continued.

"Sean?" I called out. My voice sounded awkward in the silent hallway. "It's me."

The creaking stopped. I thought I heard footsteps and waited, but the door stayed closed. "Sean?"

Nothing.

I thought of Kayley. I was due to visit that afternoon and I needed some shred of hope to carry with me or I was going to lose it and break down in front of her. That gave me the courage to knock again, hard. "Sean?"

The door suddenly swung open. He must have been standing right up against it, watching me through the door viewer. "*What?*" he growled, exasperated.

I swallowed. He was stripped to the waist and his whole upper body glistened with sweat. His chest and biceps were pumped and rock hard, even larger and more intimidating than normal. He looked...*primed,* loaded with adrenaline and ready to pounce. He'd been working out, I realized. That's what the creaking had been. He was glaring at me, those postcard-blue eyes harder than diamond, and I took an instinctive half-step back. "Sorry," I mumbled.

"Stop saying you're sorry!" That Irish accent again, like a silver blade flashing. Then his tone softened a little. "What is it?"

He'd braced one arm against the wall and I couldn't drag my eyes away from it-the veins standing out hard, the solid thickness of it, like a tree branch big enough to climb on. "I need your help," I said. "I'll pay you."

He was breathing hard. He ran a hand over his forehead and I saw the little jewels of sweat fall. His hair was damp with it. "Help with what?"

I swallowed and then raised my chin bravely. "I want to grow dope."

For a second, he just stared at me. Then his hand shot forward and grabbed the front of my t-shirt, bunching it. Just like in my fantasy.

I felt my whole body go weak.

He tugged me forward, almost lifting me off my feet, and hauled me inside his apartment, kicking the door shut behind me. For a second, I thought he was going to push me up against the wall. I grabbed for his hand with both of mine, but I wasn't sure what I wanted to do: break his grip or pull myself in tighter. Desperate fear and heady arousal slammed together in my chest—

He spun us around and pushed me away from him, sending me staggering into the middle of the room. "*What?!*" he spat.

I almost ran. His eyes were so brutally hard, so angry...but then I saw the flicker in his expression. Just for an instant, there'd been something else there. Concern.

It was almost as if he was *trying* to be angry with me.

I glanced around. The place was so masculine, all gray and silver and white, with nothing but hard edges. He'd torn down the walls and made it one big room, except for a door that I assumed led to the bathroom. I saw a weights bench, the iron plates chipped and worn from use. His guitar and amp rested up against a wall, his hammer next to them. I could smell the heady tang of leather and saw a black jacket thrown across the back of a chair.

There wasn't a single living thing in the apartment apart from us. No pets, no plants.

I swallowed and looked him in the eye, trying to ignore the gleaming nakedness of his chest. "I want to grow weed," I said. "I mean...a *lot* of weed. A crop."

He shook his head in disbelief. "*You?*"

For a second, it felt as if he'd punched me in the stomach. I mean, I knew I didn't amount to much, a college dropout with a job going nowhere and close to zero in the bank. But I hadn't expected him to put me down like that.

And then I saw the way he was looking at me. He wasn't sneering at me. He was shocked, but he looked more...horrified. As if he thought I was better than that. The pain disappeared and was replaced by a warm flush, radiating outward.

"It's not crazy," I said. "At least...not as crazy as it sounds. I *know* this stuff. I have a degree in botany—well, nearly. I know about indoor, intensive growing—that was my specialty. I read up on marijuana this morning—compared to a lot of plants it's really not that hard." I took a deep breath. "One crop—one *big* crop—that's all we'd need. It's April now. We could have it grown by September, sell it, and net half a million in profit."

"Half a million dollars?" His face turned stern. "What kind of trouble are you in?"

It had been hard with Stacey. It should have been even harder with Sean because I barely knew him. But when I closed my eyes and started to speak, it felt...right. I didn't feel as if I was in a stranger's apartment. I felt a warm, dark, comforting presence, as if was really listening instead of just hearing me.

"My sister is sick," I said. "Really sick. Half a million is how much money I need to save her. I've got six months to raise it." I swallowed. "Her name's Kayley. She's only fourteen. She doesn't deserve—"

"I know."

I opened my eyes, surprised.

"I've seen her around the building with you," he said. "The blonde kid."

I blinked. He'd been watching us? Watching *me*? Why would he—

He looked away, as if embarrassed. "I'm sorry," he said. "That's...it's fuckin' awful. But you need to find another way."

I shook my head. "There is no other way."

"You'll get killed! You've got no idea—*literally no idea*—what you're getting into. You're too...*good*."

"I know! That's why I need you! You're—" I cut myself off, but it was too late.

He raised one dark eyebrow. "*A complete bastard?*" he finished for me. I went to protest, but he shook his head. "No, it's okay. That's fair." He gave a wry little smile, but it didn't completely hide the flicker of pain in his eyes.

I put my hands out towards him as if trying to calm a wounded animal. "Look, I know plants. I can do that part of it. But you're right, I don't know anything about being a criminal."

He shook his head. "You are *so far* from being a criminal this would be funny, if you weren't going to wind up dead in a ditch."

"Then help me! We can be partners! I'll cut you in. I swear to God, it'll be the best damn crop of weed you've ever seen. I'll grow it; you sell it and protect me."

He dropped his gaze to the floor and it stayed there while he thought. He crossed his arms, biceps bulging, and I barely dared to breathe while he debated it. Then he finally lifted his head, looked me in the eye, and said, "No."

"*No?* Why? I'm not asking you to do this out of charity! I'll pay you!"

He shook his head. "It's not about the money."

"Then what? You'll happily take cash to smash things up, but not to help someone? What's the matter with you?"

His big hand landed on my shoulder and then I was being pushed towards the door. "More than you want to know," he muttered. And pushed me out into the hallway. The door slammed behind me.

I stood there gaping. Up on the roof, he'd been almost warm. Now he was back to being the Sean everyone talked about in hushed tones: brutal and cold. *The Irish,* a lot of people called him. *The Irish smashed up some place last night.*

And now I felt like he'd done the same to me. I'd peeled back my armor to reveal my one, fragile hope and he'd shattered it, told me that I was on my own and that I was nuts for even trying.

Well, fuck him.

If he wouldn't help me, I'd just have to do it myself.

10

SEAN

That night, I had a job. Perfect, because I needed to take my frustration out on something other than myself. The whole way there, I could feel the anger building up inside, bubbling out of the raw slash of pain. The shell I've built around myself, the muscles and the tattoos and the attitude, that can stand up to anything. I'll take a baseball bat to my kidney and fight on. I'll take a punch to my jaw, spit out a tooth and smile. But when the pain comes from inside...that's harder to handle. I can't deflect it away because it's already inside me, folding back on itself, and growing stronger and stronger while the thoughts play on endless loop in my mind.

I didn't help her.

I didn't help her because I can't. Because I'm no good for anything.

Because everything I touch, I break.

The only thing I'm good for is smashing shit up.

I stopped the car half a block away because I needed to get my head together. The big V8 rumble died away and the street was silent except for the cicada and a few kids playing on their bikes.

I went around to the trunk and got out my hammer. And the kids fled.

As I hefted the hammer onto my shoulder, blinds were slamming down all along the street. A woman grabbed her cat from the front porch and raced inside her house, her eyes huge with fear.

It's not the worst thing in the world, having everyone afraid of you. It can even be kind of fun. But you can't control it. Reputation billows out from you like smoke, impossible to corral. It bothered me that the woman thought I'd hurt her cat, or hurt her. But that was the price of what I did and I'd always accepted it before, even welcomed it. Scared people keep their distance.

Louise, though...she was scared of me but she'd been brave enough to approach me. She'd knocked on my damn door.

And I'd pushed her away.

The anger swelled, filling my heart and lungs.

I knew I was doing the right thing. The *only* thing. I couldn't support her crazy scheme. The idea of her locked up in a federal prison, or shot—or *worse*—by a gang didn't bear thinking about. But that meant she was going to have to watch her sister die. I'd seen the blonde-haired little thing plenty of times around the block and my stomach knotted at the thought of that bundle of energy lying in a hospital bed. I was going to have to see Louise's face as the months passed, watch her change as a piece of her was slowly, agonizingly torn out.

And I was going to have to watch it all from a distance. Hell, she'd hate me. She'd blame me because I didn't help her.

I set my jaw and picked up the pace, stalking along the street towards the target house. The rage was crashing around inside me like a living thing, now.

It needed to be let out.

I reached the house, lifted the sledgehammer from my shoulder, and gripped the shaft in both hands, knuckles white.

This was going to feel good.

The door was steel with a good, solid lock. But I'd done this many times and tonight I was driven by more than just my usual anger. I swung and landed the head of the hammer right at the lock. The steel caved inward like cardboard and the door flew open, bouncing on its hinges. Bright white light streamed out of the doorway and the sidewalk lit up with the shadows of hundreds of swaying marijuana plants. Then two tall, bulky figures were crowding into the doorway.

"Shit," I heard. "It's The Irish."

The one who'd spoken darted back inside, probably to grab a weapon. The other one tried to come out to meet me, which was a mistake. I stepped forward and drove the head of the hammer into his stomach, knocking the air out of him. He staggered back inside and knocked over a table of plants. I followed, moving slowly.

Inside, it was like every grow house I'd ever seen: tables crammed with plants and powerful lights hanging down from the ceiling. The windows were covered in newspaper but they hadn't done much else to hide the fact they were growing there.

I swung the hammer in a whistling arc that sent it through one of the overhead lights, through the plants, through the table and into the floor below. Sparks spat across the room and dirt showered my chest and arms. That section of the room plunged into darkness. The destruction felt good. I was making my mark.

The guy I'd hit was still holding his stomach and groaning. The other one was backing away from me, his face deathly pale. I started to advance towards him, table by table.

"You're right in the middle of Malone's territory," I told them. Then I swung the hammer again splitting the next table in two and sending a light shade skittering away across the room. "That was very fuckin' stupid."

The guy put his hand out towards me, still backing away. "Look," he said quickly. "We can make a deal." I pegged his accent as Central Europe. Serbian or Croatian or something like that—it didn't really matter.

I swung the hammer again, this time going sideways and demolishing the legs of three tables at once. The table tops and plants crashed down and the floor became a carpet of dirt and leaves. I could feel the plants scrunch under my boots as I walked towards him. Everyone I crushed helped me vent a little more of my anger, but it did more than that: it savagely silenced the voices that had been taunting me from inside. *The only thing I'm good at is smashing shit up? Fine. Then watch how good I am.*

"Tell Malone we'll pay!" said the one I'd hit. His voice was a labored croak.

"We'll pay!" agreed the other one. He was still trying to back away, but then he ran out of room, his back against a dresser. I knew he probably had a weapon in there, a knife or a gun. They always do. And they always think they can buy me off. But once someone's hired me, I'm loyal.

The guy next to the dresser finally managed to get a knife out of its hiding place. A big ugly thing with a six inch blade. He held it up in front of him defiantly.

I advanced on him again, the hammer resting casually on my shoulder. "Put it down," I told him.

Instead, he shoved it towards me, slicing at the air. "I'll fucking cut you!" he shrieked, his voice cracking in fear.

I took another step towards him. He pressed back against the dresser, his face deathly pale, swiping the knife in vicious little arcs to keep me away.

I gripped the hammer and started to swing it back....

The knife fell from his fingers. His legs wilted and he slumped to the floor on his ass, his hands up in front of his face. "Please!" he begged.

He'd come to rest with his legs splayed. I swung back the hammer and I saw his mouth drop open in horror as he realized what I was about to do. His scream filled the air as the hammer whistled down right between his legs.

There was a crunch of wood and the head buried itself in the cheap floorboards between his thighs. I'd aimed it so perfectly, the top of the head was just brushing his balls. He stared at the hammer, speechless with relief.

I smash things. Sometimes I have to hurt people. But I'm not a sadist.

My voice was calm, the anger gone. "You ever grow in this

neighborhood again," I told him, "and next time it'll be an inch higher."

I waited for him to nod. Then I grabbed him by the collar and hauled him out into the street. When I'd dragged his friend out as well, I took the little bottle of gasoline from my pocket and emptied it over the debris, then lit a match and threw it in. By the time I was halfway back to my car, the whole house was burning.

I should have felt good. I should have felt like hitting a bar—that was my normal routine, after finishing a job. But I didn't. All I could think about was Louise. I'd vented the anger but the anger, it turned out, was the easy part. Now it had blown away, I could see where it had come from: that throbbing wound inside me that had been left when I let her down.

I couldn't remember the last time I'd given a shit about anyone. But I was really starting to care about this girl.

11

SEAN

I didn't see her again for a few days. Then, one evening, I came down the stairs to find her in the lobby, struggling towards the elevator.

She had two huge white plastic sacks in her arms, gathered to her chest like twin babies, and she was teetering under the weight. Every few steps, the sacks would threaten to slip out of her grasp and she'd have to grab for them again. She was far too preoccupied to notice me.

She just barely managed to make it to the elevator and hit the button. I winced.

"It's broken," I muttered.

She snapped her head around, startled, and dropped one of the sacks. It went *whump* on the floor, narrowly missing her foot. Then, struggling to pick it up, she dropped the other one.

"Let me give you a hand," I said.

She ignored me, crouched, and tried to pick up the first sack. That meant that, as I approached, I was looking down on her and *fuck me*...she was wearing a scoop-neck top and the view I had of her pale cleavage was amazing. Smooth white skin and her breasts were the most perfect shape, just waiting for a hard hand to slide down the front of her top and cup them....

For all my good intentions, I still wanted to bang the hell out of this girl.

She hefted both sacks and stood, her knees trembling a little under the strain. Then she headed towards the stairs.

"Ah, come on," I said disbelievingly. "It's ten floors."

She ignored me and put her foot on the first step. I silently shook my head at her stubbornness...but I had to admire her determination.

She stepped up to the second step. I started up the stairs behind her.

"Please stop following me," she said tightly.

"I'm just walking up the same stairs. It's a free country."

"Weren't you on your way out?"

"I forgot something."

I saw her grit her teeth and then she started a steady march up the stairs, with me one step behind her. At the top of the first flight, she stumbled and nearly dropped both sacks, but recovered. She straightened up and tossed her hair back as if to say, *see? I'm fine!*

She was only a little thing but God, she had spirit.

She marched up the second flight of stairs. Each step was a little slower than the last. By the time she reached the top, she was barely moving.

"I'm going up to nine anyway," I said. "I might as well take one of them."

She was panting but trying not to show it. "What are you now, neighbor of the year?"

I just held out my hands for a sack.

She looked up at the stairwell above her...and with a despondent sigh she pushed a sack towards me. I took it, trying not to make it look too easy.

As I'd thought, the label said it was some sort of chemical fertilizer. I really hoped it was for her house plants.

We moved on, making faster progress now that she could heave her sack in both hands. She managed another four floors before she ran out of steam. I stopped beside her. She was red-faced, now, and her legs were shaky, but she was still doing her best to hide it. She gave me a glare, as if daring me to doubt her. But I could tell she was wiped out.

"When we get to your place, you're going to need your hands to open the door," I said carefully. I wasn't used to this diplomatic shit, but I was doing my best. "Why don't I take the other one?"

She just looked at me with hate-filled eyes...but then her exhaustion overcame her anger and her shoulders slumped. She didn't offer the sack, but she didn't resist when I scooped it out of her arms, either. My forearm accidentally brushed across the soft swell of her breast and I felt my cock go rock hard in my jeans. *Jesus,* this girl did it to me *every single time.* Just looking at her now, with all that shining red hair cascading down her back and those big, green eyes —I didn't care if she hated me. I was imagining pushing her back against the stairwell wall, kissing her hard as I unfastened the belt of her jeans, hooked her panties down, and pressed her thighs apart—

"What?" she asked, bemused.

I realized I was staring at her. I hefted a sack onto each shoulder and set off up the stairs. "Nothing."

When we reached her apartment, she opened the door and then turned around, blocking the doorway. "Just put them down here," she said. "Thank you."

I didn't put them down. I had to know what was going on—was she growing somewhere? "Let me carry them inside."

"I'll be fine. *Thank you.*"

That's when I caught a faint scent wafting from her apartment. "Ah, no," I groaned, my stomach tightening. "You couldn't be that fuckin' daft...."

Before she could protest, I pushed past her. Since she was trying to block the doorway, that meant muscling her out of the way. I tried not to think about how good she smelled, or how soft her skin was as it brushed against mine.

Inside, everything was long drapes and too many cushions—you could tell women lived there. And I've never seen so many things growing: plants in pots, plants on shelves, even plants on the window ledges. But the normal plants weren't what were making the smell.

Right in the middle of the room, arranged in neat rows, were about thirty marijuana plants.

"Are you kidding me?" I said to myself. I dumped the fertilizer sacks on the floor and spun to face her. "Are you *fuckin' kidding me?!* You can't grow *here!*"

She quickly shut the door. "I don't have anywhere else!" She crossed her arms defensively.

"So you do it in *your apartment?* You're going to just haul everything up here: fertilizer, lights, the *plants*...oh, Jesus, you carried those up here! How many people saw you?"

"None! I brought them up one at a time, in boxes."

"And you're going to do that for the other—how many do you need, to make half a million?"

She shifted from foot to foot and looked at the floor. "A few hundred."

I looked around. "There's no space! And what about the smell? I could smell these out in the hallway and that's thirty plants, at the start of the season. When it's two hundred, fully grown, you'll be smelling it a block away!" She stared at the floor. "And what happens when the super comes around to fix a leak? What happens when your sister comes home?"

She finally snapped her head up and glared at me. "If I don't do this, she's not *coming* home!"

We stood there glaring at each other. Those big green eyes were blazing at me, her chest was heaving and her lower lip was stuck out in an angry, sullen pout.

I'd never wanted to kiss a girl so much.

"You can't grow here," I said again. The anger was ebbing away, to be replaced by a sense of impending doom. I wasn't going to be able to talk her out of this. I could see that now. She was going to grow, no matter what I said. She was going to wind up dead or in jail...unless I helped her.

I let out a long sigh and tapped the nearest pot with my foot. "Can you really grow this shit? Do you know what you're doing?"

She tilted her chin to look up at me and her eyes narrowed. Hopeful, but cautious: I'd disappointed her once already. "Yeah," she said at last. "Yeah, I know what I'm doing."

I looked around at the plants and ran a hand through my hair. Then I let out an enormous sigh.

It was the only way.

"Okay," I grunted. "I'll help you."

She bit her lip and nodded quickly, thanking me. I wasn't ready for how that made me feel: like a hot bomb going off in my chest.

"But on one condition," I told her, as gruffly as I could. "We do it my way. You do the growing but when it comes to the other stuff, you do exactly what I tell you."

She swallowed. "I'll do exactly what you tell me," she repeated. In her voice, it sounded like the most erotic thing imaginable.

I had to keep my distance from her. The deeper she got involved with me, the more chance there was I'd destroy her life the way I destroyed everything else. This had to be a temporary alliance, a business relationship. Nothing more.

The next six months were going to be fucking unbearable.

I took a deep breath and sealed my fate. "Alright then," I said. "Let's grow some weed."

12

LOUISE

The next day, after my shift at the garden store, I went to visit Kayley. I'd already decided that I wasn't going to tell her about the plan. If she knew what I was doing she'd start talking sense into me, repeating all the things that were already keeping me awake at night: that I'd get caught, or shot, that people would find out what I'd done and hate us. I wasn't sure I'd be able to so easily push all the protests aside, when they came from her. And even if I did ignore her and go ahead, all she'd have to do would be to threaten to go to the cops and then I'd have no choice but to shut down. She had to stay totally oblivious.

I'd thought I was going to have to fake happiness with Kayley, but it was surprising how easy it was to slip into it. We'd spent so much of our lives together, there was a kind of inertia that the disease couldn't stop. We talked about boys at school and getting her a new backpack; about whether she was allowed to watch that cop show, *Blue & Red*, on Netflix (no, way too much sex and violence); about new Ben and Jerry's flavors we'd like to see.

And then I made the mistake of mentioning last year's vacation. We didn't have a lot of money, but I tried to scrape together enough for us to go somewhere each summer: last year had been camping in the Los Padres forest. Kayley grinned excitedly. "This summer—" she started.

And then she stopped. And her lip trembled.

I pulled her quickly into a hug. "Hey," I said, stroking her hair. She was starting to tremble. "*Hey!* It'll be fine. We'll just make it fall, instead of summer."

She gulped and nodded. But when she eventually pulled back from me, her face was white. "Can we plan it?" she asked.

I looked at her, thrown for a second.

"Can we plan it?" she asked again. "Really plan it?"

And then I understood.

"Yeah," I said. "Absolutely." We got out her phone and started planning where we were going to go, once she'd recovered, and what we were going to do when we got there. Every meal. Every last detail. Because both of us needed to feel like it was really going to happen.

While we were browsing hotels, she suddenly said out of nowhere, "This isn't bullshit, is it?"

For once, I didn't pull her up on her language. "No," I said firmly. I grabbed her hand and squeezed. "It's not bullshit."

And I told myself it wasn't.

I'd been wavering since the talk with Sean the night before. I knew I needed his help and I was glad of it. But getting mixed up with him changed the whole feel of the thing. When it was just me doing it, in my apartment, I could almost kid myself I wasn't doing anything wrong. It felt just like growing any other plant. But as soon as I started working with him, it felt like I would become part of the whole system, a drug grower connected with dealers and enforcers and God knows who else.

I knew it made sense. I knew I couldn't operate in a vacuum if this was going to work. I knew I'd been kidding myself that I could. But none of that made it easier. By even talking to Sean, I was getting myself—and by extension, Kayley—involved in a world I'd always swore I'd stay away from. Sean was everything my folks had warned me about when I was a kid. I'd always been a good girl and men didn't come much worse.

Except...sometimes, when I looked into his eyes, he didn't seem as ruthless as everyone made out. I was still scared of him, but less than when he'd first grabbed my arm, up on the roof. I was having trouble imagining him actually hurting me. But I was having no trouble imagining him doing other things to me.

I flushed and hoped that Kayley didn't notice. Whenever I was around him, my mind slipped into fantasy mode. Each touch of his hands was enough to send me into a downward spiral that always ended with him on top of me...or me on top of him...or him behind me. I was finding that I was permanently, shamefully wet when he was close. No man had ever done that to me.

What was maddening was that sometimes, just occasionally, I'd feel his eyes on me, a lick of heat traveling up and down my body, or he'd narrow his eyes in that certain way, when we were arguing, like he wanted to take me over his knee. I'd get just the tiniest hint that maybe he wanted me too. Then it was gone again, too quickly for me to be sure I hadn't just imagined it. If he hadn't been interested in me, it would have been easy: I could have written off my fantasies as just that, fantasies, and pushed them down inside. But the little hints of interest were just enough to keep them bubbling up to the surface, every damn time.

Hence the wavering. Could I really become a criminal, like Sean? And could I even function, working side-by-side with him for six long months? What if something...*happened?* What if the hints were real and he made a pass at me? Hell, what did I mean, *make a pass?* Sean wasn't the sort of guy who'd *make a pass,* he'd just throw me down on the ground and—

I pressed my thighs together.

Nothing was going to happen. I wasn't going to get involved with him. I wasn't going to bring someone like that into Kayley's life: no way. I'd take cold showers three times a day if I had to. Sean and I would be just business and, at the end of six months, we'd go our separate ways.

I pulled Kayley close and kissed the top of her head. For her, I'd make it work.

After the hospital, I headed straight for Sean's apartment and knocked on his door. A moment later, he opened it...and froze.

"What?" I asked. I looked down at myself. I wasn't wearing anything out of the ordinary, let alone sexy, just a green scoop-neck top and blue jeans.

He glanced away for a second, then back at me. "Nothing. Come in."

He wasn't topless, this time, although the black tank top didn't cover much. It almost made him look bigger, drawing attention to his tight waist and the way he seemed to flare out in an X from that point, up to the broad, muscled chest and shoulders and down to his hips.

"You want coffee?" he asked, and walked through to the kitchen area.

I trailed behind him, a little thrown. I'd never thought about him doing something *normal*, like eating breakfast or drinking coffee. I guess until that moment, I'd only seen him as a criminal, smashing stuff up or picking up women in bars and pounding them into the mattress so loud I could hear it through my floor. I knew now he played guitar. What else did he do? Did he have friends? Family?

He leaned against a wall. I hopped up onto the counter and perched there, then took the mug of coffee he poured for me. "You—" He caught himself and started again. "*We*...are going to need a grow house. Somewhere we can give over entirely to growing."

I nodded and sipped, looking surreptitiously around. I suddenly wanted to know more about him. There were no family photos that I could see...actually, there were no photos at all.

"It's got to be in a neighborhood where people won't ask too many questions," Sean told me, "but close enough that it's not a pain in the arse to drive to, because we're going to be there a lot. And we need to be on the right turf."

"Turf?" I asked disbelievingly. "Like, *West Side Story,* 'you're on our turf,' turf?"

He nodded.

"It's really like that? I mean, I know about gangs and stuff, but...."

"If we grow in someone else's area, our place will be trashed. Or burned. Or reported to the cops. *At best.*"

"At *best?* What's 'at worst?'"

He looked away, suddenly unable to meet my eyes. "It won't happen. I know a neighborhood that's quiet, now. We can grow there."

My stomach churned. From the concern in his eyes, he was worried specifically about *me. God, what the hell am I getting into?* And then I thought about how I'd been going to try to do all this on my own, without six-foot-something of criminal muscle on my side. I winced.

He drained his coffee. "You ready to go house hunting?" he asked.

God, we're really doing this. It wasn't just taking the step of finding a grow house; it was the fact I was heading out with him, trusting him to take me who-knows-where for who-knows how long. Until now, I'd only ever seen him for a few minutes at a time. This was like our first proper date.

He led me downstairs and around the side of our building to an alley. His car was a glossy black 1960's era Ford Mustang and it loomed with almost as much evil, muscular charm as Sean himself.

"You park it *here?*" I asked, looking around. The thing must have been worth a fortune. Without answering, he opened the door. "You don't even *lock it?!*" I couldn't imagine my car lasting an hour if I parked it in a dark alley, and my car is a piece of junk. "Why doesn't it get stolen?"

He just looked at me and then I got it.

It didn't get stolen because everyone knew who it belonged to.

I climbed in. The inside was just as impressive as the outside: old, but every bit of chrome was shining. "I thought you'd drive something European," I mumbled. When he turned to look at me, I said, "You're Irish, right? I mean, originally. You sound Irish."

He nodded. "Born in Ireland. Ended up here." He went quiet for a moment, staring at the steering wheel, and I stayed quiet, too, hoping he'd say more. Just when I thought he wasn't going to, he ran his hand over the dash and said, "It's been with me a long time. I like it because it's American. I wanted to fit in." And then he shook his head, as if he thought he was being stupid.

Before I could say anything, he turned the key and the engine roared into life, the V8 throb echoing off the walls of the alley and booming back to us, making the whole car shake. It was deafening and over-the-top and wonderful. Sean reached down for the gear shift...and everything stopped.

I was suddenly aware of just how close we were, in the car. His hand, gripping the knob of the gear shift, was inches from my knee. He could grab that just as easily and my whole body stiffened minutely as I imagined the warmth of his palm through my jeans, the way his fingers would squeeze hard before he swung his whole body across the car and onto me, a leg pushing between my thighs, his other hand sliding up under my top—

The car didn't move. His hand just stayed there on the gear stick. *What's he waiting for?*

Unless...he was staring at my knee, imagining the exact same thing.

My breathing started to speed up. I told myself I was being crazy. *Of course he's not thinking about grabbing you.* I waited three more breaths and then forced myself to look up at him.

He looked up at the exact same moment and we stared into each other's eyes. The expression on his face made a slow-motion explosion go off in my chest, the embers falling down to ignite a new fire in my groin. He looked...*hungry.* As if he was barely restraining himself from pouncing on me. And he looked angry, as if it was all my fault, as if I was teasing him into it. *But I'm not doing anything!*

I heard the gears shift as he finally moved the stick. Only then did he break my gaze and look out through the windshield. We surged forward.

And drove into hell.

13

SEAN

Normally, driving the Mustang makes me forget everything else. For me, the low rumble of the engine, soaking through the steering wheel and into my body, is better than any massage, no matter how many oiled-up women you throw in.

But that afternoon, as we cruised through the streets, all I could think about was who was sitting next to me. Even when I wasn't looking at her, I was more aware of her than I'd ever been of any woman. I could hear every soft breath she drew, smell the warm, spicy scent of her skin, hear the scrape of her denim against the leather as she shifted position....I'd been in bed with women and thought about them less. And when I *did* glance across at her, pretending I needed to check the door mirror...it was hard as hell to look away again. This girl had done a number on me. Some sort of goddess-of-nature witchcraft, maybe.

It didn't matter. It didn't matter how much I wanted to grab hold of her, drag her onto the back seat and ram those jeans down her legs, push between her thighs and bury myself inside her. It was bad enough that she had to get involved in my world to save her sister. I wasn't going to mess her up even more by letting her get involved with *me*.

Arriving was almost a relief, because it distracted me from thinking about her. I heard her intake of breath as she got her first look at our new home.

I'd taken her to the neighborhood where I'd scared off the Serbians. Malone's turf, and I knew him well enough that I could make that work. He'd insist that we sold through him, but that was cool—we had to sell to someone.

In the daylight, it looked even worse than at night. Single story houses built so cheaply that they started leaking and rotting the second they went up. Chain link fencing, sometimes with barbed wire. No one gave a shit about mowing their lawns here, so every yard was overgrown. Sometimes there'd be a plant in a pot, but it was always yellow and sickly or just plain dead, left behind by some previous resident when they'd seen sense and gotten the hell out.

"God...." said Louise from the seat next to me. Our apartment block was bad, but I don't think she'd realized how much worse things could get. We drove past gang members sprawled in lawn chairs, watching us pass with one hand on their guns. We passed pit bulls and Dobermans who ran at the car, snapping and snarling at us before their chains brought them up short. Many of the houses were boarded up. Of the ones that weren't, maybe half were occupied by the kind of people you really didn't want to mess with. The other half were like fortresses, with bars on the windows and reinforced doors, their occupants living in fear of the first half.

"We really have to grow *here?*" Louise whispered.

"People won't ask questions," I told her. "The cops aren't welcome, here." I pulled over and pointed to a rental sign. "How about that one?" Like all the others, the house had been white once. Now it was every shade from gray to green, bleached by the sun, and stained by mold. The houses on either side were derelict.

Louise looked up and down the street. "Why that one? That's like the worst one on the street."

"We're growing in it, not living in it. We *want* the worst one. The realtor'll be desperate to rent it and they won't care who to." I punched the realtor's number into my phone, then passed it across to Louise. "You call," I said. "They'll trust a woman."

The call gave me another chance to drink her in. It wasn't just that gorgeous face with its delicate cheekbones and that full lower lip. It wasn't just the body with its perfect curves. It was her whole manner: the softness of her voice, the way she looked so serious when she listened to the realtor's reply, the way she nodded and bit her lip as she thought. She was classy, a world away from the women who flung themselves at me in bars. She didn't belong in this place any more than a Ferrari or some exquisitely carved violin.

Louise gave me back the phone. "We can look round it tomorrow morning," she said. Then she shook her head. "But how the hell are we going to pay the rent? I mean, it's cheap compared to my apartment but I'm flat broke. The hospital bills are eating everything up." She looked up at me with big eyes.

I'd been worried about this. It wasn't that I didn't know a solution; it was that I didn't like it.

"You need a loan," I said. "Enough for the rent for six months. That way it's taken care of and you don't have to budget for it every month. And it'll be cheaper if you pay six months up front."

She shook her head again. "I've been calling loan companies since this started. If I take every loan I can get and max out my cards, I can just barely pay the hospital bills Kayley's insurance won't cover. I'm going to be up to my neck in debt. There's no more credit left."

My guts tightened. "Not that sort of loan."

14

LOUISE

Sean drove us to a strip mall that had long since died. At first, it looked as if every business was closed down, their windows boarded or broken. But there was one other car in the parking lot: a gleaming Audi. It was parked in front of a small single story unit, the sort of place that could have housed a dental surgeon or a lawyer, and that place looked as if it might still be open. There was no sign on the door, though, and the blind across the window meant we couldn't see inside. There was no clue as to what sort of business it was.

Sean parked and then sat there staring at the place as if he'd rather walk off a cliff than through the door.

"What?" I asked. "What is this place?"

He looked at me, then looked at the office in front of us. "Just...do as I say in there okay?" I'd never heard his voice so tense. Tense with anger, as if he was having to count to ten, over and over again, just to hold himself in check.

We got out and Sean slammed his door so hard it hurt my ears. He stalked in ahead of me, glaring from side to side like a soldier entering enemy territory.

Inside, there was a waiting room. One guy was sprawled in a chair, flicking through a magazine. Another lounged against the door that led through to the back room. Both of them were in suits, but they didn't look like they belonged in them. They were both heavy-set, bulky with muscle under a thick layer of fat. The sort of guys who barely seem to have necks.

They must have known Sean, because they both sneered at him when he walked in. Their expressions changed when I came in behind him. I felt two pairs of eyes work their way down my body. Crude, but practiced, as if they'd done it plenty of times. I shrank away from them a little. Sean stepped forward aggressively. "Tell him we're here!" he snapped.

The one guarding the inner door knocked, leaned inside and muttered something: *The Irish* and then a lengthy description of me that ended in *-itch*. I saw Sean's biceps swell as his hands tightened into fists. I put a hand on his back, acting on instinct, and saw his lungs fill as he took a slow, deep breath.

The man at the door nodded us inside. Just before we went in, Sean leaned close and whispered in my ear, "Get enough for everything we need. Lights, chemicals, all that shit. Not just the rent. You don't want to have to come back to this guy."

I swallowed and nodded.

The inner office held just a desk, a few chairs and a safe. There were also a few large potted plants, the leaves luxuriantly green and healthy. They made me feel better for a second. Then I saw they were plastic.

Behind the desk, tapping at a laptop, was a man who was...*wrong.*

I knew it as soon as I saw him. Anyone would have: the aura of it pervaded the room like a bad smell. I felt a physical urge to turn around and run. The scariest thing of all wasn't how strong the feeling was, but the knowledge that everyone who came in here must feel the same way...and yet, given that the guy was still in business, they didn't run; they stayed. That's how desperate his customers were.

That's how desperate *I* was.

He wasn't frightening, physically. He was a little overweight and, standing up, he couldn't have been much taller than me. He was maybe fifty, with a bald spot that was growing and gold-rimmed bifocals. His shirt had dark sweat patches under the arms. He looked most of all like someone's dad. There was nothing in his appearance you could pick out that was threatening...and yet being in his presence was almost unbearable. To not run, I had to fight every instinct I had.

I sat down.

Sean sat next to me. "This is Murray," he told me. "He'll give you a loan."

Murray grinned at me. "Absolutely." He kept grinning. He wouldn't stop grinning. It was the sort of smile a wolf might give a young fawn, just before it went for its throat.

"Tell him how much you need," said Sean.

"Twelve thousand dollars," I said shakily.

Murray just kept grinning at me. He looked right into my eyes and—

Guys mentally undress you. That's what they do. Every woman's had it. But this wasn't that. This was deeper and dirtier. More violating. He wasn't just undressing me, or even imagining fucking me. He was sizing me up like a piece of property. Figuring out what I was worth.

He nodded. "Sure," he said. "For how long?"

"Six months," I told him.

He turned to the safe, spun the dial and opened it to reveal stacks of banknotes. He slapped two thick bundles on the desk, then counted out some more bills. "Twelve thousand," he said. "I'll give it to you for six months at four hundred percent."

I stared at the money. It was more cash than I'd ever seen in my life. Everything that we needed to get going. But... *"Four hundred percent?"*

"We'll take it," said Sean. I whipped my head around to gape at him, but he gave me a warning look. Murray chuckled. "We'll take it," said Sean again.

I remembered what he'd said outside, but this was insane. I shook my head, leaned across to Sean and whispered. "Have you any idea how much that is? That's, like, *thirty thousand dollars,* by the time we pay it back!"

"Twenty nine," said Murray smugly.

"That's crazy!" I said. "No way!"

"Just take it," grated Sean. I could hear the rising anger in his voice.

Murray sat back in his chair, still grinning. "I could offer you a much better rate—" he started.

Sean leaned across the desk towards him. "You shut your mouth right now," he said in a low, dangerous tone.

Murray smirked at him. "You want me to call the boys in here?"

"She'll take the four hundred percent!" Sean snapped.

"Don't you think she should at least hear her options? It's *her* name on the loan."

"What?" I asked. "What are my options?"

"There are no other options!" snapped Sean. "Let me handle this!" I could see the muscles of his back standing out through his tank top: he was a heartbeat away from taking a swing.

Murray threw his head back and laughed. He didn't look scared at all. I realized that this was fun to him. He was baiting Sean—he wanted him to lose it and hit him, just so he could have the fun of watching his heavies beat him up. It was going to happen unless I did something. "Sean's right," I said quickly. "Four hundred percent is fine. I'll take it. Where do I sign?"

Murray laughter died away. He shook his head, a man denied his ultimate prize, but he didn't stop grinning. Sean sat down, still glaring at him.

Murray printed off a document and slapped it down in front of me. While he took copies of my driver's license, I read it thoroughly. *Twice.* With Sean looking over my shoulder. But it was just a standard loan agreement, save for the ridiculous interest rate. I signed, my hand shaking, and Murray pushed the cash across the desk to me. I scooped it into my purse.

"See you in six months," said Murray cheerfully. "Or before."

Sean glared at him, pulled me to my feet and swept me out of the room, then out past the two heavies and into his car. Then he just sat there clutching the wheel, knuckles white.

"Sorry," I said quietly. "I should have just agreed as soon as you said." It was hitting me now how close we'd come to disaster. Another few seconds and Sean would have been in a fight with Murray's two heavies. Even if he'd won, we sure as hell wouldn't have gotten the loan.

Sean nodded silently. "It's okay," he muttered at last. "You didn't know."

"What...was it?" I asked tentatively. "What was my other option?" I thought I had a pretty good idea. "Did he want to have sex with me, or have me give him a blowjob or—"

Sean spun around to face me. There was more anger in his eyes than I'd ever seen and his hand crushed the steering wheel so hard I thought he was going to break it. It was intimidating...but not frightening, because it didn't feel as if he was angry *at me.* "No," he said in a strained voice. He turned away and started the engine.

"Worse than that?" I asked hesitantly.

He put the car in gear, but didn't drive off straightaway. "Promise me something," he said. He looked round at me again and this time he didn't look angry: he looked scared. I'd never seen anything scare him before. "Promise me you'll never go back there."

I nodded slowly. "I promise."

We moved off. It took several minutes for the mood to ease, which gave me plenty of time to think about what had just happened. He obviously hated Murray, had hated introducing me to him. But that alone didn't explain how angry he'd gotten at the thought of me being ensnared by the creep. But I knew what would.

I didn't know exactly what Murray had been trying to bargain me into, but it was obviously sexual. What if Sean was protective because he wanted me for his own? Was he expecting to bed me...did he think that was his right, in return for helping me?

What was really scary was...I wasn't sure how I felt about that. I knew I should be outraged but the idea of him fucking me had been scalding my brain since the first time I'd met him. And the darker idea of him fucking me *and me not having a choice about it* was, if I was totally honest with myself, also pretty hot. *I need him,* a little voice inside me murmured. *I'd have to do anything he wanted....*

God, I'm disgusting.

Was that it? God, that *was* it, wasn't it? That totally explained why a bad boy like him would help me. I was going to be his sex slave for the next six months. I turned and stared at him, making it obvious, so that he couldn't help but notice. I wanted to get it over with. I wanted him to know that I knew. I wanted him to just turn around and lay it out for me, and then pull over by the side of the road, order me into the back seat and tell me to take my clothes off and—

He turned around to look at me.

I forgot how to breathe.

"*What?*" he said. "You've been staring at me for five bloody miles."

My heart was hammering away and my face was scalding hot. "I —" I swallowed. "I just—"

"What?"

We stared at each other. *Am I your sex slave?* I nearly blurted. But looking into his eyes, I knew I was wrong. There was lust there, for sure. But there wasn't the edge of cruelty I remembered in Murray's eyes. I couldn't believe he'd force me into sex. I dropped my gaze, my face going scarlet. "Nothing."

A lot of things flooded through me: humiliation, relief...and just a tiny bit of disappointment.

We drove on in silence, my brain working overtime. I'd just remembered something else, from Murray's parking lot. After the anger, there'd been that other look he gave me, when he got me to promise I wouldn't go back there. He'd looked *scared.* There was only one thing that explained him getting angry *and* scared.

He was protecting me.

As crazy as that sounded, the guy whose reputation was built on breaking things and scaring people was trying to shield me from the worst of his world. As if he didn't want me tainted by it. Was that it? I looked across at him but his expression didn't give anything away.

The idea that he felt something for me made my chest go unexpectedly light. Was it possible? *Him?*

"You keep staring at me, I'll make you get out and walk," he muttered.

"Sorry," I said in a small voice. I faced front.

But I kept stealing glances at him the whole way home.

15

LOUISE

"School work?" asked Kayley in dismay. "You're kidding, right?"

I shook my head and handed her another pile of worksheets. "You're missing a lot of school and you're going to be missing a lot more. I want to make sure that big brain of yours gets a workout." I smiled and tried not to stare at how pale she looked, how sickly. I knew it was just the side effects, that the chemo was doing her good, long term. But part of me wanted to just rip the needle out of her arm and whisk her home.

Kayley studied a pack of worksheets on the Civil War. "I hate you," she muttered.

I leaned in and gave her a hug in response. It went on a lot longer than I'd intended: I just couldn't let go. "Okay," she said at last, her voice muffled by my hair. "Enough, already."

I let her go. But right at the last second, as I pulled back, she awkwardly clung to me again.

"You okay?" I asked, keeping my voice carefully neutral. "Like, the food's okay and everything?"

"Sure. Except they only have lime jello. You know how I feel about lime jello."

I looked into her eyes and I could see the fear there. But I could also see the determination: she really, really didn't want to break down and cry and she begged me with her eyes to help her.

I nodded, stood up and slung my purse over my shoulder. "Okay. I'll see what I can do about the lime jello. And do the worksheets. When you get back from Europe, I want you to slot straight back in as a grade-A student, you hear me?"

She made a big show of sighing and rolling her eyes but she looked relieved...just as I'd intended. I wanted to convince her—okay, convince both of us—that this was just temporary, a glitch. That before the end of the year she'd be a normal teen again, heading back to school.

Because the alternative...that didn't bear thinking about.

The next morning, we went to look round the grow house. Just as Sean had said, the realtor was desperate to rent. In less than an hour, the paperwork was complete, we had handed over the money, and we were standing holding the keys in the middle of the empty house.

"We can fit about eight tables in here," I said, pacing out the living room. "And another two in the kitchen—I want to keep the sink free so I can hook up water lines. And another four in each bedroom..." I was muttering mostly to myself. "It's almost a pity there are walls. It'd be easier if it was one big space, like a warehouse."

Sean nodded. "I was thinking the same thing," he said. "Should be easy enough." He knocked experimentally on a wall.

I gaped at him. "I wasn't *serious!* We can't knock the walls down, we're renting this place! There are rules in the lease! We're not even meant to redecorate!"

He blinked at me. "I reckon we're not meant to grow dope, either."

"But...what happens in six months, when we move out?"

He tilted his head to one side and he gave me a look that told me just how naive I was being. And yet it didn't feel patronizing at all. It felt as if he thought my innocence was adorable. "You let me worry about that," he said.

Fine. This was why I'd asked for his help in the first place, after all, because he knew all this stuff. I checked out the windows. "We'll need to do something to stop the light getting out."

"A lot of people cover them with newspaper," said Sean. "Or use blackout blinds. But it looks obvious. Who has their blinds shut all day, every day?"

"So what do we do?"

For once, he looked almost...*shy,* like he was admitting a weakness. "I've got this idea," he muttered. "Might not work. But I'm gonna give it a crack. Okay?"

"Of course," I told him.

He nodded quickly and went off to his car to get his sledgehammer. I gathered up the few items the previous owners had left us: some scarlet, fake velvet drapes in the living room, a saucepan with no handle I found in a kitchen cupboard and a solitary coffee mug. A few moments later, the demolition began.

I knew what he was famous for, of course. I'd imagined, plenty of times, how he must look swinging the thing. But imagining isn't the same as seeing...or hearing.

At first, it was fine. I stood there open mouthed as he tore through the place. Huge chunks of plasterboard went flying, wallpaper flapping at their edges. Cinder blocks shattered, chunks of stone and clouds of dust arcing out across the room. The muscles of Sean's back bulged and flexed hypnotically under his tank top as he swung, his tight core powering him round. I couldn't take my eyes from his hard ass as it stood out under his jeans.

But as he worked, the mood changed.

It wasn't that he got angry. That would have been okay. Everyone likes to unleash some healthy rage when they do something like knock down a wall. But you do that with a silly grin on your face— you yell and scream and it's cathartic, but then you laugh at yourself.

Sean wasn't laughing. I could see the rage throbbing through his body, see it in the way he gripped the hammer and the way he pounded it into the walls with single-minded determination. It pulsed out of him like a heat haze and, every time the hammer struck, it reverberated through the room and soaked into every surface. This wasn't just demolition; Sean was ripping through the house the way a hurricane rips through a town, changing it forever.

I called out—I'm not even sure why. Maybe to get him to slow down. Maybe so I could tell him I was going to wait outside. Mainly, though, I just wanted to check that I could stop him, that he was still in control. And immediately, I wished I hadn't.

Because he didn't stop.

Either he didn't hear me or he was so used to ignoring the pleas of the people whose home or business he was destroying that he tuned me out. The air was full of choking dust, now. Sean stopped for a second to peel his tank top from his gleaming body and I wanted to yell again, but I was too busy coughing. Through the dust, I saw something: I'd thought he had no tattoos aside from the sleeve, but now I saw there were some on his back: twisting black lines that fanned out like flames from between his shoulder blades. In the circular space where all of the lines converged, there was another tiny tattoo no bigger than my thumbnail, and it didn't match the style of the lines at all, as if it had been drawn at a different time. A shamrock.

The destruction started up again and this time I got really scared. It wasn't just that he was angry, that the destruction was letting something dark and dangerous pour out of him like a river. It was that he was enjoying it. His lips were drawn back in a tight, hard smile, a look of savage victory. By destroying, he was winning—or he believed he was. The sight of it chilled me: I'd never seen anyone take such pleasure in carnage before. *And this is the guy I've teamed up with. The guy I've let into my life.* "Sean!" I yelled between choking gasps.

No response. He'd completely forgotten I was there. I was starting to really choke on the dust, now, my fear was making me hyperventilate and that was making the coughing worse. Sean was between me and both doors and I didn't dare get in his way. I had to snap him out of it. I darted forward through the clouds of dust to bang on his shoulder and—

Too late, I saw the head of the hammer swing back towards my head—

I let out a cry as the iron head came straight towards my face, heavy and fast enough to shatter bone. I ducked and twisted, losing my balance, and slapped Sean on the shoulder, all at the same time. The hammer whistled past my face close enough that I felt the waft of air against my eyelashes, and I wanted to throw up. Then I thudded into his wide, solid back, my feet skidded between his legs, and I was on my back on the floor, looking up at him.

He turned and looked uncomprehendingly down at me. The raw emotion in his face made my chest tighten: not just anger but hate and shame, all spilling out of him. My fear of him eased a little. *What the hell's going on inside him?* I had this overwhelming urge to tell him *it's okay.*

And then he came back to himself. His jaw dropped open and he flung the hammer down on the floor and fell to his knees over me. "Ah, Christ! Did I hit you?" The anger in his eyes evaporated in a second, to be replaced by sick fear. He started patting my body. One hand stroked my head. "Did I hit you?" he asked again.

I shook my head, panting at how close he'd come. "Not quite," I croaked, and coughed on the dust. We were both covered in it and more was settling on us as the air stilled. It clung to the sweat on his body, painting him gray, until he looked like a huge stone statue hulking over me. I tried to speak again but the dust had caught in my throat and I couldn't stop coughing.

He swept his hands under me and scooped me up, then marched over to the back door and out into the sunlight.

I drew in a huge gulp of warm, clean air, then another and another. The fear eased along with my breathing. And then he was setting me down on my back on the warm, sun-drenched grass.

He knelt beside me and took my cheek in one palm, using his thumb to rub away some of the dust. "Jesus, I'm sorry," he said. "I didn't mean to—" He looked off into the distance and his hands curled into fists. I could see the anger rising in him again, this time at himself.

I reached up and took his hands in mine, curling my fingers around his fists. "It's okay," I said. "You just scared me a little."

He suddenly looked down into my eyes and I saw the fear and shame there. As if scaring me was the last thing he wanted. Then he jumped up and started to walk away, slapping the dust from his clothes.

I got to my feet and ran after him. "It's just a job," I said. "I mean, I get it. You have to be scary. Scaring people's what you do. I just hadn't seen it before."

He didn't turn around, but he shook his head. "It's not just a job," he muttered. "You know that." He glanced over his shoulder at me. "You saw that."

I swallowed and nodded. It was quiet, in the long grass behind the houses, and the air was thick with the smell of wildflowers. No kids played on the street and few people had a reason to drive through the neighborhood so there was almost no traffic. If we closed our eyes, we could have been in a meadow somewhere. "Maybe you don't have to be like that," I said.

He turned and spread his arms wide, showing me his huge, dust-caked body. "This is what I am!" he snapped. "This is *who* I am! I break stuff. I scare people. I don't know how to do anything else." He stalked away.

"Maybe you could learn," I offered to his retreating back. But I had no idea if he even heard me.

I gave him some time to cool off before I went back inside the house. Now that the dust had settled—literally—I saw how cavernous the space was. You walked in the door and did a double-take at how far away the opposite walls were.

We needed supplies, so we drove to the nearest hardware store, still covered in dust. We barely talked on the way, Sean keeping his eyes on the road and me chewing nervously on my lip. Nearly hitting me had changed things: I was at arm's length again...maybe for good.

At the store, we filled three shopping carts with stuff: the security doors I understood, but Sean bought wood, wallpaper, even window blinds. I didn't get it: were we going to redecorate?

Back at the house, Sean went to work and I spent the rest of the day planning out the rows of plants: how could we pack the most in without overcrowding them? I got so absorbed in it, it was evening before I looked up and saw what he'd done.

Each of the house's windows was now covered by a floor-to-ceiling box of false walls, like a tiny room only a few feet wide. I frowned, not understanding at first. Then I saw that the wallpaper he'd bought was gone. "Wait," I said, pointing, "from the outside, does it look...?"

He turned to look at me and I saw that the brooding anger had faded away. I even got a hint of a smile. "Let's go see."

We went outside and looked in through the nearest window. It looked great: through the half-closed blinds we could see the wallpapered wall a few feet beyond...and nothing else. There was no hint that the house was now just an empty shell inside, and there would be no way anyone could see a plant. "That's brilliant!" I told him.

He shrugged self-consciously but I could tell he was proud. "Ah, it's not."

I threw an arm around his shoulders and pulled him close to my side. "Are you kidding? It's *so* much better than just papering over the windows. That'd look suspicious. This looks...*normal.*"

He shrugged again, but he allowed himself a tiny smile. It looked great on him...but, at the same time, it made my chest crush inwards: I got the haunting impression that it was the first time anyone had ever praised him for anything.

I wanted to say: *See? You can build stuff, not just smash it.* But I didn't know how to put it into words. It didn't help that I was suddenly distracted. Now that I'd pulled him up against me, I was very aware of the hard press of his body, all the way from shoulder to ankle, and how it would only take the smallest twist of our bodies to be pressed thigh to thigh, chest to breast, lips to lips. He didn't say anything, but his shoulder tensed under my hand. I felt him turn his head and my scalp prickled as I felt him looking down at me. If I lifted my head and looked up into his eyes, would something happen? Would he grab me and—

It was all too much, too fast. I dropped my hand from his shoulder and stepped quickly away. "We should get on," I croaked. I walked back into the house and forced myself not to look back. If I looked back and he was looking at me...I wasn't totally sure I'd be able to control myself.

Back inside, he swept up the piles of dust and debris and I pretended to be measuring for the tables. Inside, I was going over and over what had just happened. Had we been seconds away from a kiss? I was simultaneously giddy with the thought of it and berating myself for even thinking of getting involved with someone like him.

When I'd got myself together, Sean was installing heavy metal security doors to replace the existing ones. "Do we really need those?" I asked, worried.

He looked at me seriously and nodded. My stomach flipped over. It was a reminder of what we were getting into. People were going to want to break in. Steal stuff. Hurt us.

And he understood those people because he was one of them. *Jesus, and I'm standing here fantasizing about him.* I crushed the feelings down inside. *Get it together!*

Another hour and the house was ready: one big, empty, secure space. It was perfect...but with the windows boxed off, all the light was artificial. And with the security doors in place, it felt more industrial than homely.

That's what this is, I reminded myself. *A factory. A factory for making money.* I'd be hunkered down in here for most of the next six months. I glanced around, suddenly claustrophobic despite the space. Then I looked down at my dust-covered, sweaty body. "I wish we'd kept the bathroom," I muttered, thinking out loud.

Sean looked up. "We did."

He led me down to the end of the house, where he'd made another of the tiny rooms to cover the bathroom window. He'd almost halved the bathroom's size, but he'd managed to keep the toilet, shower stall and sink. There was no door, so he had to move aside one of the wood panels to let me in. "Thought you'd want somewhere to wash," he told me.

I looked from the shower to him in astonishment, then delight. Having a bathroom would make the place a lot more comfortable. And I needed a shower right now—my hair was matted with dust and it was caked on my skin and even inside my clothes. But... "There aren't any towels," I realized.

"There are curtains," said Sean. "From the lounge."

I looked at him blankly.

"The...*drapes*," he said, having to grope for the American word. "From the *living room*." He unfolded one of the big, scarlet drapes and threw it to me.

I didn't need telling twice. I got inside the tiny room and waited while he propped the wood panel back in place. There was almost no floor space: I had to undress in the shower stall and hang my clothes on the sink. But it didn't matter: sluicing the dust from my body felt amazing. The water turned gray for a while, there was so much dirt, but soon I was clean and luxuriating under the spray, letting it beat on my tired shoulders.

I started to think about Sean. I'd already had to rework my opinion of him countless times. Just days ago, he'd been the scary guy in the elevator, the notorious thug everyone avoided. I'd seen too much to believe that's all he was. I'd caught glimpses of who he used to be...or maybe who he had the potential to be. And I liked that person.

But none of that changed who he was. Seeing that cold, deadly anger in full force as he'd torn the house apart really had shaken me. It didn't feel as if he'd ever hurt *me*...the horror in his eyes when he'd nearly clipped me with the hammer told me that. But he hurt other people...plenty of them. And he was a criminal, part of a world I barely knew.

I froze. *That isn't true anymore, is it?* I'd leapt right into that world. Technically, now, *I* was the criminal. I was the one growing half a million dollars worth of weed. He was just hired help.

Was that why I was drawn to him? Was I just trying to find support, or prove to myself that his world wasn't all bad? But even before deciding to grow, I'd been attracted to him. I'd lain in bed, imagining our bodies twisting together. I'd thought about how it would feel to kiss my way across the broad expanse of his hard, solid chest, to run my hand down his pecs, sliding down over his side and then over his abs, a slalom course that ended at his cock. I'd thought about how he'd grunt at the touch of my hand and shove me savagely back on the bed. Those powerful thighs of his, hard with muscle, levering my legs apart. His body pushing between them, God, no chance of fighting back at all, even if I wanted to. His hands on my shoulders, pressing me down into the bed, as he—

I registered a strange sighing sound and a change in the light, but it wasn't until I heard the crash that I turned around.

The wood panel Sean had propped in place had toppled over and was now lying on the floor. That meant one whole side of the bathroom was missing, and Sean and I were standing facing each other, both of us gaping at the other one.

Except he was dressed. And I was naked and dripping wet and—

Oh Jesus, my hand was between my thighs.

We both stared, our mouths open and our lips moving soundlessly. And then Sean's eyes narrowed. The look he gave me made every inch of my exposed skin blaze, as if I was standing naked in front of a furnace. And as it soaked into me, I reacted: I felt my nipples tighten and a deep, hot ache explode in my groin, turning instantly to slick wetness. I couldn't move. Two, three seconds ticked past, and with every shuddering breath I took, I could feel him drinking me in, burning my image into his mind forever.

And I liked it. I'd never been looked at that way before: like I was a painting or a statue, like I was something he could look at forever and still never get enough.

Then I suddenly came to my senses and twisted away from him. Covering myself wasn't so easy: my makeshift towel was on the sink and there was barely room to open the shower door to get it. For a few seconds I had to stand there with my naked ass towards him, one arm hooked around the door, flailing for the drape, while the other clutched at the dial to turn off the water. Only when I finally had the scarlet drape wrapped around me did I turn around. I wanted to see if he'd averted his eyes.

He hadn't. He was staring at me transfixed. I gulped, aware that the drape was clinging to my body as tightly as any Hollywood red carpet dress.

Sean walked slowly towards me, lifted the panel and slotted it back into place. His eyes never left mine, not until the false wall finally separated us again.

I let out a long, shaky breath and slumped against the wall of the shower stall. I knew I had to dry myself, put my clothes on and get out of there. I knew I had to walk out there as if nothing had happened so we could get back to being business partners. I knew I had to dunk all these feelings back under the black waters of my mind and hold them there.

I knew all that. But for long minutes, I just stood there staring at the panel Sean had put back in place...and wishing it would fall again.

When I finally got myself under control, I threw on my clothes, said goodbye to Sean and almost ran to my car, then sat behind the wheel shaky and weak. *That was just the first day in the grow house,* I thought. *How the hell am I going to manage six months?*

16

SEAN

I woke up and frowned.

Most of the time, I don't remember my dreams and that's a blessing. There's bad shit down in the depths of my memory, rooted in too firmly to ever extract. When I'm awake, I can mostly keep it contained, bricking it up behind sheer willpower. A little of it always escapes, a toxic drip, drip, drip of blackness that sours my mind and feeds my anger, trying to lure me into losing control completely. But mostly, by day, I'm its master. At night, things reverse. It lurks in the dark places, waiting for me to drop into sleep so it can grab the other me. The scared kid.

At four AM in the darkness, we're all scared kids.

I don't remember what happens, but sometimes I wake up in sweaty, twisted sheets and that wall I built is lying in ruins, my past so close that I can reach out and touch it. And it takes an hour of wailing away on the guitar or smashing someone's place to pieces before I feel like me again.

This time, though, I wanted to remember. This dream had been *great.*

This time, I'd dreamt of her.

There were after-images of her in my mind, the sort you think will be clearer if you close your eyes and focus on them, but the more you concentrate the more they break up and blow away. I could still feel sunshine on my skin...yeah, there'd been lots of sunshine, streaming through that red hair of hers. And her legs...long, graceful legs, bare under a long skirt. She'd been barefoot. Barefoot in a fucking meadow, that's where we were. And I'd been...we'd been...

I screwed my eyes shut, but it was gone. I cursed hard enough to strip the paint from the walls.

It wasn't like I should need dream-Louise. I had plenty of images of real-Louise filed away in my head: her in that green scoop-neck top, for one, all that soft, pale cleavage and her bewildered by all my staring. Her lying in the grass, beautiful even covered in dust, my heart in my throat because I'd come so close to killing her.

But mainly, her in the shower.

I'd seen just a taste of her and it was maddening. Smooth skin, milky-white and gleaming with water. Her breasts, the ones I'd hungered after so badly, were just perfect. The water had slid down over the soft globes like it was caressing them, making them shine and glisten, dripping from her rosebud nipples. I've never wanted to fill my hands with a woman's breasts so much. I could already feel them, wet and heavy and soft under my palms, the nipples rubbing across my fingertips.

Her stomach, soft and smooth and with that cute little navel I wanted to kiss and lick until she squirmed against me. She had that gorgeous womanly shape: tight on the waist, flaring out at the hips. And between her thighs....

I'd been imagining what lay between her thighs ever since I first caught sight of her. Every man wonders, when they see a redhead. When that board had dropped and I'd seen her, my eyes had dropped to her groin in less time than it takes to blink...but my view had been hidden. By her hand.

I still wasn't sure what to make of that part. There was a chunk of my ego that wanted her to have been playing with herself, thinking about me. But I knew it was more likely she'd just clapped her hand there to hide herself.

It didn't matter. Getting so close to seeing every part of her, even that most secret one, just made my cock even harder for her. I needed her naked and under me like I needed to breathe...and yet I had to keep fighting that urge.

That was why I tried to hang on to those images of dream-Louise. Because my dreams were the only place I could be with her.

We spent the day setting up the banks of lights. I'd told Louise to spend the extra money to get low-energy LED bulbs: I'd known plenty of growers get caught when the power company got suspicious about the huge amount of power they were drawing. We hung them from the ceiling so they pointed down at the tables. When we switched them on, the tabletops became desert-sun bright.

That evening, the plants arrived. Louise had very carefully reached out over the internet and struck up a friendship with some guys from the Netherlands, talking about gene lines and heritage and cloning and other shit that made them all sound like they were evil scientists in a sci-fi movie. They'd hooked her up with their guy in the US and he'd agreed to sell her a batch of seedlings. He pulled his van into our garage, opened the doors and we were staring our future in the face.

"That's it?" I asked. "They're tiny."

"They're tiny *now*," Louise told me. "Wait till they're near the ceiling. This place'll be a jungle."

I had my hammer ready in case the deal turned bad, but as soon as the two of them got talking, I knew we had nothing to worry about. This guy was like her: a plant nerd. This was the science end of the business, where everything was happy and fun. It was down at the other end, the selling, where things got ugly. Some time soon, I was going to have to introduce Louise to that part of it, too, and the thought of that made my stomach twist into knots.

I helped Louise carry the trays of tiny plants, each one only the size of my finger, through to the house. Louise carefully lifted the first plant from the tray, set it down on a table and hunkered down to look at it. "So fragile," she said. She was so close to it that the words made the leaves tremble.

I squatted down on the other side of the table, because I figured I should get a look at the core of our new business. Our faces were maybe a foot apart, the tiny seedling rustling in the breeze whenever one of us talked. We had to practically whisper, or we'd knock the damn thing over. "That's going to be worth thousands of dollars?" I asked.

"That guy's stuff is the *best*. Trust me, he's an undiscovered talent. I did my homework and this strain has *so* much potential to just pump out THC." Her gaze flicked to me. "THC's the stuff that—"

"—gets you high. I'm not a *complete* fuckwit."

She blinked. "I didn't think you were. Sorry, I just—"

I had to interrupt her again, because if she kept being nice to me I was going to lean across and do something I regretted. "If it's such hot shit, how come we can afford it?"

She grinned: a slow, satisfied smile that I *really really hoped* was the same one she got after she'd just come her brains out. "Because it's so tough to grow. You need to treat it really carefully and get everything just right...*but,* if we do, I think it can be great. Like, off-the-charts great."

"And you can get it just right." A statement, not a question.

She nodded. Then blushed. "I mean, you know, the stuff I did in college gives me a big advantage. Most of the growers don't have that background—they're just fumbling around in the dark. It's not *me*. I'm nothing special."

I just stared at her. She honestly believed that. She flushed again under my gaze, but I couldn't look away.

"I should start planting," she said at last. "I've got a lot to do."

I moved back a little from the table and watched as she took the first pot, filled it with a carefully-measured mix of soils and fertilizers, and transferred the seedling into it. There was something incredibly restful about watching her work: the seriousness of her expression as she measured, the total joy in her face as she sunk her pale fingers into the dark earth. I could tell she was completely absorbed—I'd ceased to exist. And that meant I could watch her as much as I wanted. I could take in the hanging curls of her copper-colored hair as they bounced against her cheeks and the smudge of dirt she left on her nose as she brushed them out of the way. I could watch her creamy breasts bounce and sway in her scoop-neck top as she leaned over the plant and imagine running my hands over her ripe, curving ass through the tight denim of her jeans.

I would have happily watched her all night but, after the fifth plant, she suddenly remembered I was there and said, "You don't have to stay. I'll be here for hours."

I nodded and headed for the door. I knew the smart thing to do was to leave—I was too into her, too close to losing control and doing something stupid. I put my hand on the door handle. And then, out of nowhere, I heard myself say: "Or...you could show me what to do and I could help."

17

LOUISE

He looked as surprised as I felt, as if he hadn't realized he was going to say it until the words were out. We stared at each other for several seconds.

"Okay," I said at last. I'd brought a couple of stools from my place just so we had something to sit on. I pulled up one for myself and sat down, then pulled up one for him right next to me.

Sean walked around the tables and sat down. We were so close, we were almost touching.

I slid a seedling and a pot along the table to him, the scrape of plastic on wood very loud in the silent room. "Start by measuring out the mix," I told him. "One cup of this, half a cup of this, one cup of this." I demonstrated. *Why are my hands shaking?*

"Make a hole with your fingers," I said, pressing two fingers into the cool, soft earth. Next to me, I watched him form two fingers into a probe. "You probably just need one finger," I mumbled. "Your hands are big."

He eased his thick finger into the soil. I swallowed.

"Is that deep enough?"

"Yes. Plenty deep enough."

He stopped.

"Now ease out your seedling and carefully clear most of the dirt away from the roots."

He lifted out his seedling and started to knock at its roots with a finger.

"Gently! You don't want to damage the roots."

He frowned. "I'm not good at gentle." He turned a little and caught my eye. My heartbeat had turned into a bass drum boom that shook my whole body—slow, but gathering speed.

"I'll help you," I said. I stood, scraping my stool on the floor, and stepped behind him, putting my arms around him so that I could guide him. But immediately, I realized my mistake: he was so big, I couldn't easily reach around. Not without getting very, very close.

Too late now. I stepped right up to him. My pubis grazed his back through my jeans and I caught my breath. As I leaned forward, my stomach and then my lower chest and finally my breasts made contact with his back. I slid my head next to his, our cheeks inches apart. I could smell the clean, outdoor smell of him, like the air after a storm, and feel his back rise and fall beneath me as he breathed.

"Just brush at it," I told him, trying to focus. The roots were like tiny hairs and I was staring at his thick, powerful fingers as they touched them. I stroked the roots with my own fingers to demonstrate. Every time I moved, even the slightest amount, my breasts shifted against his back. I could feel my nipples hardening, pressing out through my bra and top to rasp against his muscles. He tried brushing again and immediately, I was hypnotized by the sight of his two big fingertips stroking along the roots— "Careful," I mumbled. "It's really sensitive."

"Sensitive?" His voice was a rumble I felt through my whole body.

I flushed. "Delicate."

He carefully put the seedling down.

My voice sounded almost drunk. "Why are you—"

He twisted around, his back and then his front sliding across my breasts. And suddenly his lips were almost brushing mine.

18

LOUISE

Even that almost-contact was enough to send ripples of excitement straight through my body, all the way to my toes. I hadn't fully understood how much I'd been needing him—aching for him—until that second. My whole body stiffened against him and I felt the heat of him throbbing into my groin and breasts.

I'm not sure if he leaned closer or I did. We were now so close I could feel his breath against my lips and with every slow exhale I sank deeper into an intoxicating darkness where anything could happen.

And it hit me that I couldn't let it.

I staggered sideways, away from him. We stared at each other and I saw the dark, animal lust in his eyes.

"I have to go," I croaked. And ran.

19

SEAN

*S*hit.

I was still reeling from the almost-kiss. My whole body was coiled and tense with the need to grab her, hold her.

Another half second and I would have been kissing her. Another ten and I would have slammed her down on the table and torn that scoop neck top right down the middle, baring her to me.

But now everything had gone wrong. Before I could even get up, Louise had slipped out of the door and off into the night. The thought of her out there, alone, was what finally gave me enough of a jolt to shake off my stupor and jump up—so fast I knocked over the table. The seedlings we'd been so carefully planting crashed to the floor, spilling fantails of soil.

Outside, I looked up and down the street but there was no sign of her. *Shit!* She didn't have her car with her—I'd driven us here, today. What if someone had been watching the house and had grabbed her when they saw her alone? What if she'd run into some gang who didn't know she was with me? What if—

On my second check of the street, I finally saw her: walking on the dark side of the street where the streetlights were broken. Her natural reaction was to hide herself away, to disappear, not realizing that just put her in more danger. Out here in the darkness, her pale skin made her look even more vulnerable. We needed to talk...but first, I needed to make sure she was safe.

I raced across the street and caught up with her. "Louise!"

Her shoulders tensed but she kept walking. That's when I grabbed her arm.

She yelped, pulled up short and spun around, eyes wide with fear. My heart leapt into my throat. I didn't want to be that guy—not with any woman but especially not with her. Both of us looked at my big, clumsy hand encircling her slender arm. I opened it, releasing her, but now there was a dirty mark on that smooth, milky skin from my soil-covered fingers.

"You can't walk home alone," I muttered. "It's not safe."

She was breathing fast, looking up into my eyes with an expression I couldn't read. *You're safe with me,* I wanted to say. *I swear, you're safe with me.* But I'd just proved she wasn't, hadn't I? I'd betrayed her trust and tried to kiss her, and she'd run, just like I'd always feared.

"I can take care of myself," she said, her voice quavering a little.

"Not in this neighborhood!" It came out harsher than I'd meant it to. "Come on, I'll drive you home." I took a step back towards the house but she stayed stubbornly where she was. "For fuck's sake!" I snapped, "Let me take care of you!"

We stood there staring into each other's eyes. I felt my gaze soften. She glanced away and then cautiously back at me, as if wondering whether she could trust me again. *Jesus, I'm an idiot. What have I done?* I wanted her more than ever, but seeing her out here in the street had brought back all my fears. What if she decided she needed to go it alone, after this? I thought of what was coming: meeting a dealer, protecting the crop as it grew. She'd last a week, without me. *Just please let her come with me,* I offered up to whoever was listening. *I swear I'll never try anything again.*

Louise let out a long breath...and started walking back towards the house. I fell in beside her, my legs shaky with relief. I was only just realizing how much I'd come to care for her—it overpowered everything else, even the need to kiss her, to touch her, to have that luscious body twisting and writhing against mine.

I quickly locked up the house and we climbed into my car. We didn't talk at all on the way to our apartment block, or on the way up the stairs, or even when we got to her front door. As she went inside, I opened my mouth to say something...but I couldn't find any words. I was replaying the nearly-kiss over and over in my head. I'd thought she'd wanted it but then she'd run. Had I driven her away forever? Did she hate me?

The door closed behind her. *Fuck. I wish I knew what she was thinking.*

20

LOUISE

I pressed my back against the door. I had no freaking idea what to think. God, I'd wanted him so bad. I hadn't let myself admit how much until he nearly kissed me. It had been building for days and I was at least as much to blame for it as him. I'd done the one thing I'd been promising myself I wouldn't. I'd jeopardized everything. I couldn't get involved with someone like him. I was just a tourist in his world: six months and I'd be out, back to my normal, safe world with Kayley. I couldn't bring him into my life...however good it felt. We needed to somehow get back to being just business partners.

Then I looked down and saw the dark mark on my arm where he'd grabbed me. Something about it made the heat swell inside me and then plunge down to my groin. The essence of what he was, brutal and dangerous, was what kept me backing away from him. But it was exactly what drew me in, too. Jesus, what if I *hadn't* pulled away? Would I have wound up on his lap, feeling the hard press of his cock through his jeans? Would he have tipped me back, my hair hanging down to the floor as he tongued my breasts?

I pressed my ass hard against the door, imagining him kissing me...then his hands cupping my breasts and squeezing, then sliding down my body...one hand going under my jeans and then my panties like *that,* stroking through the hair and the sensitive skin beneath, leaving me gasping. And then further down, his thick wrist stretching out the front of my jeans, those strong fingers hooking underneath, finding me, parting me, like *this*—

There was a loud knock at the door. Since I had my whole body grinding up against it like a cat in heat, the vibration went right through me. I jumped away from it, pulling my hand from my jeans and panting in shock. I put my eye to the door viewer and—

Oh Jesus, he's still there! He'd been standing there the whole time!

I felt my face heating up. Had he heard? Had I moaned something? Had I been banging my hips against the door?

I slowly opened the door a hand's width, putting on my best poker face. But as soon as I looked into his eyes, I went weak inside. I thought he was going to push open the door and grab me right there. *God, does he know what I was just doing?*

He seemed to wrestle himself under control. When he spoke, his voice was carefully neutral. "What time do you want to start, tomorrow?" he asked. "We've got a lot of planting to do."

I just stared at him.

His eyes said *please.*

He'd realized it had been a mistake. And he wanted me to know that he knew. He was trying to tell me that it was all going to be okay, that he would keep his distance.

I nodded slowly. "Okay," I said. Then, "Two. I'll meet you there."

I saw the relief on his face...but I could see the frustration there, too, only just outweighed. "Okay," he said.

I closed the door. We were back to just business partners, exactly as I'd wanted.

So why did it feel like I was having something ripped away from me?

21

LOUISE

April

The days quickly became a routine. I'd visit Kayley at the hospital so I could be with her for her chemo. I sat beside her as the chemicals flowed into her body, trying to distract her with books and videos and chat. I held her hair out of the way and stroked her back while she threw up. I sat there silently raging, wishing I could *do* something, wave a wand, and magically make her better. And when the visit was over, I never wanted to leave. I had to keep telling myself that the most useful thing I could do was grow the crop, make the money, and get her to Switzerland. So I'd drive to work, do my shift, then drive to the grow house.

There, I'd check every plant in turn. The seedlings were growing steadily, soaking up the light from the huge banks of lights and drinking in the filtered water and carefully-measured fertilizer I gave them. Monitoring them and adjusting the mixes took hours but I found I relished the challenge. I even rigged up sensors to send a text message to my phone if the temperature got too high or too low. This was the one thing I could do to really help my sister, the one shot she had. So, goddamn it, I was going to do it right.

Then, about a week into April, the hospital called and told me I needed to get there *now*. I rushed over there, tires squealing, heart in my mouth.

Dr. Huxler stopped me outside Kayley's room. "I'm sorry," he said. "I didn't think it would start this soon. Normally it takes at least a couple of weeks, but the treatments we're giving her are so aggressive...."

"What? What's happened?"

Then we heard a sob from inside Kayley's room. I pushed past him and opened the door.

Kayley was sitting up in bed, her eyes red and her lip trembling. She must have been crying continuously, all the time the hospital was summoning me and all the time I was racing across the city. I could actually see the wet patch down the front of her nightshirt where the tears had soaked through. And she was surrounded by—

Oh Jesus.

I ran to her and pulled her into my arms. Little locks of blonde hair bounced off the bed and onto the floor.

"I look—" She was too upset to get a sentence out. She had to force the words out between big, gulping sobs. "I look like a *freak!* And—And the rest's—It's all going to fall out—"

I shushed her and pulled her even tighter against me. What could I tell her? That it wasn't so bad? That it was temporary? "We'll figure something out," I told her.

"A *wig?* I don't want a wig!"

I hugged her close. "I know. I know you don't." I patted her back. "We'll get through this. We'll get you through this and go to Switzerland and everything will be okay."

But I kept thinking of the plants, still just fragile seedlings. Kayley's entire future was locked up in those slender stems. One mistake, one disaster: a fire, someone robbing us, the cops—hell, even if I just got the fertilizer a little off. That was all it would take.

I'd do everything I could. I'd spend every waking hour at the grow house.

But that brought a new problem: the more I was at the grow house, the more I was around Sean.

22

LOUISE

May

Sean stopped by every few days. Even though it was me looking after the plants, there was always something that needed doing: a leak in the roof or a faulty light, a sack of fertilizer that needed carrying in from the car. He kept to our unspoken agreement: he didn't try to kiss me again.

But that didn't stop him looking.

I'd hear the low throb of the Mustang in the street outside and my heart would beat faster. Then the heavy thud of his boots on the sidewalk and the creak of the door. If I was busy checking plants, I wouldn't even look up at first, but I was aware of every little thing he did. I could feel him staring at the tight denim stretched over my ass if I was bending over. I'd feel his gaze slowly stripping me, layer by layer, melting my clothes away and caressing my body in languorous sweeps. By then, I'd be so hot and jumpy that I *couldn't* look at him, so I'd keep my eyes on my work, walking around the tables and checking plant after plant as his eyes ate me up.

I knew he was thinking about what he wanted to do to me and I was imagining, too. Whenever I had my back to him, I thought of suddenly feeling his hands on my waist, skimming up the sides of my top, lifting it a little and then darting underneath and squeezing my breasts. He'd pull me back against him and I'd feel the hard outline of his cock between the cheeks of my ass, grinding against me as I writhed in his grip. Then, unable to restrain himself any longer, he'd shove me forward against the table, the wood digging into the front of my hips. A hand would press into the middle of my back, bending me over it, and then he'd yank my jeans down hard, ripping the buttons from their stitching. I'd have just a few seconds to process what was happening as I lay gasping and panting with my cheek pressed to the wood. I'd feel the cool air of the room on the damp folds of my sex and then the hot, weighty pressure of his cock and—

Sometimes I'd whip around to face him, right at that moment in my fantasy. I'd look him in the eye as he penetrated me in my mind and I knew, *knew* he was imagining the same thing. We barely spoke, hours and sometimes whole afternoons passing without a word. But in my head he was growling and panting and finally gasping, my earlobe between his teeth, as he finished inside me.

I thought it would get easier but it got harder instead. Every day he was there turned into a marathon of self control. He was watching me...but I was watching him, too. I'd drink in the hard muscles of his legs and ass whenever *his* back was turned, or peek between the leaves of the plants as I was working and lose myself in the smooth swells of his pecs under his t-shirt, tracing their curves with my eyes the way I wanted to with my fingers. I imagined Sean on top of me, underneath me, behind me, up against the wall. I day-dreamed about his lips on my body so vividly that I swore I could feel them, working their way millimeter by millimeter across my chest, my nipples growing hard under my top as his tongue lathed each one.

I knew things were going in a dangerous direction. After a week, we were like two caged animals. I felt like we needed to be separated for our own safety.

I tried to defuse things by talking to him, but that made things worse.

At first it was innocent enough—the same sort of conversation you'd have with anyone if you spent enough time with them. Movies and food and safe subjects like that. He'd become even gruffer, since we nearly kissed, so it was me doing most of the talking. One day I told him about the candy I used to eat as a kid, stuff like Pixie Sticks. "I love those things," I told him. We were just chatting. It was fine.

Except, the next morning when I visited Kayley, she was running a fever. She'd picked up an infection, something that would have been no big deal normally, but the medication she was on had left her vulnerable. I stayed with her as much as possible over the next few days, falling asleep by her bedside until the nurses chased me away. I barely ate. Sean told me he could look after the plants, but I stumbled bleary-eyed to the grow house every day anyway, because it was better than sitting worrying in my apartment alone. And just as I was losing it, just as I was at my lowest point, I came in to find a clumsily-wrapped package sitting on one of the tables.

Sean was across the room, messing with the hinges on one of the security doors. He didn't say anything or even look up as I opened the package. But inside was a whole box of Pixie Sticks. I looked at him, but he kept his eyes on his work.

The next day, Kayley's fever broke and everything went back to normal. But little things like that kept happening: like I noticed my wreck of a car was running better and realized that, while I'd been looking after the plants in the house, he'd sometimes been out in the garage, swapping out a filter or changing the oil. Or I'd pull a double shift and get to the grow house late, having not eaten, and he'd grunt that there was an extra turkey and cheese sandwich if I wanted it. Or once, when I was so caught up in the plants and the hospital and my job that I barely went home for a week, I suddenly realized I hadn't watered my plants on the rooftop. I ran up there, expecting to find them all dead...and found someone had done it for me.

He never acknowledged any of it and that made it even harder. When I was around him, the fantasies wouldn't stop: those big hands tangled in my hair or the press of his chest against my breasts. But now, when I was alone, I started to miss him. The days when he didn't visit felt lonely. And at night, after I'd tossed and turned and finally run out of willpower, after I'd played with myself to visions of him thrusting deep inside me, I lay there and imagined him spooning me from behind.

He was changing, in my mind, from some dark, bad boy lover I fantasized about to a real person—just as dark and just as dangerous but someone who'd *be* with you for more than just one night. Which was insane, because a guy like Sean didn't do relationships. And I knew that. But I'd still wake on a morning in the empty apartment and look down to the floor, imagining him in his apartment downstairs, and have a crazy, momentary wish that he was there beside me. I wondered who he was sleeping with, down there. I suspected he'd started going to the homes of the women he picked up, because I hadn't heard him bring anyone back recently.

At the end of May, Doctor Huxler said Kayley could come home. The initial round of treatment was finished and he told me quietly that she'd feel better for a while. "But don't make the mistake of thinking she's cured," he warned me. "Remember, this is only a holding action. Soon, she's going to start going downhill. Slow at first, then fast. Four months and she'll need the Swiss treatment."

I nodded and told him I was taking care of it. I thought of the plants, still with so much potential for disaster, and felt sick.

The chemo had taken most, but not all, of Kayley's golden hair. It would grow back eventually, but for now she'd chosen to wear a *Sex Pistols* cap I'd found on the internet. The first night she was home, she wanted movie and a pizza. I went into the kitchen with my phone to order the pizza...then stopped. Normally, I'd fight her on it, saying the pizza was unhealthy and expensive. Of course, now I didn't care about any of that, I just wanted to indulge her...but if I did, would that give away how worried I was about her? Spoil her because she was so ill and risk her knowing, or be tough on her to reassure her that everything was normal...and risk her thinking I didn't care?

I got stuck in a loop with it—it wasn't just that it was a hard decision, it was that there was no one in the world I could ask for advice. Mom and dad were gone and I'd been so busy at the grow house that I'd barely seen any of my friends for months. Even Stacey thought I was being cold because I was so secretive about where I was all the time. I got more and more worked up and, just when I thought I was about to hurl the phone at the wall in frustration, I broke down in tears. They came out of nowhere, all of the stress just pouring out, and I couldn't keep them quiet. I let out a fractured, moaning sob.

Kayley's voice from the living room. "Louise?"

Shit. I heard her jump down off the couch. I looked around, eyes full of tears...and then grabbed the handle of the refrigerator. I hauled open the door, shoved my hand in and then slammed it on my fingers.

Kayley ran in to find the refrigerator door open and me crying and nursing my throbbing hand. *"Motherfucker,"* I spat, showing her the rising red marks.

"I'll get some ice," she told me. "And that's a dollar in the curse jar."

I watched her with eyes full of tears. The grow house had to work. I couldn't lose her.

23

SEAN

June

I'd sworn to myself, after I nearly kissed her, that I was going to keep my distance...and I did. But not seeing her made me crazy: I was addicted and I'd start jonesing after just a couple of days.

I'd find excuses just to be at the grow house and then sit there watching her, imagining every filthy thing I'd like to do to that pale body...and she just carried on working, oblivious, probably thinking about roots or nutrients or something. Surrounded by plants, she looked even more like some goddess of nature. I'd never seen her look so totally at home...I just wished it could be in a proper garden instead of a windowless grow house. Somewhere she'd be safe. Like one of those stately homes I'd been taken to as a kid. That'd suit her, being lady of the manor. God knows she was classy enough.

I did what I could for her. Little stuff. I couldn't stand by while life ground somebody like her into the dirt. So I helped her out and quietly drove myself crazy, torturing myself by putting myself in the same room as her week after week.

Then, one day in June, it all went wrong.

It was way too hot for so early in the year, even in California. One of those days where the sun really pounds down on you, where you can almost hear your skin hissing and reddening and the asphalt in the streets goes sticky under your feet. It wasn't too bad in the air conditioned house, but I'd been walking outside, checking for anyone sizing up the house. When I got inside, I pulled off my tank top and went and stood right in front of the air conditioning unit so that the cold air was smacking right against my shining body.

Bliss. I closed my eyes and let out a long groan and slowly rotated, letting the air chill every part of me. I had to back up, so it could hit all of me, and eventually I felt myself knock into a table.

I heard an intake of breath behind me and twisted around, opening my eyes. At first, I thought maybe I'd knocked something over, but everything looked fine. Then I saw Louise staring at me, her hand to her mouth.

"What?" I grunted.

"What happened to you?" she whispered. She was staring at my back.

Shit.

She'd seen the burns.

They're pretty well hidden by my tattoos. That's the idea of them —all those snaking lines and the black ink make the circular, puckered scars disappear. But when I'd backed up against the table, the lights had lit me up, hundreds of watts of pure white light shining right at my skin, and revealed everything.

I looked back to Louise. Her eyes were wide with shock...and something else I never wanted to see: pity.

"None of your fucking business," I spat. It was out before I could stop it, a reflexive defense. I pulled my tank top back and stalked outside into the sunlight. If she called after me, I didn't hear it over the roar of the Mustang's engine and the screech of the tires.

That day woke me up. It reminded me of what I was and why we couldn't be together. It didn't matter how much I wanted her: I wasn't going to taint her or put her at risk by getting any closer. Sure as *fuck* not close enough that she'd figure out where all my anger came from.

I stopped hanging out at the grow house. Louise was doing just fine with the plants, I reasoned. She didn't need me there at this stage. I buried myself in work, taking on as many jobs as I could fit in.

A few weeks later, at the end of June, I was in the back of a car with Lennie, traveling to a job. I prefer to drive myself, but sometimes the people who hire me like to come along to watch.

Lennie's one of the bigger dealers. Thin, under his suit, and sort of jumpy, but he's got all this long black hair and big dark eyes so women flock around him. Right now, I was sitting with him in the rear of his huge old Lincoln Town Car as it cruised down the street. He had a blonde next to him and she was running her hands all over his chest through his shirt, her fake boobs almost falling out of her dress. Normally, I would have enjoyed the view. Now, all I could think about was how much better Louise would look in that dress, with her pale, natural breasts, and how amazing those cool, soft hands would feel as they explored my body....

"Lennie," I said. "Could you get me a meeting with Malone?" I'd only met Malone, the big distributor, a couple of times. Normally, the jobs came from either the dealers or the growers, well below his level.

Lennie was looking at the top of the blonde's head. She was unbuttoning the top of his shirt, now, and starting to press her lips against his chest in hungry little kisses. "Why the fuck would you want to see Malone?" he mumbled.

Working for these people is kind of like being their attack dog. They respect you for your abilities, but they don't expect their animals to talk back...or even talk, period.

"I've got word about some product," I said. "Weed. A lot of weed. Really good stuff."

Lennie grunted and shifted in his seat. His shirt was undone halfway, now, and the blonde was kissing his nipples. "You rip someone off, Irish?"

"I know a grower. A new one. It's just business, Lennie. More weed for everyone—that's good, right?"

The blonde was massaging his cock through his pants, but Lennie's eyes were suddenly on me. "You're trying to do a *deal?* With *Malone?*" He gave me a patronizing grin and shook his head. "That's a fucking dramatic leap up the food chain. Why don't you bring this grower to me? I can make the introduction." He leaned back in his seat, humping his groin into the blonde's hand a little.

I knew what he was saying: *all you're good for is smashing stuff.* I said nothing, just sat there and soaked it up. But I let my fingers play up and down the shaft of my hammer like it was the fret of my guitar.

Lennie's smile faded along with his hard-on. "But sure," he said quickly. "Sure, if you want to see Malone, I can make that happen."

I nodded. "Thanks, Lennie." I leaned my hammer back against my shoulder and relaxed my hands.

With the threat gone, Lennie tried to regain control of things. "You okay, Irish? You seem different. Woman trouble?" He looked down at the blonde, who was drawing his hardening cock out of his pants. "You want to find yourself a girl like Marissa here. Marissa knows how to have fun."

I gave a non-committal grunt. I'd thought staying away from Louise would make it easier, but it was like a sickness, a hunger...the longer I went without seeing her, the more she was in my mind. I hadn't ever had that, before. Women had always been replaceable, to me, as I'm sure I was to them. But now...I hadn't picked up a woman since that day I'd shared the elevator with Louise. I hadn't wanted to. The women in those bars I used to go to just seemed...plastic, somehow. Faded and almost translucent, next to the Technicolor reality of Louise.

I wanted her. And yet I knew I couldn't have her, not unless I wanted to fuck her life up the way I fucked up everything else. Getting involved with her would drag her down into my world, and that would be like seeing a priceless marble statue sink into a swamp. One time wouldn't be enough and yet more would destroy us both. Because a girl like her would want more—deserved more—than just sex. But *more*—even if I could offer that—would mean her getting much closer than I could let her. I rubbed my back, where the scars were. *What the hell am I going to do?* I'd gone from barely feeling to being a mess of emotions whenever I was around her. This was a world I just plain didn't understand.

I realized the car had stopped. Lennie was looking at me expectantly. We'd arrived outside the biker bar—some hapless motorcycle club who'd been dealing coke in Lennie's territory. *A message needs to be sent,* he'd said. Already, the bikers had seen the car pull up and they probably recognized it as Lennie's. Five or six of them were gathering outside the bar.

I climbed out.

"Oh fuck," one biker said, his face going pale beneath his beard. "He brought the Irish."

This, I understood. This was my world, the one I didn't want Louise anywhere near. I lifted the hammer almost lazily, spun in a circle and smashed it into the rear wheel of one of the Harleys parked outside. The first blow is always the most important. This one caved in the wheel and sent the bike toppling onto the one next to it, setting off a domino effect. The bikers jumped back, cursing, mad as hell but too scared to approach.

I could feel the anger unwinding in my chest, coming to life like a waking dragon. I slammed the hammer down into the next bike and the front forks crumpled. A biker howled as he saw his baby ruined. I've smashed a lot of things in my time and I've learned the fastest ways to cause the most expensive damage.

I swung the hammer down on a bike's fuel tank and it felt fantastic. One swing dented it. The second brought the stench of gasoline and a rapidly-spreading dark puddle on the concrete. I was in my element now, the adrenaline flooding my veins, the anger burning bright.

"Jesus!" yelled one of the bikers. "Enough!" He and another guy finally ran at me. I swung the handle of the hammer into the stomach of one, hard enough to leave him doubled-over and winded. The other guy I dodged and then pushed backward, using the head of the hammer against his chest, so that he was out in the middle of the street. The other bikers followed, snarling and cursing but not brave enough to try rushing me again.

"You stop dealing," I growled at them. "Or you keep it off Lennie's turf."

"Alright!" snapped one of them. He had a President patch on his jacket. "We get it!"

I stepped back towards the bikes. And took out a lighter.

"Aw, come on!" pleaded the President. "We got it!"

I looked from his agonized eyes to the pile of gasoline-soaked bikes...and something happened: I saw the scene as Louise would. And suddenly, the anger slunk away, an animal forced back to its cave, and I just felt disgusted at myself.

"It's your lucky day," I muttered, and put the lighter back in my pocket. Then I stalked back to the car, where Lennie was grinning at the devastation I'd caused and the blonde was wiping her mouth.

The car moved off with me sitting brooding in the back. I couldn't even enjoy the one thing I did well, anymore. Staying away from Louise wasn't working.

I had to see her.

24

LOUISE

The grow house had changed. With summer properly underway, it was stifling inside. It wasn't so much the raw heat —we couldn't let it get *too* hot, or the plants would die—but the lack of windows. Combined with the thriving plants, the whole place was starting to feel like a jungle: a few howler monkeys and a leopard prowling around and the picture would be complete. I knew the conditions were ideal for the plants...but that didn't make them comfortable to work in. I'd stripped down to a spaghetti-strap pink top and an old pair of shorts. I didn't normally like baring that much skin, both because I'm shy and because with my skin I burn in about thirty seconds flat. But I figured it was okay since I was out of the sun...and there was no one there to see me.

Since that day when I'd seen his scars, Sean had virtually disappeared. He put his head around the door once a week or so to check on me, but that was it. Every time I thought back to what had happened, I winced. I knew better than to try to ask him about it— his reaction had made it pretty clear it was private. All I could do was wait for him to open up, but I had a feeling that was never going to happen. And if he kept me shut out, that was going to come between us.

There is no "us," I reminded myself. We'd nearly kissed, once, because we'd let things get out of control. That's all it was.

Except...on those rare days I *did* see him, I couldn't stop looking at him. He'd barely be there, just a minute or maybe two, but I'd drink in every smooth, tanned inch of him.

My gaze would start at his shoulders—I didn't dare make eye contact—and trickle down his whole upper body like a drop of water on a glacier. It would hug the broad swells of his shoulders, following the delicious in-and-out as his arms narrowed and then flared again at his biceps. It would dance along the veined hardness of his forearms, picking up speed as it neared those big, powerful hands, the ones that could so easily grab me. And then, at his waist, where the hem of his tank top flapped in the breeze from the air conditioning, it would reverse course and go up.

Here, things varied a little. If he was facing the air conditioning unit and the breeze was flattening the thin cotton against his muscles, my gaze would do the same. It would skim up his body, molding the black material into every crease and valley of him, and I'd imagine I was doing the same thing with my cheek, feeling the heat of him through the cloth as I stroked each hard ridge.

Sometimes, though, the breeze would catch his tank top in just the right way and it would balloon away from his body for a second, an inviting dark tunnel that, if I *just so happened* to be crouching down beside one of the plants for a second and looked up in *just* the right way, let me catch a glimpse of his abs. Then my gaze would go up *under* the cloth, fueled by my imagination, and I'd be able to almost feel his body under my palms as they slid upward, moving slower and slower, hitting each hard band of muscle like a note on a rising piano scale. I'd imagine it all so vividly that I could actually feel the tight fabric against the backs of my arms as I slid my hands higher, until my palms were smoothing over his pecs and I had to stand so close to him that my breasts were brushing his body. And then his arms would suddenly lock around me, his hands on my ass, and—

And then I'd look away and redden, the heat throbbing through me. A moment later, he'd be gone, back in the Mustang before the engine had even cooled. The memories, though, would stay with me the rest of the day and the combination of the sweltering heat outside and the dark heat inside left me practically rubbing myself against the furniture. I'd never felt anything like it. I'd thought I'd been addicted before, but now I was in full-on withdrawal.

I wanted him. Before, that had been a secret, shameful admission to myself and it had felt like a safe little fantasy because, obviously, *no way* would he want me. The biggest thing I was risking, by lusting after him, was humiliation if he found out. But ever since the nearly-kiss, things were different. Now I knew that there was a real risk of something happening. He could obviously control his feelings: for now, he was keeping his distance...but if he figured out how much I wanted *him*....

He could grab me in the time it took to blink.

He could push me up against the wall without effort. He could lift me off the ground and hold me there while he stripped every stitch of clothing from my body. I could kick and struggle all I liked, but I wouldn't be able to escape...and I wouldn't want to.

That was the scariest thing: not that he'd lose control, but that I would. It was so, so, tempting to look at that hard body and those cobalt-blue eyes and to think of him as a normal guy. And then I'd remember where he was going, when he drove off. I'd think of that whole world he belonged to, the one I'd worked so hard to keep Kayley and me away from. A cold, dark world, with sickeningly strong gravity that pulls in anyone who gets too close. I was already flying way, way closer than I should, drawn in by its promise of quick money. As long as it was just business, I told myself that I could still break away. But once I let Sean into my life, once I let the darkness wrap itself around every inch of my body and invade me...then, there'd be no escaping it. I was going to be drawn down by that world's gravity and crash. And neither I nor Kayley would ever get back to our world again.

I had to stay the hell away from him. I closed my eyes for a moment, drilling that into myself.

When I opened my eyes again, he was standing there, the door still swinging closed behind him. He was breathing hard, as if he'd almost run up to the house, but now he wasn't moving at all.

He'd stopped as soon as he saw me.

We stared at each other and for a moment the only things that moved were our chests as we took slow, shuddering gulps of that oven-hot air. Then he stalked closer, lithe as a jungle cat, and my breathing got faster with every step he took. He slammed his hands down on the table between us and I flinched, even as the sudden nearness of him sent a surge of excitement through my body.

"We have a problem," he growled.

25

SEAN

I hadn't known what I was going to do, the whole way over there. Four times, I'd turned off down side streets and started to head home...but every time, I'd cursed and changed my mind and steered back towards the grow house. Even as I was getting out of the car, I had no idea what I was planning, once I got inside.

Then I smelled it, and suddenly I had an excuse to be there. It was almost a relief, despite how serious the problem was.

"It's the plants," I told her. "I can smell them from outside. Fuck, you can smell them halfway down the block!"

Louise looked around her. Seeing those big green eyes blink in bewilderment made my chest ache—God, she looked so innocent! "I don't...I mean, sure, they smell, but not *that* much..."

"You've gotten used to it," I told her. "You're here too often. You don't realize it, but it reeks in here...and outside."

She pressed her lips together and nodded. Then, before she answered, she licked her lips. I wasn't ready for how that sent a jolt of electricity straight to my cock. I glanced away, afterimages of that quick, pink tongue playing over and over in my mind. "What do we do?" she asked.

"Filters," I managed. "We need charcoal filters over the air vents."

I sighed and ran my hand over my face. "I knew we would. I kept meaning to do it, but..." *But I haven't been around enough.* I was meant to be protecting her. What if one of the neighbors had smelled the scent and tipped off the police? "I didn't think we'd need it yet," I said, then waved at the plants. "They've grown so fast, this month..." I did everything I could to avoid her eyes, but somehow wound up looking at her anyway. "Good job."

"Thanks," she said. A breathy little whisper that drove me absolutely insane. Fuck, she looked so *right* standing there, surrounded by plants. Like a farmer's wife raising her crop, all good and pure and natural. She was wearing some skimpy little barely-there top, just a couple of bootlaces and a few handfuls of pink fabric that put the whole top of her breasts on display, creamy and ripe and rising with each breath...fuck it, was she *trying* to make me lose it?

"I'll go to the store," I said. "I can have it all set up in an hour."

She nodded, but neither of us moved. The thick, pungent scent of the weed seemed to hang in coils around us: every breath was full of it. And it was hot, too. The combination of the smell and the heat and Louise in that top...and the place was so private, every window covered, no one watching what we did. It felt like an opium den or a Parisian brothel, temptation inevitable unless I left *right now.*

"You want to see?" she asked. Her eyes seemed bigger than normal, her pupils huge. "You want to see what I've been doing?" I could hear the timid pride in her voice. She'd spent all these weeks working, I realized, and there was no one in the world she could share her achievement with, no one to give her praise...except me.

I swallowed and went to say, *no.* But nothing came out. And then she was beckoning me closer, walking away from me towards the corner of the room and—

Fuck.

I hadn't seen it when she was standing behind the table, but she was wearing cut-off denim shorts that hugged the lush curves of her ass, the frayed edges teasing at her skin, inviting me to feel just how soft and smooth and warm it was. Without any conscious effort, my legs carried me after her. The plants were so big, now, that there wasn't much room between the tables. She slipped easily through the gaps, but my shoulders brushed through the leaves on either side as I passed. Everything was so soft and green and delicate and I was so big—I was scared I was going to break something.

She brushed her hands through the leaves of a plant. To me, it looked just like all the others, but she said, "This one? This is going to be the best of all of them."

She bent slightly at the waist to look closer, and I caught my breath as her ass thrust out towards me and a narrow slice of skin opened up between the bottom of her top and the top of her shorts. I'd never thought someone's back could be sexy. But Louise's lower back, smooth and arching and glistening just a little with the heat...that was the sexiest thing I'd ever seen. My hands twitched with the need to run them straight up under her top, my thumbs pressing either side of her spine, my fingers wrapped around to stroke her sides. All the way up...and then my thoughts grew darker, imagining her on all fours in front of me, my cock disappearing between her thighs as I drew her back onto me.

"I got the mix *just* right," said Louise, jolting me back to reality. "This is our yardstick, now. Look how big the leaves are. Feel them."

I blinked and swallowed, my eyes flicking from that entrancing crescent of skin to the plant.

"Feel them," she insisted. And she suddenly grabbed my hand.

I caught my breath at the feel of her smooth, cool skin against my calloused fingers. She was so delicate, next to me: it took two of her slender fingers to equal one of mine. I had to step closer, as she drew my hand towards the plant, until the hard bulge of my cock in my pants was almost brushing her thrust-out ass. And she was completely unaware, of course. God, how did she do this to me? How could a blonde in some bar work her body all over me, giving me a full-on clothed lap dance, and I'd mentally shrug, but Louise could have me hard as a rock just from being close? Even over the heady smell of the plants, I could still detect the soft, clean scent of her, natural and magical. I wanted to bury my face in her and breathe nothing else.

"See?" said Louise, drawing my unresisting hand through the leaves. "It's not just the color, or the shape. They *feel* healthy." She turned to me and bit her lip guiltily and I damn near lost it. "I know it sounds dumb. It's hard to describe, but...can you feel it?"

"Umm-hmm," I grated.

She must have heard something in my voice because her eyes locked with mine and she let go of my hand. She slowly straightened up, turning to face me as she did so. Everything else in the world ceased to exist: all I knew about were those big green eyes as they came closer and closer and her sigh as she exhaled. All that red hair was spilling down over her shoulders like gleaming, liquid copper and I've never wanted to run my fingers through something so bad.

My hands hurt. I realized I was digging my nails into my palms to keep from grabbing her.

"I don't know about this stuff," I told her. I could hear the hoarseness in my voice, like I'd just sprinted a mile. "But...they look good." I took in those moss-green eyes, the soft lips that drove me crazy. "They look really good."

She nodded.

"Now I've got to go to the store," I told her, each word a Herculean effort.

She nodded again. And...was there a hint of sadness in her eyes? Disappointment?

I turned away and forced myself to walk towards the door. I was almost there, almost safe, when she called out to me. "Wait! I almost forgot—I got you something."

I spun to face her, mad as hell. Didn't she realize what she was doing to me?

"It's...outside," she said in a small voice, jerking her thumb at the back door.

Outside. Outside where there was air, and there were people. Outside, nothing could happen. I nodded quickly, crossed the room and flung open the door.

Air. Good, clean, fresh, wholesome air. In the shadow cast by the house, it was blessedly cool. After the stifling house, it was like jumping into a mountain lake. I knew I couldn't just stand there with the door open, not with the reek of grass flooding out, so I stepped forward to let Louise out behind me. I heard her shut the door and then I slowly turned around to face her. With every breath, my mind was clearing. I figured that, out here, everything would be okay.

But when I faced her again, I had a new problem. It was easier to hold back the lust but hiding beneath that had been something even stronger. God, she was beautiful. And then she made it worse. She bent down and picked up a plant from beside the door, holding it out towards me. "It's for you," she told me. "It's a rose." She looked at it shyly. "I figured you'd want something...y'know. *Manly* and covered in thorns. And it's Irish. *Irish Blood,* they call it. Made me think of you."

I stared at it. This was the last thing I'd expected. It was bad enough that she was a constant fucking temptation, but...was she *being nice to me?!*

"I've got no idea what to do with this," I mumbled.

"That's because no one's taken the time to teach you."

This was different. This wasn't like the simple battle between my need to fuck her and my need to protect her. We'd suddenly moved into a whole new and unfamiliar arena. "Umm..." I said. But I couldn't think of a bloody thing to say to get out of there without hurting her feelings. Normally, I'd just get angry. But every time I reached for my anger, those big green eyes made it slip away.

"C'mon," she said, and knelt down on the grass, next to a patch of dirt.

I knelt slowly down facing her, my body dwarfing hers. The ground was pleasantly cool against my knees. I couldn't even remember the last time I'd sat on grass. And the ground wasn't dusty and dry, here, it was soft and even a little damp. She'd found a good growing spot, even in the middle of this hellhole of a neighborhood.

"Dig a hole," she told me. She reached behind her. "I brought a trowel, or—"

I shoved my hands into the bare dirt between us, forcing my way through the soft earth until they were wrist-deep, then pushing them outward. An image swum into my mind: my hands pushing her pale thighs apart in just the same way.

"...or you could just use your hands," said Louise, her eyes huge.

Being outside hadn't cooled my lust at all. It had just brought everything into sharp focus. And the way she was treating me was defusing my anger, the only thing that had helped to keep me in check.

"Now take the plant," she said, holding it out towards me. "Careful of the thorns."

I gazed past it, straight into her eyes. "I can't do this," I muttered.

"Yes you can," she said, her voice growing softer. Then, "I believe you can."

This is stupid. This is fucking stupid, just get the thing in the ground and get out of here. I grabbed the stem in my fist, not caring about the thorns that stabbed into my flesh, and slammed the roots into the hole. My whole body had gone tense, every muscle quivering—

But suddenly, Louise was beside me, her hand between my shoulders. All the tension eased away—however much I tried to cling onto it.

"Cover up the roots," she told me. "Gently."

I bulldozed the piles of dirt inward with my palms until the hole was filled.

"Pat it down a little," she whispered. Her mouth was almost at my ear, each word tickling.

I put my palms on the mound of soil and patted at it, feeling stupid. But then her cool hands were on top of mine, the smooth softness of them sliding over my knuckles, and my patting died away. And then we were just kneeling there, me like a hulking beast and her like some foolish maiden wrapped around me, her red hair blowing against my cheek, her hanging breast brushing my side.

I need to get angry. I need to get angry right now.

"It's okay," she breathed, so softly I wondered if I was imagining it.

I told myself that she couldn't possibly understand, that she had no fucking idea what was inside me. But then she said, "See? You can grow stuff. Instead of just tearing it down."

And her hand slid down my back to the place where the scars were.

Suddenly, my anger came back, a flash of heat that filled my whole body. I grabbed her wrist and wrenched, tossing her over onto her back and, before I even knew what I was doing, I was on top of her, my knee between her legs. *"What are you doing?"* I yelled. *"What the fuck are you doing?"*

Her eyes were big and liquid, but she was staring up at me in defiance. She was scared as hell, but trying to put up a front. "I just want to help you," she panted.

"I don't need your help!" I yelled. "It's *me* helping *you!* There's nothing wrong with me!"

We stared at each other, both of us breathing in ragged gasps. I knew she must be terrified. I wanted her to be terrified, because then she'd stop.

"Stay away from me," I told her. "Or I'll—"

I stared into her eyes...and I couldn't say the words. Not even for her sake. I couldn't so much as think about doing her harm.

"No you won't," she whispered.

My hands were flat on the ground on either side of her head. I felt my fingers claw into the dirt. *"You don't want this,"* I told her.

She took two big, shuddering gulps. "Yes I do."

The look in her eyes, the concern she had for me, siphoned off the last of my precious anger. And then I lost control completely, leaned down and kissed her.

26

LOUISE

I'd had the rose stashed away out back for days in the hope he'd show up, watering both it and the ground to keep it all ready for him. I'd just wanted to do something nice for him, to apologize for asking about the scars. Then, when he'd been about to walk out, when I thought of him getting in his car and driving back to that world of violence....

I couldn't let him go.

I'd watched myself kneeling down on the grass with him and touching his back, like putting my head between a lion's jaws. I'd screamed at myself not to do it. But the need to help him, to find that man he used to be, the one someone had cruelly scarred, was too strong.

And now I was facing the consequences.

It was a brutal, hard kiss, his strong lips mashing down on my softly panting mouth, a kiss that forced me open and damn well took me whether I wanted it or not.

And I wanted it. Oh, God, I wanted it. My lips flowered open and I welcomed him in. I even reached up to slide my hands into his hair—

He grabbed my wrists and slammed them down into the dirt, and I went weak inside.

As he kissed me, the muscled chest I'd fantasized about so many times was pressed against my chest, warm hardness grazing my aching nipples through the thin layers of cloth. One knee was thrust between my legs and I could feel the outline of his cock, rock-hard and burning hot, against the top of my inner thigh.

Both of us were panting for air through the kiss, him caught between anger and lust and me caught between lust and fear. I wasn't scared that he'd hurt me; I was scared of the cliff I was about to jump off of, the descent into blackness if I let this happen.

Let this happen? I wanted it to. Needed it to.

The kiss changed. His tongue found mine and drew it into a dance, hard and fast and building rapidly, exploring my limits and demanding to know how much I could take. Testing me, *wanting* it to be too much for me so that he could release me and end this. But every touch of that expert tongue against my sensitive flesh whipped the hurricane inside me faster and faster. I welcomed him in with a groan of pleasure that vibrated against his lips. And with every second that I let the kiss continue, I could feel him getting more and more out of control, his whole huge body growing hard against me.

He broke the kiss and glared down at me, those scalding blue eyes hooded with lust. He leaned down and caught my upper lip between his teeth, biting gently, and I groaned again. I pressed up with my wrists, needing to move, to respond, but his hands were like iron bands. And that only made me hotter.

He gazed down at me for a second, eyes locked on mine, and then darted in again, this time pushing my head to the side and finding the edge of my jaw with his lips, kissing the line all the way up to my ear, making me squirm and thrash under him with every burning contact. And when he reached my ear, he hissed into it. Molten air that carried syllables of brimstone, left rough by the Irish in his accent. "Is this what you want?" He nipped my earlobe in his teeth and I moaned. "This isn't a fuckin' game, Louise. I don't care how innocent you are, I'll pound you into the dirt."

The coarseness of it made me catch my breath...but I wasn't ready for how it made the black heat rise up from my groin, spreading and building. "Yes," I managed, almost a whimper.

He growled again and suddenly rolled us over so that I was on top. My hair flew out in a cloud and my legs slid around him, my knees on the cool ground. His groin pressed up against me, both legs between mine, now, and I could feel his cock even more clearly, throbbing against my inner thigh. I realized with a lurch that I was straddling him and I lifted myself to slow things down just a little.

That's when his hands clamped down on the cheeks of my ass, pulling me down on him. The softness of my groin ground against his cock and both of us groaned. Even through our clothes, I could feel my soft lips pressing against that heavy, thick hardness and, as he dug his fingers hard into my ass and dragged me up and down a little, I felt myself opening, moistening. I panted and tried to move myself, but his hands were too strong, his fingers like rock through the thin denim. He was in control. He dragged me up and down his length again and pleasure rippled outward from the contact, making me buck and wriggle.

I realized my hands were free and grabbed for his shoulders, running my fingers over the muscles I'd gazed at for so long. He was solid and heavy, the feel of him addictive under my palms, the sense of raw power that throbbed from him overwhelming.

He rolled us again, slamming me down on my back in the dirt. I could feel damp earth on my knees where they'd pressed into the ground and I knew my pink top was probably the same. We were getting filthy and I didn't care, the heat howling inside me, now, demanding release. We stared into each other's eyes again....

And then he grabbed the spaghetti strap of my top and the strap of my bra in his fist and my stomach seemed to slam down into my shoes. *Oh my God he's going to—*

There was a ripping sound as threads gave way and suddenly one of my breasts was bared, the nipple throbbing at its sudden exposure. Sean stared down at it...and I saw the animal lust in his eyes. I groaned as his hand lifted and then squeezed the soft flesh, his thumb caressing the nipple. Then his mouth was on me, his tongue bathing my skin and swirling around the stiffening peak. My hands were still free but I couldn't move them: the sensations were too much. My knuckles rubbed against the cool ground and my fingers spread and strained as his tongue darted around the base of my nipple. When he took it lightly between his teeth, I began to pant and press my groin up towards him, swirling my hips. The pleasure was radiating out from where his mouth touched me in quick little earthquakes that I felt all the way to my fingertips and toes, and every shudder raised the heat inside me another notch.

He lifted his mouth from me. The breeze wafted over my slickened flesh and I gasped. Then his thumb was rubbing across my hard nipple again, making me groan and arch my back. "I've been wanting to see these since the day I first saw you," he told me. The words were like burning hot harpoons, digging into my mind, and dragging me down into the dark heat below. "All the time I've been with you, I've wanted to do *this*." And he yanked the other strap, snapping the top and bra on that side, too, and baring me completely.

I cried out as his mouth found my other breast, tossing my head on the ground, hair flying. Then he lifted his head again and both hands went to my breasts, squeezing and rubbing them in a slow rhythm. "Best I've ever seen," he growled down at me. He squeezed a little harder and I tipped my head back, eyes screwed closed and chin tilted up towards the sky. I couldn't believe we were doing this outdoors, where some neighbor might see us. But as his thumbs worked at my aching buds, I forgot even that, my mind carried along on a current of pleasure that was moving faster and faster and leading inexorably *down*.

He leaned down and kissed me again. The first time, the kiss had gotten more and more out of control, testing me. This time, it got steadily slower and more deliberate. I was kissing him back as hard as he was kissing me, twisting and moving, exploring his lips and tongue with my own. Every time I brushed the tip of my tongue against his or nipped at his lips with my teeth, he responded: a groan, a shifting of his body atop mine, a tensing of his massive chest. I'd never had that before with a man, never had that feeling of power. The realization that he wanted me that much was intoxicating.

Sean broke the kiss but kept his mouth very close to mine. He slid one hand down my body: over my ruined top, down to the bare skin where the fabric had ridden up over my stomach. He brushed his palm lightly over that place, just barely making contact, and I could feel every microscopic hair standing to attention. I groaned and arched my back again, wanting him closer, firmer, harder. I wanted him so much, I forgot to be embarrassed at how I was responding.

I felt his palm rotate until his fingers were pointing towards my feet. Then the hand slid further down, down to the frayed edge of my shorts. I kept my eyes closed but drew in a slow, fractured breath as the tips of his fingers played with the denim and then with the waistband of my panties. I could feel those blue eyes blazing down on me, savoring my anticipation. The tips of his fingers slipped under my shorts and lifted the waistband of my panties and I gasped as the thin fabric stretched away from my body...God, I could feel how wet I was.

"I've been thinking about this, too," he said, his voice a whisper, the words felt as much as heard, tiny kisses as our mouths stroked together. "Thinking about how you'd feel. Whether you'd be wet for me. Are you wet for me, Louise?"

I couldn't answer. The heat was roaring in my ears now, furnace-hot. The feel of his heavy body on mine, the way he was touching me, the sound of his voice...it was all rushing me towards a climax and the thought I might actually come, right here, outside, left me reeling. His fingers slid lower and then they were caressing the soft curls of hair and—*God!*—the tips of them were sliding over the lips of my sex, already sticky with my juices—

My eyes flew open and I was looking up into cobalt-blue pools that blazed like fire. "You are, Louise. You're wet for me." His hand moved lower, knuckles rasping against my panties, and I moaned and thrashed in anticipation, feeling myself approaching my peak. Two fingers stroked over the line that separated my lips and I cried out and rolled my hips. Then the fingers were spearing up into me, spreading me. "Jesus, you're soaking," he told me, and the fierce heat grew even stronger, pushing me towards the edge. The fingers slid deeper. Second knuckle. Third. Hooking inside me and rubbing that secret place—

My eyes closed again and my arms suddenly locked around his shoulders as the climax hit me. I rocked against him, grinding my groin into his hand. His thumb brushed across my clit and I trembled and shouted a wordless cry of pleasure. My knees came up, my sneakers dragging across the dirt, and I shuddered and shuddered against him.

And then everything went wrong.

27

SEAN

I felt her spasm and tremble around my buried fingers, wet and hot and perfect. As she finally relaxed against me, I drew my fingers from her. God, she was so soft there, the hair like silk. I popped the button of her shorts and put both hands on the waistband: one good tug and I'd have them down over her hips and off, her panties, too. And then I'd finally get my first glimpse of what she looked like there. My imagination had been going crazy for months.

I'd dreamed of her a thousand different ways: light pink lips and dark pink, hair every shade from the copper on her head to the brown of her eyebrows, all of it framed by that soft, pale skin. A thousand ways...and all of them perfect. I was going to drag those shorts off her—tear them off, if I had to—and then I was going to bury myself in that lush body, feel that heat around my aching cock. I wanted to see her gasp and pant and dig her nails into my back as I pounded her bare ass into the dirt.

She opened her eyes and stared up at me, the liquid green of a forest clearing. So innocent.

I froze.

"What?" she asked, sounding worried. The sound of her voice

made it even worse: soft and sweet and almost apologetic. She was worried *she'd* done something wrong.

I sat slowly back on my heels, looking at what I'd done to her with fresh eyes: her pale skin smudged with mud, her hair mussed, her top and bra hanging in shreds, breasts still shining from my mouth.

I'd been about to not just fuck her but *pound* her, down here in the dirt, getting her filthy, tearing her clothes...as if by doing that I could somehow bring her down to my level. Part of me had always been turned on by the gulf between us: the thought of taking someone so pure and leading them down into dark, moaning pleasure. But now that I saw what I was doing....

I couldn't do it. The only thing stronger than my need to fuck her was my need to protect her. It was almost as if I was seeing myself through someone else's eyes. I didn't *want* a guy like me fucking her.

"I'm sorry," I muttered, getting to my feet.

"W—*what?!*" She half-sat up, then felt her ruined top and bra fall around her waist and tried to cover herself. Suddenly, it hit home that she was outside and she looked around fearfully, clutching the rags to her breasts. "*What?* What are you—"

I shook my head helplessly. And saw the tears well up in her eyes. *Ah, shit!*

She jumped to her feet, glancing down disbelievingly at her ruined clothes and dirt-smudged body. "Don't—"—her breathing hitched—"don't you...want me?"

Part of me died inside. This was destroying her and it was all my fault. "Yeah. Jesus, *yeah!* But...this is wrong. You can't get tangled up in my life."

She had her arms crossed over her breasts, now, holding the shreds of white and pink fabric against her. Tears were spilling down her cheeks. "I already *am!*"

I shook my head fiercely. I hated to see her cry but with every tear I was more sure. "You need a good fucking man," I snapped. "Not me." And I marched into the house, straight through it and down to the road, not stopping until I reached my car. I walked as fast as I could, but I still couldn't outrun the choking, helpless sob behind me as she really started to cry.

In the Mustang, I started the engine and then pounded my fist on the dash so hard the plastic cracked. *Fuck!* I wasn't mad at myself for stopping. I'd done the right thing. I was mad at myself for letting it go so far.

I slammed the car into gear and roared off down the street. No matter how hard it was, I had to make sure nothing like this ever happened again.

28

LOUISE

I heard the Mustang roar off down the street and that gave me the confidence to hurry inside the house. I didn't want him to see me like this. I wasn't sure I ever wanted him to see me again, period.

I was a mess. There was grass in my hair and mud on my knees and calves. My top and bra were ruined and filthy with dirt where we'd rolled around. But the worst damage wasn't visible.

What the fuck had just happened? After weeks—*months*—of us both lusting after each other, suddenly he'd decided it couldn't work? And he'd waited until he had me half-naked and panting under him, still flushed from the freaking orgasm?

The worst part was that, however much I raged about it, however much I hated him for it, I knew he was right. He'd given voice to exactly what I'd been worrying about. I'd been thinking all this time that we shouldn't get involved, that giving into it would be the worst thing possible, connecting Kayley and me to a world we should stay the hell away from. I'd known this...but it was Sean who'd called a stop to things. He'd reduced me to such an aching hot mess that I would have gone ahead and had sex with him...and loved it. He was the criminal and I was the mom and yet *he* was the responsible one.

Well done, Louise. Well freaking done.

And what now? My stomach lurched. *What if he doesn't come back?* I had no idea how to go about selling the crop, or how to protect it as harvest time grew near and it became more and more valuable. By letting things get out of control, I might have just jeopardized the whole plan. I might have just thrown away Kayley's only hope.

I braced my hands on the edge of a table and leaned over it, shoulders silently heaving as I wept. I could hear my tears falling onto the leaves of the plants like rain.

Idiot! You freaking idiot!

And then there was the least important thing of all: my own shattered pride. I knew he'd done the right thing, but that didn't stop the rejection hurting. It wasn't just the physical side...when we'd been planting the rose I'd thought I was actually getting close to him. And that just made me feel even more stupid, for letting those sorts of feelings creep up on me when we were so obviously, completely wrong for each other.

I knew things would change, now. The next morning, I found out how much.

29

LOUISE

The next day when I arrived at the grow house, Sean was waiting for me, leaning against a table with his arms crossed. I knew immediately that we weren't going to talk about what had happened the day before.

"I've fitted the filters," he told me. "You can't smell the weed from the outside, anymore." Then he nodded towards the corner and I saw the mattress. "I'm going to start sleeping here," he told me. "Every day, the crop's worth more. Someone could just roll a truck up and take the whole thing. And at night, this place is completely unprotected."

I looked around. When he put it like that, it *did* feel very vulnerable. But this was about more than just that. "So you'll be here at night...but not during the day?"

He nodded. "You're here in the day. And if someone tries to break in, they'll do it under cover of dark."

I stared at him. I nearly said, *But I'll never see you.* But that was the whole point. He was separating us.

I kicked at the mattress. "Doesn't look very comfortable." I could hear the bitterness in my voice.

I could feel his eyes on me. "I'll be okay." Then his voice softened. "It's simpler, this way."

My guts twisted. I wanted to scream at him that I didn't want it to be *simple.* I wanted the way he made me feel, when he touched me, when he whispered in my ear in that granite-and-silver accent. Even with all the complications they caused, those moments we'd had were better than...*this!*

Then I looked up and saw his eyes. The pain I saw there made my chest ache...and underneath that, the burning throw-me-down-on-the-table-and-fuck-me lust, stronger than ever. Every muscle in his body was coiled, a panther ready to spring. He was only just holding himself back.

Being around me was tearing him apart. He was just trying to do the right thing, what he thought he needed to do, to protect the crop *and* me.

I closed my eyes. "Fine," I said. And stalked out to my car, not looking back. I told myself that he was right, that it was better this way. That getting the money and saving Kayley was the only important thing and to hell with my feelings.

I didn't know that the new arrangement would put me in more danger than ever before.

30

LOUISE

July/August

Two months flashed past. Between mornings at my job, afternoons at the grow house and checking in on Kayley at the apartment, things became a blur. I was a machine, existing only to feed and water the plants, my sister, and, when I remembered, myself. I stopped caring about dates and measured time in *things*: three more bags of fertilizer until I had to go to the store, two of coffee, one of Kayley's favorite instant oatmeal. I was trying to treat her in any little way I could because the inexorable slide Dr. Huxler had warned me about had started. Each day, she looked a littler paler, a little weaker.

I was so focused on the changes in Kayley, I didn't realize how big the plants had gotten until I saw Sean one day, right at the end of August. I'd only run into him a few times since the new arrangement began: normally, he'd be gone when I arrived at the grow house each day and he'd show up to sleep there after I left. One afternoon, I stopped by in the late afternoon to drop off some supplies and found him standing there in the middle of the room, gazing around in awe.

Immediately, it was like someone had thrown a switch in my

body. My chest went light, my head clouded and that slow, dark twisting began in my groin. The feelings hadn't shrunk for being ignored; they'd grown stronger than ever. He was facing away from me and I marveled at the movement of that sculpted back as he breathed.

A floorboard squeaked and he spun around. I saw the shock in his eyes...and then the way it changed to raw, almost uncontrollable heat. There were two tables between us and, for a moment, I thought he was about to smash them out of the way to get to me.

Then his eyes flicked to the side. I could see the tension in his forearms and shoulders, every vein standing out. "You've done good," he muttered.

I could barely speak. "Thanks."

His eyes returned to me, searing into me. "They look great."

I felt myself flush, feeling his gaze stroke down my neck and then down, down, down. "So do you," I blurted. Then, as I realized what I'd said, "You're early."

"You're late."

"I got stuck in traffic." I dumped the bag of fertilizer I was carrying on the floor. "What's your excuse?"

That seemed to snap him out of his reverie. "I'm not staying," he said. "I just stopped by to check on the place. I can't be here tonight." He headed for the door.

"What? Wait!" I reached out and grabbed his arm as he passed.

He slowed to a stop as my arm drew tight. It was such a ridiculous sight, like a battleship being pulled up by a rowboat. He looked down at my pale hand on his bronzed forearm as if I had all the power in the world.

We were standing so close, his trapped forearm was a hair's breadth from touching my breasts. I could feel the heat from his body throbbing into mine. But something was wrong—his face was drawn and tight with worry. "Why can't you be here tonight?" I asked. "You're here every night."

He wouldn't meet my eyes. *Another secret,* I thought. "I just can't. Something I have to do."

"Everything okay?"

"Yeah," he muttered, in a way that meant *no*. "But I've got to go." He looked down at my hand on his arm. I slid it off him and he started forward.

"Well...okay, I'll sleep here," I said. "I can get Stacey to crash at my place with Kayley."

Immediately, he whipped around. "What? No! I'm not having you here by yourself!"

"What about the house?"

He sighed. "It'll be fine. It's just one night."

I frowned. This wasn't like him. What the hell was so important that he'd put the grow house second? And that could stress him out so much? "Then why do *you* have to be here every night?"

He shook his head and I could hear the frustration in his voice. "Louise..."

"What if tonight's the one night we get robbed?"

He suddenly grabbed my forearms and shoved me up against the wall, so hard the air was knocked from me. "Fuckin' hell, Louise: *no*, okay? *No*. Just be told. What if someone *did* break in? What would you do?"

I just gaped at him. My feet were off the floor. His anger would have been terrifying...if I hadn't been able to see how worried he was about me.

He gently let me down and released me. "It's too dangerous," he said in a softer tone. "Okay?"

I swallowed and nodded. "Okay."

"Go home. Promise me."

I nodded.

"Louise!"

"I promise!"

He turned to go. Then stopped in the doorway as if about to say something. *Tell me! Tell me what's going on,* I screamed in my mind.

"I'll see you around," he muttered. And left.

Fuck. My mind was spinning. Something was obviously up with him, but what? He'd closed me out again.

I turned in a slow circle, looking at the plants. The longer I stood there, the less I wanted to leave them there undefended. What if someone *did* break in? If we lost them all now, there was no time to start a new crop—we needed the money for Kayley's treatment in a month.

But I'd promised Sean.

I stood there debating for a full half hour before I finally called Stacey and asked if she could come over to my place and be there for Kayley.

"Sure," she said. "Is it a date?"

"No!" As if I'd leave my sister to run off and sleep over at some guy's place! "No, nothing like that. Just a...work emergency."

"At *night?* You work in a garden store!"

I closed my eyes and gripped the phone so hard in my fist the casing creaked. "Stacey...I'm sorry. I can't get into it right now. Will you just watch Kayley for me?"

"Yeah," she said in a hurt tone. "Of course."

I thanked her and ended the call. *Dammit!* I was keeping things from her just like Sean was keeping stuff from me. She deserved better.

I went out to grab takeout. *It won't be so bad,* I thought. There was a mattress and some blankets and a bathroom. I spent half my life in the grow house anyway: what was one night? And the chances of anyone breaking in on that particular night were tiny. Right?

I sat at a red light, tapping my fingers on the wheel. Sean's words came back to me. What would I do, if someone did break in?

When the light went green, I turned away from the takeout place and towards a Wal Mart. First, I bought some kitchen knives and then, after trawling through the sporting goods section, I found an aluminum baseball bat. Then I finally grabbed the takeout and headed back.

Stupid, I thought, as I sat cross-legged on the mattress with the knives spread out in front of me. *I'm being stupid. Nothing's going to happen.* I made a mental note to hide everything the next morning, so that Sean didn't see it. He'd go berserk if he knew what I'd done.

At ten, I called home to say goodnight to Kayley.

By eleven, the traffic noise outside had stopped and the house was deathly quiet. *This is fine. I'll just sleep.*

At midnight, I was still lying there staring at the ceiling, willing the hours to pass, my body wracked with tension. *How does Sean do this?* I kept expecting to hear footsteps outside or the sound of breaking glass.

I thought about running for the car. I could be home in ten minutes, back to my safe little burrow. I could apologize to Stacey, hug the sleeping Kayley and everything would be great.

And the weed would be sitting here undefended. What if someone was sitting out there *right now* waiting to see if I left? What if me being here was the only thing stopping them?

I lay there for another few minutes, my mind switching back and forth. And then I heard the noise, faintly at first, so faint I couldn't make out what it was. A rising and falling tone. I scrunched up my forehead, listening as it got louder. Wait...it wasn't...no...

Shit!

Sirens.

31

LOUISE

People talk about the paralysis of fear. I know now what they mean. I sat bolt upright on the mattress and then froze there, listening, as the sirens came closer.

Run, I thought. There was still time. I could run for the car. If I left right now....

But I didn't run. I sat there, digging my fingers into my knees, praying that I'd hear the sirens change in tone as they turned off down a side street. But they just keep coming.

Run! Too late to get the car started and out of the garage, now, but I could run out of the front door and be walking down the street when they got there. *My house, officer? No, not mine, I was just out for a walk. I don't know who lives there.*

But my car was in the garage. The house was rented in my name. Even if I was gone when they got there...the fear clutched at my stomach, freezing liquid lead. *This is not happening, this is not happening....*

The sirens entered our street, so loud that I couldn't think. All the windows were covered with Sean's fake walls, but there were enough tiny cracks that the darkened room still lit up with red and blue flashes.

Run! Out of the back door and hope they haven't surrounded the house. Get a good lawyer. *At least I'd have a chance!* But by then it was too late: the lights got brighter and brighter, the sirens hurting my ears. *They'll go past. They'll go right past and it'll all be okay—*

Tires screeched, right outside, and the sirens went quiet. The whole room was alive with moving, fan-shaped red and blue patterns as the lights bathed the front of the house.

Fuck! Fuck, fuck, fuck!

Car doors opened and slammed outside. Voices. Radio crackles.

I squeezed my eyes shut. *Mom!* How had everything gone so wrong? *I was just trying to save Kayley!* Now I was going to jail and Kayley was going to die scared and alone.

Footsteps. I tried to convince myself they weren't coming my way.

Three heavy, authoritative bangs on the door. "LAPD!"

I looked around in horror at the knives and baseball bat around me. If they kicked the door down and saw this, they might shoot first. "Coming!" I yelled, and threw the weapons into the far corner of the room, under a table. Then I ran to the door, undid the locks and opened it, ready to face my fate.

A dark-haired young cop stood there, his gun drawn. "Ma'am? We have a situation out here. I want you to stay in your house and keep away from the windows."

I just blinked at him.

"We have a suspect on the loose in this street and he's armed. Just stay indoors." And he raced off down the path. Across the street, I could see more officers knocking on other doors.

I slammed the door, put my back to it and then slowly slid down until I was sitting on the floor. I could barely breathe. I'd come *so close* to being caught. If I'd opened the door a few inches wider, if the lights had been on, if the breeze had been different and the cop had smelled the weed.... And there were still tens of cops out there, just a few feet away.

I sat there in the darkness, every muscle and tendon in my body tight with tension. Every footstep on the street outside might mean another knock at the door. Every murmur of one cop to another transformed in my mind to *do you smell weed?* What if the filters Sean had fitted didn't work as well as he thought?

After an hour, the cops found their man, hiding behind some garbage cans in someone's backyard. They left without a single shot being fired. I finally slumped in relief, a limp, exhausted wreck.

Minutes after the sirens had died away into the distance, I heard the rumble of an engine outside and then footsteps. *Sean!* He'd come after all. He was going to be mad as hell when he found me here, but I was so glad to see him, I didn't care. I was going to throw my arms around him and—

I pulled open the door to greet him.

It wasn't Sean.

32

LOUISE

There were two of them and the first thing I realized was, *they weren't surprised to see me.* They grinned when they saw my face. They weren't expecting the house to be empty and they weren't expecting Sean.

"Who—" I started.

One of them stepped forward and shoved me hard in the stomach. I folded at the waist and staggered back, winded, catching myself against one of the tables. My eyes were on the floor as I tried to heave in air, but I heard the two of them stroll in and shut the door behind them.

"Jesus," said one of them. A heavy accent I didn't recognize, vaguely European. When I managed to look up, they were looking around at the plants in wonder. "So that's what he's doing."

I had no idea what was going on. When they'd pushed their way in, I'd thought they were there to rob us, but they sounded surprised. If they hadn't known this was a grow house, why were they here?

I finally managed to straighten up and get a better look at them. Two men, bulky with muscle, both with shaved heads. One of them pulled out a knife—a huge, ugly thing with a blade as long as my hand. *Oh Jesus!* "Who are you?" I croaked.

"We know your boyfriend," said the other man. "He paid us a visit. So now we're paying you a visit."

I swallowed. "He'll be back. He just stepped out."

One of them shook his head. "He hasn't been here all night. We've been watching this place. Would have been in here an hour ago, if the fucking cops hadn't showed up."

Oh Jesus. I'd had the police there. I'd had the police *right there* at my door and I'd wished for them to leave. My stomach turned. This was the world I'd chosen. I was a criminal, now, and the police don't protect us.

Sean's words came back to me: *what would you do, if someone broke in?* My plan seemed so stupid, now. The knives and the baseball bat were in the far corner of the room, where I'd thrown them. *Idiot!* And the men were looking at me in a way that made my skin crawl. When I'd bedded down, I'd kept my top and bra on, but it had been too hot for jeans so I was standing there bare-legged in my panties. I swallowed and looked around at the plants. "Take them," I said. "Take everything."

They laughed. And that's when I realized they weren't interested in the weed.

They were there for me.

33

SEAN

It hadn't taken as long as I'd thought. She hadn't needed me to stay the night. A little after one, I was ready to go back to the grow house. I shook my head tiredly. All that arguing with Louise, and I'd be there most of the night anyway.

I hadn't had a chance to eat since lunch. I figured I'd grab a pizza on the way and eat it when I got there.

But on the way to the pizza joint, something nagged at me. That argument with Louise...she wouldn't normally give in that easily. The girl was stubborn as hell.

At the next intersection, I changed course and swung by our apartment block. Louise always parked her rusty old Japanese car in the same place.

But tonight, it wasn't there.

"*Shit,*" I muttered, and drove straight for the grow house.

34

LOUISE

There was nowhere to go. There were only two doors and two of them—a man was always between me and escape. We'd taken out all the walls so I couldn't run for a bedroom and lock myself in. I backed away across the huge room, but every time I took a step, they took a step.

"Please," I said, my voice shaking. "Please!"

They weren't even running. They knew they had me trapped and they were taking their time, enjoying the game. "He wrecked our grow house," said the taller of the two men. "Destroyed it. So we're going to destroy *you.*"

My back hit the wall. I was at one end of the house, looking down the long rows of tables. "Please!" I begged, my voice cracking.

The other man laughed. "Nice of him to leave us a mattress," he said, nodding at it. "Maybe he knew we were coming."

My insides turned to water. *Oh, Jesus, no....*

I bolted between two of the rows of tables, trying to put something, anything, between me and them. The one with the knife strolled down the row towards me. I turned around, but the other one was waiting for me at the opposite end.

I jumped across a table and made a run for the front door, but they darted that way as well. I dropped to my knees and crawled under a table, thinking I could maybe make it to the back door, but they just flipped the table over, exposing me and sending the plants crashing to the floor. I was screaming, hysterical, and they wouldn't stop laughing—

And then I heard the crunch of the fallen plants as the man with the knife walked over them, stems crunching sickeningly. I tried to scramble away but, before I could move, he'd whipped his arm around my waist and hauled me to him, the denim of his jeans rasping against my bare legs. I kicked and yelled and clawed at his arm...and then the knife was at my throat and I went deathly still.

The other man stepped up in front of me, sandwiching me between them. "When your boyfriend gets back," he told me, "he's not going to want you anymore. We're going to fucking *ruin* you."

Tears were streaming down my face as he reached out to tear off my top. This was my punishment. This is what I got for leaving my nice, safe world and teaming up with criminals. I shouldn't have tried to change Kayley's fate, should have just accepted it and wept at her funeral like a good little girl.

No. The thought of that made the anger well up inside like lava rising in a volcano. *Fuck that.*

I spat in his face.

Sean opened the door just in time to see him slap me.

35

SEAN

I'd arrived at the grow house all ready to storm in and yell at Louise for being there alone. Then I'd seen the unfamiliar car outside and it was like my stomach dropped through the ground. I'd never felt that sudden, sickening lurch before. I'd never cared about anyone enough.

I ran, not even stopping to close the car door. I burst into the house to see the two Serbians holding Louise. There was a loud *crack* as the one in front slapped her across the face.

The rage slammed into me, a moving wall of heat that soaked into every cell.

I was moving before I was even aware of it, long strides eating up the distance between us. The guy who'd slapped Louise looked up and saw me and I saw his vengeful grin collapse. He ran out from behind the table, fists raised—

I was dimly aware that I'd left my hammer in the car.

I didn't need it.

I swung back and punched him under the jaw, leaning in and giving it everything I had. He went soaring backwards like a car that's just met a semi-truck coming the other way. Before he'd even landed, I'd turned towards the other guy.

He was still holding Louise, keeping her between us, the knife to her throat. Tears were streaming down Louise's cheeks and her eyes were huge and locked on me. She was terrified.

Dear God, I was going to kill these men.

The guy was yelling at me to stay back—he was barely less scared than Louise, now. When he'd backed up enough to reach the wall and I still kept coming, he finally realized threats weren't going to work. He pushed Louise in one direction and ran in the other, towards the door.

I caught him just as he reached it and slammed his head into the metal. He crumpled to the floor.

The room was suddenly still. Louise and I stared at each other, both of us panting. Then she was running towards me.

I folded her into my arms and she pressed her wet, sobbing face against my chest. I thought the pain inside me would ease, knowing she was safe, but it got worse. This was my fault.

"I thought they were here for the weed," she managed between tearful gulps of air. "But they said they knew you. They were getting revenge...."

I hugged her even tighter. Rocked her, too. Inside, I was planning all the things I was going to do to the two Serbians when they woke up...*if* they woke up. But most of my anger was reserved for myself. I'd brought this down on her. Me.

"It'll be okay," I promised her. And I swore inside that it would. I'd never go near her again. Never get close enough that her soft skin and copper hair and those lush green eyes could draw me in. Because I'd woken up to something. The way I'd felt when I'd realized she was in danger....

Somewhere along the way, I'd fallen for her. It wasn't just me lusting after her, anymore. Maybe it never had been. I knew I wouldn't be happy unless I could *be* with her. And that was impossible: tonight was evidence of that.

"Come on," I told her. "I'll take you home."

One more month, I thought. *One more month. I'll see her as little as possible, we'll finish the crop and save Kayley. And then I'm out of her life forever.*

36

LOUISE

S ean drove me home in my car and saw me to my door. When I asked what he was going to do with the two guys, he said he'd take care of it, and that I never had to worry about them again.

I didn't have to ask what that meant. And however much my stomach turned at the thought of it, I'd be lying if I said a little part of me didn't light up with the dark glow of vengeance.

Stacey's face fell when she saw me. I couldn't tell her anything, which only made her worry more, and Kayley had woken up and was pale-faced with concern, too. Eventually, Stacey and I managed to get her back to sleep and I dozed fitfully on the couch, leaning against Stacey's side.

In the morning, I made up a story about a bust pipe at the garden store causing a flood, and all of us being summoned in to help clear it up, and a guy at work saying something that had upset me. I wasn't sure either of them bought it and I hated having to lie to them. It seemed like I was lying more, every day, just to keep the grow house covered up.

When I returned to the grow house the next day, the two guys were gone and Sean had put the plants back on the tables. I taped up the ones with damaged stems—with proper care, I hoped they'd survive.

A week went by and I didn't see Sean at all: I was there in the day and him at night. I told myself it was better, this way. I'd seen the darkness that surrounded his life. I'd been right all along about the danger that came with being close to him.

But none of that stopped me from wanting him. It was more than just lust, now. I needed him in my life.

Then, one day, the alarm on my phone went off, triggered by the sensors at the house. I checked what the numbers were telling me, my jaw going slack in disbelief. Then I ran for the elevator and tapped out a text message to Sean on the way down.

PLANTS ARE DYING.

37

SEAN

I screeched to a stop outside the grow house and ran for the door. Louise's text had been short on detail so I burst in ready for anything...except what I found.

Louise was stretched out on the floor, naked.

Almost naked. She was in bra and panties except—

She was wet with sweat and they'd gone almost translucent.

"Close the door!" Louise yelled. Her voice was muffled because her head and shoulders were inside a large metal box screwed to the wall. I slammed the door behind me.

That's when I noticed the heat. It was scorching outside, one of the last really hot days of the summer. But inside, it was like an oven.

"It's the air conditioning," said Louise. "It broke, probably some time this morning. The place has been getting hotter and hotter all day, until it got hot enough to set off the alarm. The plants are dying." I could hear from her voice that she was on the verge of tears, and she was venting it as frustration. "What took you so long?"

"I was on the other side of town," I lied. "On a job." I didn't want to tell her the real reason. It had been maybe an hour since she'd sent me the message—had she been inside the grow house ever since, with the temperature like this? No wonder she'd stripped off. I didn't think I'd be able to bear it more than a few minutes in here.

I hunkered down beside her. Every little movement was an effort: the heat was *ferocious*. It made it difficult to think, and the fact I was staring at her nearly-naked body made it even harder. Jesus, her breasts were *right there,* a foot from my face, the dark shadow of her nipples visible through the soaked fabric of her bra—

I dug my nails into my palms and forced my eyes away. "Can't we—"

"Call an engineer?" she snapped. "Look around you."

"Shit. I could open the doors."

I still couldn't see her face, but I saw the tips of her hair toss as she shook her head. "The smell."

She was right. The charcoal filters worked for the air vented through the air conditioning system, but if we opened the doors then big clouds of marijuana-scented air were going to waft right down the street. And I wasn't even sure it would do much good—there was barely any breeze outside to move the air. We needed air conditioning.

"Do you...know what you're doing?" I asked.

"No!" she snapped. But I heard that edge in her voice again, the fracture that was seconds away from cracking open and spilling tears. "I'm figuring it out as I go along, but at least I'm *doing* something, not just standing there—"

I heard her take two big gulps of air, almost sobs. Everything we'd worked for was about to be wiped out. I laid a gentle hand on her ankle and her body tensed....and then relaxed a little.

"It's okay," I said. "We'll fix this."

Another two long gulps of air. Then I saw her hair move as she nodded.

"I'm going to come in there with you," I said.

"There's not a lot of room."

"Do you want help or not?" The heat was slowly cooking my brain. I was getting frustrated already and I'd only been here a few minutes. She'd been here...what, an hour? No wonder she was losing it. And every time I glanced down at her nearly-naked body, I came close to losing control in a whole other way.

I peeled my tank top over my head and dropped it on the floor.

"What are you doing?" she asked.

"Taking off my clothes, what do you think? I'm dying in here." I pulled off my jeans and then, in just my jockey shorts, lay down beside her. To get my head inside the air conditioning unit next to hers, our bodies were going to have to be touching. I scooched closer and she jerked as my hip contacted hers. *Jesus.* I lay there propped up on my elbows, looking down the length of her gorgeous body, every pale curve glistening with sweat. And down between her thighs, where the thin fabric of her panties had soaked through, I could see the shadow of—

"Are you coming in?" she asked, her voice tight, "or not?"

I swallowed and lay down. Then I had to slide my body along the floor to slot in next to her. My leg slid against the side of her leg, hard against soft, both our bodies heated and slick. I could feel my cock swelling and rising. The nearness of her, the touch of her body like this, was driving me wild.

My head slid into the box and then, finally, I could see her. We were side by side, like two lovers lying on their backs in bed, staring up at the ceiling. Except we were looking at tangle of multi-colored wires and, higher up, curving insulated pipes.

"It's a wiring problem," said Louise, her voice shaky.

I twisted my head to look at her. "How do you know that?"

She bit her lip. "I don't. I'm just hoping for the best. If it's anything other than wiring, we're utterly screwed. A loose wire, maybe I can find and fix."

She had a small flashlight in one hand and a screwdriver in the other and was poking determinedly through the nest of wires. I felt my chest grow tight. Goddamn it, even now she wasn't giving up. This girl was amazing.

That's why she deserves better than a thug like you, who's going to get her killed.

"What can I do?" I asked.

She nodded towards my side of the box. "Trace the wires. See where they go. I haven't done that side yet."

I stared up into the rats nest of wires and started following them with my finger. We lay there barely moving, barely breathing, like a couple of lizards baking in the sun. Eventually, I said, "Are the plants okay? The ones those bastards broke?"

She glanced at me. "They look okay, don't they?"

I nodded. When I'd come to the grow house each night to sleep, I'd seen the patched-up plants, their stems carefully wrapped in tape and they seemed to be doing fine. "But...y'know. You're the expert," I said. "And sometimes, you can't tell by looking." I held her gaze long enough to confirm that it wasn't the plants I was talking about.

"They'll be okay," she said at last. Then she stared straight up into the wiring. "Now those guys are gone. And they'll never come back?" She made it into a question.

I put a hand on her arm. "Damn right. Guaranteed."

She nodded. "Then they're okay."

I nodded too and we went back to work. Knowing she was alright let me relax a little...but that made me even more aware of how close our bodies were. And thinking about the Serbians had only reminded me of how much I needed to protect her from my world. Half of me wanted to just dive on top of her; half of me wanted to run out of there before I could. But the only way I could help her was to stay exactly where I was, balancing on a knife edge.

"Here," I said suddenly. "I think I feel something."

"Where?"

"*Here.* I've got my finger on a wire and it feels...rough."

"Rough?"

"Chewed."

"*Chewed?*"

"Shine the torch on it," I told her.

She tried, but there was no room. "Move out, let me move in," she said.

"I won't be able to find it again!" I was keeping my finger jammed against the suspect wire. "I only found it through blind luck!"

She took a deep breath...and suddenly lifted her body and slid herself atop me, her back to my chest. I caught my breath as her ass settled onto my groin. My heart was thumping like a pile driver in my chest. I could feel the tension in her body, too, both of us trying to hold back, to stay icy cold.

But it was *so...damn...hot*. There were so many reasons to stay away from her...but the feel of her against me was making them tissue paper in an inferno.

Louise shone the torch up into the wires. Her voice was strained. "Goddamnit, it *is* chewed," she said. "A freaking raccoon or something's been at it." She reached out with her left hand for something, groping down by our legs. Every tiny movement made her ass grind against my rock-hard cock and I gritted my teeth, seconds from snapping and grabbing her. "Pass me the wire cutters!" she said urgently. "I can't reach!"

I groped and found them. My head was spinning—the heat, the feel of her against me...holding back was the hardest thing I'd ever done. I passed the wire cutters up and—

My forearm brushed across her bra-clad breasts. Both of us froze, her nipples standing out like rocks against my arm. Her breathing fell into line with mine, becoming rapid pants.

It was just—

—too—

—*much*—

I grabbed her waist and twisted her, slippery as a mermaid pulled from the sea, so that she was facing me. And suddenly we were kissing, kissing like the only air in the world came from each other's lungs, kissing like we hadn't seen each other for a thousand years. I've never, ever kissed with such raw desperation. We couldn't move or use our hands—they were all holding tools and wires. It was just our mouths: kissing, gasping, panting and kissing again in great hungry gulps.

When we finally broke, we stared at each other. Every muscle in my body had gone rigid with tension and, for the first time, there was no question of holding back or pulling away. A dam had burst inside each of us. All we had to do first was—

"*Fix the fuckin' air conditioning!*" I croaked.

She twisted so that her back was to my chest again, grabbed the wire cutters and stripped and twisted the wires. Then she poked with a screwdriver and—

"Fuck!" Yellow sparks showered down on us and—

There was a slow whine that grew into a deafening roar. I felt wind against my toes and heard Louise's lungs fill in elation. I pushed out of the air conditioning box, taking her along with me and—

It was as if we were lying on a sun-drenched mountain ledge, with the crest of the mountain just above us. Our bodies baked but we could feel the edge of the current of air as it whipped past. I lifted an arm and it was like trailing my hand beside a boat in the cool, clean water. Louise slowly sat up, her ass grinding against my cock. She slowed down as she came up towards sitting, savoring the moment...then gasped, arching her gleaming back as the air hit it.

I stared at that sensual, elegant arch, bisected by her bra strap, and I couldn't take it any longer. I had to have her...*now*.

I reached up and unclipped the clasp: Louise drew in a big lungful of chill air as she felt her bra go loose. Then my hands were closing on her waist and I was lifting her, turning her to face me and setting her down again. She gave a long, shuddering breath as her soaking panties and the softness beneath them kissed the hard bulge at my groin. Her chest was heaving, her nipples standing out through the half-off bra. I scooped it off her shoulders and she let it trail down her pale arms. Her eyes never left mine for a second.

She sat there atop me, creamy body glistening, nipples hard and getting harder in the flow of cold air. Every freezing lungful of air she took in made her rock minutely against my cock. Her copper-colored hair hung down her back and spilled over her shoulders in gleaming waves. She'd never looked more beautiful.

I sat up, bringing our faces together. The tips of her breasts kissed my chest and we both tensed at the sensation. I could feel the blood pounding in my ears and I knew it must be the same for her: we were both being carried on a wave, now, out of control.

Just as I leaned forward to kiss her, I felt her fingertips against my lips. "Wait," she croaked.

Wait? I couldn't wait. I was completely and utterly insane for this girl. I put my hands on her hips, feeling the firm warmth of her, reassuring my brain that this was real, that I had her in my hands at last. Seven seconds. I could wait maybe seven seconds. "What?" I grated.

Her voice was barely more than a whisper. "Don't stop again. Don't push me away again. Not this time." She shook her head, her red hair tossing. "I couldn't take it. Okay?"

I already knew. Sometime in that cramped, steel box, the pressure that had been building up for months had finally gotten too much. It had exploded and shattered every reason I had for staying away from her: the ones that were to protect her and the ones that were to protect myself. It wasn't a decision, anymore, it was a simple necessity. I needed her like I needed to breathe.

"Fuckin' right," I said with feeling. And kissed her so fast she barely had time to move her fingers out of the way.

38

LOUISE

It wasn't like any of the kisses we'd shared before. This was as new and fresh as the cold air rushing around us, everything I'd imagined it could be but cleaned of all the problems that had been holding us back. His lips twisted and sought and I opened, sighing into his mouth as his tongue found mine. His hands swept up my body, all the way from my hips to my neck. Then they buried themselves in my hair, sliding through the strands and stroking the nape of my neck in a way that made me gasp and arch my back.

My breasts crushed against his chest—God, just as hard and hugely broad as I'd imagined it. We were both still so hot that every contact of our bodies—every scrape of my nipples against his iron pecs, every brush of his rippled abs against my stomach—sent ripples of fire through me, soaking down to my groin. I'd tilted my head up to meet his kiss because, even with me sitting atop him, he was still taller than me. So I was panting up into his mouth when he twisted his hands, fingers pointing down my spine, and slid them all the way down the arch of my back to my ass. A long, glorious river of pleasure, like liquid gold flowing down my body, and I arched like a cat. Then his palms cupped my ass cheeks and *squeezed,* fingers digging in just a little roughly, and the pleasure turned darker, hotter—

He broke the kiss and drew back a little. My stomach lurched. *Oh shit...no, no, no, don't stop!* "What's wrong?" I asked, my voice weak.

He was staring down at me with raw, unbridled lust, those cobalt-blue eyes flaring like I'd never seen them. "Not a bloody thing," he growled. "Just lookin' at you."

He'd looked at me that way plenty of times and it had made me squirm every single time. But I'd never been straddling him before. Now, as his gaze licked down my body, it made me subtly twist and flex against the hard bulge beneath his jockey shorts. I felt him tense at the feeling and I laid my palms on his pecs to feel him better. Immediately, I went weak: the size of him, the sheer power of him, heart booming so hard I could feel my hand trembling, every muscle primed and ready. I looked down at the point where our nearly-naked bodies were pressed together, his tanned hips between my pale ones, and caught my breath. The two of us were bound together in a feedback loop: the more he looked at me, the more I moved; the more I moved and ground against him, the more his eyes narrowed in lust.

"You've got no idea, have you?" he growled. "You've got no idea how much I want you." The Irish in his accent made the words into rich amber liquor that poured straight into my brain and left me reeling...then spread out through my body as eager, nervous heat. I flushed and looked away for a second because part of me couldn't believe he was wanting *me*: the botany geek, the "mom."

In response, he pushed closer to me, putting his mouth to my ear. That meant that I could feel the vibration of every word through our chests as he spoke. "You drive me fucking insane, Louise. You always have."

I drew in a shuddering breath and he groaned in response as my breasts pressed harder against his chest. His voice was low and iron-hard, now, barely-restrained, the rumble of thunder seconds before the storm. "Your face. This hair. These breasts." He ran his palms up between us and cupped them, making me gasp, then worked outward and down to my sides. "These gorgeous fucking curves. This arse." He slapped it and I jerked. Then he was kissing me again, a long, deep plundering of my mouth that left me breathless. He drew my lower lip into his mouth, sucking on it for a second, and I writhed, crackling pleasure lashing down within me and whipping the building heat to spin faster and faster.

When he spoke again, his voice was lower still. His accent turned the words into dark, silver-flecked smoke that twisted down inside me from my ear straight to my groin. "You don't want me to stop? I'm not going to. Not this time. I'm going to fuck you like I should have done the very first time I met you." He ran one big hand up my side and caressed my neck and jaw, the pad of his thumb rubbing over my cheek. "Is that what you want?"

When I answered I barely recognized my own voice. "Yes. God, yes!"

The need in my voice must have taken him over the edge because he suddenly snarled. He lay back, pulling me down on top of him, and then rolled us so he was on top. Then he stood, scooping me up with one thick forearm under my shoulders and the other under my ass, lifting me off the floor as if I was made of air. As he came up to standing, the bulge of his cock rubbed the full length of the lips of my sex. My hands grabbed for his shoulders and found them, helplessly squeezing at the hard muscles in response.

He walked us over to the nearest table, every step making him rub and twist against me. I closed my eyes and clamped my legs around him, delighting in the solid breadth of him between my legs: I was a vine clinging to a rock face.

Then the warm wood of the tabletop was under my ass. He sat me down on the very edge and then stepped back to look at me. I slowly opened my eyes and looked up at him to see what was next.

"Jesus," he said slowly. He brushed his thumb across my cheek again. "So innocent." He was looking at me the way an artist would look at a virgin canvas, as if he couldn't believe how many possibilities there were.

I didn't *feel* very innocent, sitting there almost naked on the edge of the table, legs spread and a man between my knees. But then, as I looked up at him...suddenly, I did.

I'd gotten to know him. I'd even glimpsed beyond the outer shell he showed to everyone else. But that didn't change who he *was*. Now that he wasn't holding back anymore, I could feel that aura of darkness: he was raw and dangerous and completely outside any rules.

I wasn't innocent. But I was pure as the driven snow next to him. And that only made me want him more. I was like a bound, sacrificial maiden being offered up to a beast, unable to do anything more than gaze hypnotized at her approaching fate. I looked up at him with hooded eyes, marveling at the size of him: the hard-packed bulk of his shoulders, the broad, hard chest, the solid hips and tight waist that would let him pound a woman for hours—

Jesus. Pound *me* for hours.

"I want to know how you sound when you scream my name," he said. "I want to know how hard you claw at my back, when I'm holding you right on the edge. I want to know whether you come harder with me on top, or behind you. But you know what I need to know most of all?"

Having him say it all to me with *that* accent was like being wrapped in iron chain dipped in silver. I couldn't move, couldn't close my thighs, even if I'd wanted to. I dazedly shook my head.

"I need to know what you look like," he told me. "Here." One hand hooked into the front of my panties—

I realized what he was going to do just as he did it. There was a crack and snap of elastic and the renting of wet cloth, and then the remains of my panties were in his hand and the cool air from the air conditioning was caressing my sopping folds.

Now I *did* try to close my legs: just an instinctive reaction. But his muscled thighs were between my knees, as immovable as stone. And I felt his eyes scald their way down my body to my groin.

We looked down together at the soft pink lips and the curling copper hair above them. I could actually *feel* his reaction, his whole body stiffening with excitement. The thought that he'd been thinking about that one part of me, fantasizing about it, all this time, was hot as hell.

He growled low in his throat and pushed hard in between my thighs. The bulge of his cock, throbbing and hot as it rubbed against my lips, was a whole different experience now that there was only one thin layer of cloth between us. He gathered up my hair at the back of my head in one huge hand and tugged, lightly but firmly, tilting my head back. I caught my breath...but a whole new type of heat flashed down through my body.

He pressed harder against me and I went weak as his cock caressed me. I felt a hunger inside like I'd never known, an ache that had to be filled. "You pretend to be so innocent, but you know exactly what you want. This is what you want, isn't it?"

I wasn't capable of speech but my moan told him all he needed to know. He looked into my eyes with such a look of evil satisfaction that I went mushy inside. Suddenly, he hooked his forearms under my knees and tugged me forward a few inches, until I rocked on the very edge of the tabletop. My eyes went wide. "Wh—wah?"

He stepped back so that his cock was no longer in contact with me and hunkered lower. Low enough that I felt his next words as hot little kisses of air against my sex. "You need to lose some of that innocence. I want you to beg for it."

He dropped to one knee and my frazzled brain suddenly realized what he had in mind. "Oh God."

Then he was leaning forward, his hands on my inner thighs to spread me open and—

At the first touch of his tongue, I nearly exploded. It was like catching hold of a speeding train: zero to a hundred instantly. I was dangling from a door handle in the slipstream, helpless to do anything other than hang on as we rushed towards our destination. My back arched, my breasts pointing almost at the ceiling. With Sean down low, the cold air was free to blow right at me, playing across my dripping body like a sheet of silk.

He was brutal and gentle in equal measure. His hands were like iron, keeping my legs widespread despite my need to squeeze them shut and grind against him. But the touch of his tongue could be so light, as it traced the shape of me, that I was soon rocking and humping at the air, desperate for more. His lips, when they first opened me, were deliciously firm and controlling...but his tongue, as it thrust inside, was luxuriously slow and sensual. I began to pant for air, the heat rising fast and unstoppable inside me, taking me over inch by inch. I grabbed at the tabletop, fingernails scraping at the rough wood.

His hands worked inward, inch by inch along my thighs. His thumbs rubbed in circles at the sensitive flesh along the inside of my thighs, stirring up currents of pleasure that throbbed inward to my groin. My feet were making little circles in the air, my toes clenching. And in the center of it all, his tongue, thrusting and twisting, tasting me in a slow, insistent rhythm while his lips worked at my clit. I was being carried along on the pleasure, moving faster and faster, and I could see the edge rushing towards me.

He moved away from me for just a second, leaving me wet and throbbing, aching for more. The pause was just long enough for him to look up at me, his eyes clouded with lust, and growl, "Do it. Do it for me right now."

The words slammed into me, hurling me even faster towards the brink. When that expert tongue and those hard, insistent lips returned, it was with the added heat of him looking up at me, watching my reaction. We locked eyes and stayed like that, eyes burning into each other as I rocked and writhed and finally humped my hips towards his face, screaming his name louder and louder. I flashed past the brink. He thrust two thick fingers into me and I felt myself spasm and clutch at him over and over again, my whole body jerking and shaking.

When I finally came down, I was weak and trembling, barely able to hold myself on the edge of the table. I was so intently focused on those cobalt-blue eyes, it took me a few seconds to realize he'd stood up, and was doing something with his hands, down below his waist.

I glanced down just in time to see him push his jockey shorts down and step out of them. His cock sprang up into view, slapping against the flat of his stomach, and I caught my breath. It wasn't just long and thick but...*solid.* As if it had a weight to it, a power, beyond what it should have. I couldn't drag my eyes from it and I wasn't sure why. Was it the perfect, pink-purple head, the skin smooth and silky, or the even tan of the shaft with its elegant texturing of veins? Was it the curls of black hair at the base or the heavy balls so full of potency?

Then I got it and I went weak and heady at the thought. It was the sense of what he was. His cock somehow concentrated all that badness in one weapon of flesh designed to enter me, corrupt me. It looked powerful and brutal, beautiful and evil in the same way his Mustang did.

He wrapped his hand around his cock and drew it gently down. When it reached the point where it was pointing right between my thighs, I gave a little intake of breath. God, it was *big.* And the thought of him finally inside me...my insides went melty.

He walked towards me, the floorboards seeming to shake under his feet. I hadn't seen him completely naked until now and I couldn't take my eyes off that patch of body between the hard ridges of his abs and his thickly muscled thighs. I wanted to run my hands where my eyes were roving: the hard diagonal line of his Adonis belt, the little indents you could kiss at the tops of his thighs, those curls of glossy black hair at his groin. I've never wanted to touch a man so much.

He turned to hook his jeans up off the floor and I saw his naked ass for the first time, firm and smoothly round, so packed with muscle that it dimpled just a little. And I glanced down between my legs, thinking of him between them, and went weak all over again.

Sean dropped the jeans, pulling out the little foil packet, and started to walk towards me again. His eyes never left me for a minute as he tore the edge off the packet with his teeth. He didn't slow his walk as he rolled on the condom. Suddenly, he was between my thighs, his cock aimed right at my sex, inches from touching. I swallowed...hard. It wasn't just the size, although he was *big*. It was that aura that was rolling off him in waves. He really was the guy you're warned to stay away from: not some wannabe bad boy but an actual criminal. A man known for destroying things. If I really was any sort of innocent...he was about to destroy *me*.

And I wanted him to. Our natures—his bad, my good—had always attracted us as strongly as they'd pushed us away. Now the attraction had finally won.

His cock brushed against my slickened lips, the heat of him throbbing into me. "Oh God," I whispered.

He put his finger under my chin and tilted my head up to look at him. God, he was looking at me in a way I'd never seen before—his need for me so powerful, it was almost frightening. "Look at me," he told me. "I want to see you, when I do this."

I squirmed at the thought...but the heat inside me glowed suddenly hotter. I'd lost my virginity when I was seventeen; this felt like losing it all over again—forbidden and dangerous and achingly exciting. I held his gaze....

And felt the tip of him just part my lips. I resisted the urge to look down. The smooth, silky head, arrow shaped, eased into me, spreading me wider and wider. I felt my eyes widen in response. Inside, I was going fluttery and twitchy, wanting to take him but not sure if I could. He opened me wider. *Oh God!* My hips tried to back up onto the table but his hands suddenly grabbed them, holding me tight. The head of him stretched me, making me gasp—

And suddenly he was filling me, a long silken thrust that made me moan and grab for his shoulders. He moved closer, his hips brushing my thighs, and I arched my back as I felt him slide *deep*. He came to rest with his head almost on my shoulder and my nipples scraping against the hard muscles of his chest. I was panting and so was he. "Jesus," he said, whispering it so as not to startle me in the silence. "You're perfect." And he laid a kiss on my neck.

I could feel him throbbing and huge inside me—it almost felt as if my whole body was one tight silken sheath around him. Just having him there was sending streamers of pleasure arcing outward through my body, making me slowly writhe and twist. And he hadn't even moved, yet.

I expected him to start straightaway, to go fast and hard and deep —my whole body tensed with anticipation and just a little heady fear. But instead, his hands slid up over my hips and across my back, winding up and around, criss-crossing in a slow, deliberate massage. They covered my shoulders and then worked down and I gasped as he squeezed my breasts. His palms slid further, down over my stomach, almost to the point where we joined, and then he went out along my thighs. It was as if he was worshipping each part of my body in turn.

And the whole time, there was that big, solid presence inside me, hot and throbbing and undeniable. Every time I responded to his touch, it made me more aware of him inside me. Every time I gave a wriggle or shifted on the table, his cock would twist or slide inside me and I'd catch my breath. Every groan of pleasure vibrated down to that hardness that filled me. Even a soft sigh made me tighten a little around him. We were connected on a level I'd never known before. I closed my eyes and just absorbed it: the heat of the room against my bare skin, his hands tracing every curve of my body, and the unyielding presence of him.

With every second, the anticipation built more and more. I'd been a little scared, before. Now I couldn't wait. I swept my fingertips over his hips, feeling the power of him, and then tentatively ran them around over his ass, thinking of how hard, how fast he'd be able to go at me. I wanted it. I wanted all those ugly words that men use and women aren't supposed to like: I wanted to be *pounded* and *drilled* and *hammered*. And, before I was even aware I was doing it, I was showing him: digging my fingers lightly into his ass and making little humping motions with my hips towards him. It was only when I heard him give a dark little chuckle that I snapped to awareness...and blushed.

That was when I realized: this is what he'd wanted all along. His need to corrupt me went far beyond simply muscling his way into me. He wanted me to be ready. He wanted me to want it...no, *need* it.

He'd held back so that I'd beg...and lose a little of my innocence along the way.

His hands went back to my hips, pinning me in place. He looked into my eyes again...and drew himself from me, almost all the way. Only when the thick head was teasing the inside of my lips did he stop...and then plunge back into me.

I gave a sharp little cry of pleasure. In this position, he was going up into me and it felt like the heat inside lifted with the movement...and it didn't drop back down again. He thrust again, fast and smooth and deep, that curling black hair kissing my groin, and the heat ratcheted higher again, compressing and tightening. I wrapped my arms around his shoulders, hanging on for support as he started an insistent rhythm, a little deeper on each stroke, his hips pressing my thighs wide. Then, with one long, slow push he finally rooted himself and I clutched at his back, fingers digging in as if trying to climb him, transfixed by the feeling of him so deep.

He eased me back on the table until my back was against the wood and I gasped as he moved within me. My fingertips scampered along the tabletop and found the far edge. I clung to it—I had to grab onto *something,* just to contain the rising, expanding pressure inside me. He hooked my legs over his arms, supporting me, and began to thrust again.

Oh. My. God. In this position, he could go faster, harder. And there was something about being on my back that made it even better. Being more passive brought all sorts of forbidden fantasies out of the secret places in my head: I was an English maiden, hurled down on a table by a Viking invader, a biker girlfriend, about to be taken in the clubhouse by her brutish boyfriend, a secretary ordered to strip and lie back on the conference table by her dominant boss...

I opened my eyes and looked at the gorgeous Irishman pounding into me...and that was the best fantasy of all. Our eyes met and the helpless need he saw in mine must have inflamed him because suddenly he was going faster, harder, slamming his hips into mine, muscled thighs slapping against my ass. Every thrust was a silken, brutal perfection, smoothly filling me, completing me...*owning* me.

And every one pushed the heat higher and higher inside me, squeezing it into a tight ball of fire in my chest.

He leaned forward and began to run his palms over my gleaming body from hips to shoulders, lifting and squeezing my breasts each time he passed. I started to writhe and buck on the table, arching my spine.

The sight of him towering over me, my legs so casually thrown over his arms, his muscled hips powering into me, was hotter than anything I'd ever seen. Like me, he was glistening from the heat, little shining jewels winding their way down the sculpted landscape of his chest to rollercoaster over the ridges of his abs. But it was his eyes, blazing down at me, that made me come.

I'd been scared of him for so long, until I got to know him. Even then, I'd been scared of the idea of him losing control. But seeing him like that, huge and savage and utterly given over to his lust for me...

The pleasure tightened in on itself like a black hole...and exploded, a white-hot starburst that took away any chance of thought. My body went rigid, my legs dragging him into me, heels digging into his ass. His palms were covering my breasts and I arched up into them, crushing them into his hands, each touch against my nipples bringing new waves of pleasure. I could feel myself tightening and spasming around him and then, as he growled and slammed his hips into me a final time, I felt the heat of his release.

He leaned forward, laying breathless kisses down my neck and across my shoulders, and I rode the waves on and on until they finally subsided. It was long minutes before either of us could move, but he eventually carried me over to the mattress, kicked it across the floor so that it lay directly in front of the air conditioning vent, and laid me gently down on it. Only then did we finally separate—but only for a second, and then I felt the pressure of his body against my back as he spooned me.

We lay there with the cool air blowing over us, listening to the rustle of leaves in the breeze as the room returned to normal. Eventually, I had my breathing under control enough to say, "That was...." And then I couldn't think of a word to do it justice. Not my best speech ever.

His arm slipped around my waist and pulled me tight. "Believe me," he murmured in my ear. "That was only the beginning." He pushed a lock of hair off my cheek. "The things I'm going to do to you..."

The way he said it sent a tremor of fear through me...fear and curiosity and a twist of dark heat. "Oh, really?" I asked, trying to sound worldly and nonchalant.

He heard the quaver in my voice and gave another of those dark chuckles that made me squirm. "You've got plenty more innocence to lose," he whispered in my ear.

I squirmed against him, shocked and delighted at the same time. I was already addicted to the feeling of his hard chest against my back. And I really did feel as if I'd lost my virginity all over again—there was that same sense that the whole world had changed forever.

And just like when I was seventeen, there was that stab of fear, as the golden haze of the orgasm faded. What if that's all it was—just sex? Was that all he wanted? "So, um...you and me," I said hesitantly.

He didn't answer with words. He slipped his other arm underneath me and pulled me even tighter back against his chest, then twisted around so that he could lay a kiss on my lips. Not the desperate, breathless kiss of a lover; the slow, gentle kiss of a boyfriend.

He moved back. "Okay?" he asked.

It was better than okay. My whole heart swelled and lifted. "That's your answer?" I asked, panting a little.

"Best one I can give you." I could see the sincerity in his eyes...and the pain. "I don't *do* relationships...until now. So give me a chance...okay?"

I nodded. It felt as if we'd started to build something. It was so fragile it would shatter if you so much as breathed on it...but it was enough.

To try to fill the silence, I asked, "So...where were you, when I sent you the text? You said it was a job. They had you smashing some place up?" The thought of him taking orders from criminals made me sick, not to mention the idea of him in constant danger from men like the two who'd threatened me. But I figured that if we were going to be together, I'd better start getting used to it.

He shifted on the mattress behind me. "No."

"It wasn't smashing some place up?"

I heard the pause as he pressed his lips together. "It wasn't a job. I lied." His arms tightened around me, as if scared I'd run.

"...oh." I wasn't sure how to react—mad that he'd lied or grateful that he was being honest.

"I was taking weed to my foster mom," he said slowly. "She has MS."

I twisted around slowly to face him. "That's why you're growing the plants on the roof."

He nodded. "There's this certain strain that helps with the symptoms...it's hard to get from the medical growers and it's expensive. I thought I'd grow her some, but it kept dying on me. Until you came along."

I looked at him in wonder. He was looking after someone too? This man everyone was so scared of, who was meant to be incapable of mercy or tenderness? I grabbed for his hand. "Why didn't you say something? I can help. Hell, move the plants in here, we have room. I can turn those scrawny things into freaking *forests.*" I frowned. "Was that where you were that night? When the two guys—" I swallowed and looked away, unable to say it.

His expression hardened and he pulled me into a bear hug. "Yeah. She has times when she's okay and times when she's bad. She needed me." I felt his whole body tense as the guilt hit him. "And so did you."

I hugged him back, my arms absurdly fragile around that huge back. "You got here in time," I told him. I ran my hands up and down his back, trying to comfort him, and it gradually worked. I felt his shoulders lower and his muscles relax...

...and then my fingers touched the scars I'd seen, that day when he'd stepped under the lights, and I jerked them back. He leaned back so that he could check my expression and he must have seen me put it together: *Foster parents. Scars. Stuff he won't talk about....*

"It's not what you think," he snapped, pulling away from me.

"I didn't say—"

His look cut me off. I'd been thinking it and that was enough. "Don't try and fix me," he said. "I don't need fucking fixing." And he grabbed his jockey shorts and started to pull them on.

Shit. "Wait!" But he ignored me and stood up to pull on his jeans. "Sean!"

He froze. He'd turned away from me but I could see his massive back rising and falling as he panted, fighting down the anger.

"I'm sorry! I didn't mean to—Look, I won't ask about it again, okay? It's off-limits. We'll make it a rule." I was babbling now because I could sense I was seconds from losing him. "I'm *good* at following rules!"

He slowly turned and looked over his shoulder at me. "You *are* good at following rules," he said at last, his voice a low rumble

"Yes! So...come on." I patted the mattress next to me. "Can we make this work?"

The question hung in the air between us. I could see the battle going on in Sean's eyes as he stood there, torn between heading for the door and returning to me. He looked deep into my eyes...and something changed in his expression—a softening, as if something had just melted inside him. I thought I saw him lean towards me, about to take a step—

The silence was shattered by his cell phone ringing. Both of us jumped. Sean walked over to his jeans and dug his phone out of the pocket. Looked at the screen. Answered.

I could only hear his side of the conversation and even that was mainly muttering. But I saw the way his expression darkened and the way he kept looking at me. I recognized that look from the time we'd gone to see Murray for the loan. He was scared for me.

When he finally ended the call and let the phone hang down by his side, he just stared at me, his lips pressed together.

"What?" I asked nervously.

"It was one of Malone's people," he said. "Malone's the guy we're going to sell the crop to. He wants to meet. Tonight."

I sat up. I was still naked but the room was hot—I'd been comfortably warm until he spoke. Now, the tone of his voice made me shiver. "That's *good* news, right?"

"Yeah," said Sean. "But he wants to meet *you.*"

39

LOUISE

"Why?" I asked, my voice coming out high and tight. "Why *me*?"

"You're the grower," said Sean. "You're what counts. You're what'll make it a good crop. I'm just hired muscle."

This was the side of things I'd not wanted to touch, the side *he* was meant to handle. Sean had terrified me, when we first met, and he was several rungs below the guy we were talking about. Someone with enough money to buy half a million dollars worth of weed...that was serious gangster territory, find-your-body-face-down-in-the-river stuff. "I can't," I said weakly. "I don't want to meet him."

"I don't *want you* to meet him," he told me. And I saw his hands ball into fists. "I want to keep you as far away from him as possible. But fuckers like Malone, they get what they want. If we say no, the deal'll be off."

Shit. Now I really did feel shivery. I grabbed one of the blankets Sean used for sleeping and threw it over me, despite the heat. It smelled faintly of him, and that made me feel better. "Where? When? What's he like?"

Sean's voice was a low rumble. "His jazz club. Tonight. And he's a big, fat, bald, black fucker."

"I meant—is he dangerous?"

"I know what you meant." He came over to me and knelt down in front of me, then brushed his hand through my hair, pushing it back from my face. When he spoke again, his voice was heavy with regret. "Yeah, Louise, he's a nasty son of a bitch. But no one else around here can move this amount of dope."

"Does he know I'm a woman?"

"No. He doesn't know anything about you," he said bitterly. He'd been hoping, just as I had, that I'd be able to remain out of sight. He'd wanted to keep me insulated from all this. But now....

Now I was going to have to get closer than ever to that dark, criminal world. Or the whole plan would fail. But I was so scared...

I took a deep breath. *For Kayley.*

I leaned forward and put a reassuring hand on his arm. "You'll be with me, right?"

He gripped my shoulders with his huge hands. "*Fuck* yes."

I nodded. "Then I'll be okay." I looked into his eyes, then down at myself, at the mattress. I wanted to know where we stood, what his answer was. The phone call had interrupted us just at the crucial moment.

He gathered me into his arms, the drape sliding out from between our bodies, and cuddled me naked against him to show me that everything was alright, and I gradually relaxed. We were together and, as long as that was true, I felt like I could handle anything else. "I have to get home," I said. "I raced out this morning—I haven't seen Kayley all day."

I felt his nod against my shoulder. Then he drew back, took my cheeks between his hands and kissed me, sending a soothing glow through my whole body. "Go," he said tenderly. "For tonight, put on something dressy. I'll pick you up at nine."

40

LOUISE

At home, I fixed some food for Kayley, badgered her to do some schoolwork and talked to her about boys while throwing a load of laundry in the washer. I tried to make everything seem as normal as possible...but I was worried about her. There was only a month to go of the six Dr. Huxler had given her. Each day, her eyes seemed a little less bright. *Just hang on,* I kept willing her. *One more month.*

Meanwhile, I was reeling from what had happened with Sean. It wasn't that I regretted it: I knew being around him was dangerous, but it felt like everything had changed, now: it was him and me against the world, instead of him off on his own, not letting anyone near him. Whatever the dangers were, we'd face them together. The thing that had me reeling was suddenly being in a relationship. After years single, I was suddenly *with* someone...and I couldn't tell a damn person about it.

Add in being terrified about meeting a freaking drug lord that night and it's fair to say I was a mess. I also realized I had no idea what the hell you were supposed to wear to a jazz club and I was pretty sure I didn't have anything suitable anyway. In desperation, I called Stacey.

Being Stacey, she was at my apartment with three different dresses and two pairs of shoes in less than half an hour. I eventually settled on the third dress, a red one that managed to be classy and sexy without showing too much skin. At first, I rejected the heels—I *never* wore serious heels. But once I tried them, I found the extra height gave me a little more confidence. And I was going to need every bit of confidence I could get.

"You go have fun," Stacey told me.

I gaped at her as I realized what she must be thinking. "It's not a *date!*" I spluttered. God, she thought I was leaving my sick sister to go off and meet some guy! "It's a business thing!"

She frowned. "Louise, I've said this before: *you work at a garden store.*"

I opened and closed my mouth a few times.

She sighed and lowered her voice, making sure Kayley couldn't hear from her bedroom. "It's *okay* to have fun."

"It's not a...." I trailed off. It wasn't a date...but I *had* finally started something with Sean. She was more right than wrong. And that made me feel utterly ashamed. How *dare* I have fun? The only thing in my life should be Kayley, especially when she was sick.

Stacey must have seen my expression because she shook her head. "Stop trying to be super-mom for *one second* and think of yourself. I'm *glad* you've met someone," Stacey said. "Seriously. I hope it goes well."

I sighed...and nodded. Maybe she was right, even if she had no idea who it was I was getting involved with. Maybe it *was* okay to have some fun. "Okay," I said at last. "Thank you." Then I saw how she was looking at me. "What?"

"Nothing."

"*What?*" She had a look in her eyes you never want to see from your best friend: pity. I replayed the conversation. "What did you mean, *I hope it goes well?*"

She went quiet and it took another few seconds of studying her guilty face before I got it.

"You mean in case she dies," I said hollowly. "You mean you hope it works out because, if Kayley dies, you don't want me to be alone."

"No!" Stacey said frantically. "Not like that!" But after a second, she sighed and hung her head.

"Jesus," I said to myself. I wanted to tell her that it wasn't like that. That however much I wanted Sean, however much I liked him, the idea of him being someone Kayley and I could share my life with—I wasn't even going to allow myself to *think* about a life without Kayley —that was just....

That was crazy, right? He was a criminal. And he kept shutting me out. And yes, we'd overcome those things, for now, but to think it could last, that we could make something long term?

Crazy.

And yet I wanted it to be true. The feel of his chest against my back, the way he'd kissed me just before I'd left the grow house...it had been the first time I hadn't felt alone in years.

"You're a good friend," I said at last, and gave her a squeeze. "I don't tell you that enough."

She squeezed me back, relieved that I wasn't mad at her. "Just be careful," she told me, her voice muffled by the hug. "I hope he's a nice guy."

I closed my eyes and just held her tight for a second. Then I faked my best smile and said I'd better finish getting ready, because my date would be here soon.

41

LOUISE

I didn't want Stacey to see Sean, so I slipped out of the apartment and met him in the hallway. Thank God Kayley had dozed off in her room, so I didn't have to explain to *her* where I was going.

Sean took a long look at me, taking in the borrowed dress and the heels. Unbidden, I felt my whole body react under that ferocious gaze, icy cold and yet burning hot at the same time.

"You look amazing," he said. It wasn't like any compliment I'd been paid before. It was so simple and heartfelt—it made me *feel* amazing.

Outside our building, a full-on summer storm had started complete with charcoal sky and hard, beating drops that hurt your skin. It would be gone again within a half hour but, for now, it would soak us to the skin as soon as we stepped outside. Sean put a hand on my arm—*stay put*—and then stalked out into the middle of the street, ignoring the rain entirely, and put a hand out to stop a passing cab. Then he stalked back to me, whipped off his leather jacket and held it like a tent above my head. We jog-walked to the cab and everything except my legs stayed dry.

Inside, we both sat there brooding. I stared out of the window at the hammering rain: after weeks of dry weather, every parched blade of grass and struggling weed was straining towards the sky, desperate to receive *something.*

The cab swept into downtown, passing bars and fancy restaurants, and my fear started to build. We pulled up outside a big, slate-gray place that stood on a corner, with a neon saxophone outside. There was a line outside, people standing under umbrellas and slowly shuffling towards the door. Two doormen were checking IDs. It could have been any club—there was nothing to suggest it was owned by a...I didn't even know what to call Malone. *Drug dealer* didn't cut it. *Supplier? Kingpin?*

It brought it home to me that there was a whole other Los Angeles, a whole other *world,* lurking beneath the one I knew, a world I'd spent my entire life staying away from. "I'm scared," I said aloud.

Sean had been studying the doormen. He turned to me, but I was too busy eying the club. "Look at me," he said, his accent cleaving the air. When I focused on him, he said, slowly and deliberately, "I won't let anything happen to you. Okay?"

I took a deep, panicky breath. "Promise?"

His voice softened a little. "Promise."

We ran across the street and under the shelter of the club's awning. I went towards the end of the line but Sean shook his head and led me straight towards the doormen. Both of them squared up when they recognized him, blocking the doorway.

"Easy," rumbled Sean. "I'm just here for a meeting."

The doormen muttered into their earpieces, glaring suspiciously at Sean. I barely warranted a glance. Eventually, they heard back from whoever was on the other end of the radio and nodded us through. Another big guy in a suit directed us through a metal detector, and then gave Sean a quick pat-down and checked my purse, just to be sure. We didn't have any weapons to give up, but it still felt as if we were being made safe, in the way a creature might be de-fanged and de-clawed before being served to the king on a platter. With every step we took into the club, the outside world seemed to recede.

The main room was a huge, dark cavern with tiny, closed-packed tables and a small stage. Most of the lights were aimed at the stage, with only flickering candles lighting the tables. Every seat was full and there was barely any room to stand. Even so, the crowd parted like water when the security guards marched us through. We stopped in one corner and were told to wait behind a red velvet rope while a guard went on ahead up some stairs—presumably to announce us.

The fear had been building steadily ever since we'd pulled up outside. It wasn't just knowing that we were right in the heart of a criminal's lair, it was knowing I had to convince him that we were serious. This world was Sean's second home but I felt like what I was: a pretender. And as soon as we got in there, Malone was going to figure it out. "I can't do this," I muttered to Sean.

"You can."

"I'm not a criminal!" I hissed. I knew it was a stupid thing to say, considering the DEA would quite happily put us in Federal prison for what we'd been doing. "He'll *know,*" I told him. "He'll know that I'm just...nobody."

Sean turned to me and took hold of me by the shoulders. "You're *not* nobody," he told me, and he said it in a voice that allowed no argument. He almost looked angry that I'd said it and that made my heart flip-flop. "Look," he said. "Most of this shit is just attitude. We don't have fucking resumes. You're a grower because you *damn well say you're a grower.* Attitude. Like I have to be a scary fucker."

I swallowed. "But you *are* scary."

He glanced at me. "That still how you think of me?"

We locked eyes. "No," I said at last. "But I can't *be* scary. I'm the least scary person in the world."

"You don't have to be scary. That's not what we're selling you as."

"What *am* I?" I asked.

"The brains. And you don't have to pretend about that."

I felt my heart swell.

Footsteps descended the stairs. Sean grabbed my waist and pulled me close, his big hand sending pulses of heat through my dress. "You listen to me," he ordered, and his words were like rough-edged slabs of granite. When he spoke like that, you *listened.*

He put his mouth close to my ear and his voice changed. The words were still hard, cold stone but each one seemed to glow cherry red at its center. "You're the smartest person I've ever met. Smarter than me, smarter than Malone, smarter than anyone in this whole fucking game. You remember that."

I swallowed and nodded.

The guard returned, unclipped the velvet rope, and led us upstairs.

42

LOUISE

Malone was big, like Sean had said. Muscle-big, like he might have played football before the fat had built up. Even now, his shoulders seemed to fill most of the width of the couch, stretching out his suit jacket. And he was black—in the reflected stage spotlights and the flickering candles, his skin looked almost blue-black. But I barely registered either of those things.

The only thing that mattered was the man's sense of menace.

I'd thought Sean was intimidating, at first—sometimes, he still was. But he was scary in the way a big, strong attack dog with snapping teeth is scary. The violence he promised was somehow natural...*honest,* if that made any sense at all in a criminal world. It came from his muscles and his determination to do the job he was paid to do.

Malone put out an utterly different aura: you got the sense that he'd kill you because you'd displeased him, and the violence would be ugly and abstract, meted out by his thugs or at the end of a gun. At first, I thought of a boa constrictor, especially when I saw his huge hands, heavy with rings, which looked as if they'd easily crush a neck. But as he sat there motionless as an onyx statue, watching the stage from his private balcony, I realized what he really reminded me of: a huge, venomous spider. This club—this whole side of LA—was his web. He was powerful enough that he could simply sit there on his couch and his prey would come to him.

The guards waved us to the front of the balcony, where there were a couple of low stools. When we sat down on them facing Malone, our asses were almost on the floor and our heads were down below the level of the balcony wall. It was so that we wouldn't spoil Malone's view, I guessed. It also meant he loomed over us, even the massive Sean, and I was sure that wasn't an accident.

It took a full minute before Malone acknowledged us. When the band ended their song and the applause rang out, he finally lowered his eyes to Sean. "Mr. O'Harra," he intoned, his voice a deep bass boom that felt like it echoed off my ribcage. "What the fuck are you doing?" He said it with a lazy, poisonous malice that let us know how cruelly he'd kill us if the answer was wrong.

To his credit, Sean's voice didn't so much as waver. "I got a good deal for you. Weed. A lot of it. Fresh new supply, no problems with the law, just a nice fat crop ready to be sold."

Malone's lip curled in displeasure. "I know what you're offering, you Irish prick. I asked what you were doing. You're a fucking blunt instrument, like your goddamn hammer. You suddenly think you're sharp? Running around town making deals?"

I tensed, ready for that anger of Sean's to explode. No way would he be able to just sit there and take that. Hell, I was mad on his behalf: I'd seen how much more to him there was than smashing things.

But although Sean's shoulders set and his hands curled into fists, he said, "No, Mr. Malone. Just a one-time thing, then back to normal." He jerked his head towards me. "She's the brains."

Malone kept staring at him and I realized it was a test. He'd wanted Sean to prove his deference to his master. And Sean had sucked up his pride and done it. *For me.* To ensure the deal came off. I glanced across at him desperately, trying to communicate my thanks. He nodded.

And now Malone turned to me. It was like watching a huge stone statue come to life: only his head rotated, as if I didn't warrant moving any more of him. "And who the fuck are you?" he asked. There was a flicker of interest in his eyes: the fact I was a woman in a business run by men bought me maybe five seconds before he got bored. It was all down to me.

And I messed it up.

I swallowed. "I'm Louise Willowby. I grow stuff. And I've got—I'm growing this stuff that's going to be—It'll be really good—"

Malone held up one massive hand, palm facing me, and I stopped talking. He turned back to Sean. "You do good work," he grunted. Each word was like the launch of an iceberg, huge and unstoppable. "That's the only reason I'm letting you out of here without a beating. Jesus, I should have them take that fucking sledgehammer and break your legs with it, wasting my time like this."

Sean's eyes flared with fury and I thought he was going to spring at Malone...but then he glanced across at me and lowered his gaze to the floor. *He's scared of me getting hurt!*

Malone, meanwhile, had tilted back his head and was unscrewing the cap from a small white bottle. Physostigmine, for glaucoma—my grandma used to take the same stuff. He was taking his goddamn medication, as if he'd already forgotten about us.

As he started to drip the drops into his eyes, the guards came forward to throw us out. I thought of Kayley. All that time I'd spent at the grow house when I could have been at her side, and now it was all for nothing. We had no buyer and I was going to have to stand by and watch her die—

I jumped to my feet. "I'm a grower," I said, loud and clear. "I'm a grower, goddamn it!"

Malone kept his head tilted back, but he looked down his nose at me. The guards had nearly reached us, now.

"I'm not like the others," I told him. "I'm using stuff I learned in college, straight out of NASA, stuff that your guys won't pick up on for years. They use the same fertilizer all the time; I change the ratios of phosphorus and nitrogen, depending on the stage of the plants' growth. I raise the nitrogen while the plants are young, then switch to higher phosphorus while they're flowering, then back to higher nitrogen. That means more THC per leaf—it'll be a smoother, cleaner, more intense smoke." Hands grabbed my arms. "I know my shit so, goddamn it, *listen to me!*"

Malone slowly lowered his head to look at me. Out of the corner of my eye, I saw the nearest guard flinch at the way I'd spoken to him. Their hands tightened on my arms, digging in—

Malone lifted his hand and I was released. For several seconds he just stared at me. At last, he said, "You got a big fucking mouth. Is this weed really going to be all that?"

I swallowed and nodded. "Yeah. It's really going to be all that."

"It better be. Lennie said you want five hundred large for three hundred pounds. That's some premium shit. Is it really premium shit?"

I set my jaw and stared right back at him. "It's premium shit."

He drew in a long breath, searching for any sign of weakness in my face. Then he said, "You grow your crop. If it's really like you say...then yeah, I'll buy it."

He nodded to the guards and they hustled us downstairs and out of the club. It was still raining but nothing like as heavily as before. As we stepped out into the night, Sean and I looked at each other with the same relieved-but-disbelieving expression. Had we really...*done it?*

We had. We had our buyer.

"I'm proud of you," he told me.

I flushed. "I surprised you in there, huh?"

He looked at me steadily. "No. I knew you could do it."

I bit my lip. "I'm proud of you, too. You didn't get mad, or smash anything."

He glowered. "I nearly did, when he wouldn't listen to you. I was ready to throw him off his fucking balcony."

I put a hand on his shoulder. Just the feel of him, his warm solidness, through his leather jacket made me go heady. "I'm glad you didn't."

And then we were leaning into each other, twisting our heads to kiss. It was oddly slow and tentative: every time until now, we'd kissed because we'd lost control. Now, in the darkness, with the rain pattering softly on our heads and shoulders, I felt like a teenager working up the courage to kiss for the very first time.

With a boy she *really, really* liked.

Our lips met in a slow dance, tasting each other, experimenting. His hands slid into my hair and it was magical, one of those lift-you-up kisses I thought you didn't get once you were grown up. For a minute or maybe more, we just kissed, slow and romantic and goddamn *perfect*. When he finally drew back from me and looked into my eyes, I grinned like an idiot.

Only then did we think about the possibilities. His hands knitted with mine and he squeezed.

"You can't come back to my place," I said. "Kayley—"

He nodded quickly. "We could go to mine." He checked his watch. "But I need to go to the grow house, soon."

I put my hands on his chest, tracing the shape of his muscles. The mood was sliding, very quickly, from romantic to scorching hot. "The grow house is closer," I mumbled.

His hands skimmed down my back. "The grow house *is* closer. You could get a cab home afterwards...."

I swallowed as his hands reached my ass. I had to have him: *now.* I raised my hand in the air. "Taxi!"

We almost fell through the door of the grow house with Sean trying to work the zipper of my dress. "It's stuck," he mumbled into my neck.

"Don't break it!" I panted, clawing at the buttons of his shirt. "It's not mine!"

Sean kicked the door closed...and a white envelope that had been on the mat wafted into the air.

"What's that?" I asked, dodging a kiss.

"Don't know," said Sean. "Don't care." He kissed me, long and hard, and started to work the dress up my hips.

It took every bit of willpower I had, but I tore my lips away from him. "Wait!" I said. "Who's writing to us? Who even knows we're here?" I grabbed the envelope from the mat and tore it open.

Sean huffed and growled while I read the letter. "What?" he asked impatiently.

I read it again. And again. The words refused to change.

"*What?*" asked Sean again, worried, this time. He'd seen my expression.

"It's from the realtor," I said. "They've sold the land the house is built on. They want us out in seven days." I glanced around at the plants. "And they're coming to inspect the place tomorrow morning."

43

SEAN

We exchanged horrified looks.

"That's not possible!" said Louise, her voice cracking. "They can't just—"

"They can," I said, running my hand over my face. "They just have to give us notice—this is notice."

"But..." She looked around her. "They're not ready! We need another month!" She was getting paler and paler by the second as the full implications sunk in. I knew, because my mind was making the same connections. The money. Kayley's treatment. Kayley's *life*. She stared at me, tears filling her eyes.

And I felt that same thing I had the first time I learned about Kayley—that deep, aching swell in my chest that for so many years I'd thought I wasn't capable of. The feeling I'd been clamping down on as hard as I could, because it led to a fantasy I knew could never be real: Louise and me together and happy.

Only things were different now. I didn't know if we'd work together—fuck, I didn't know if I'd work with *anyone*. There was so much bad shit in my past that I kept locked away, I wasn't sure if there was enough *me* for a relationship. But for the first time, I wanted to try. And so I let that pressure build and build in my chest, letting myself really feel the injustice of it the way she did every fucking day.

And I got mad. Only for once, I didn't let it spill out as swings of hammer and fist. I had to be like her. For once, I had to be smart.

"We are going to move this entire operation," I said, each word slow and deliberate.

Louise looked up at me. "How? We've got nowhere else to grow! We can't rent a new place *overnight!* And even if we could, *look!*" She waved her hand at the tables, the plants, the lights. "We can't move all that by tomorrow morning!"

After all the months of grim determination and refusal to give up, she'd finally reached her breaking point. She needed someone to back her up.

I'd never fought for a fucking thing, my whole life. Only *against* things. But I was going to fight for this.

"I've got an idea," I told her, and held out my hand. "Let's go."

44

LOUISE

Sean's idea was one of those simple-but-brilliant plans that can only be born when your back's against the wall. We couldn't rent somewhere officially, not by tomorrow. So this had to be an off-the-books deal, strictly cash, no questions asked. Who the hell would agree to a deal like that?

Someone with a place that was *unrentable*.

I called Stacey and asked if she could stay the night at my apartment. I could hear the smile in her voice when she told me to go have fun—she had the day off tomorrow and was happy to hang out at my place with Kayley. "So sleep in with him," she told me. *God, she thinks I got lucky on my date!* I just wished I could tell her the truth.

We took both cars, splitting up to cover more ground. We needed somewhere big enough to house all the plants, away from prying eyes and in enough of a state that no one else would want it...while still having power, water and a roof. We trawled property ads and internet sites and, when all else failed, just drove around likely areas looking for places. We were frantic, driving to one place while calling another, swapping information between us and crossing places off our list. Since it was late evening, all the offices were closed...so we had to track down the owners' cell phone numbers and call them direct.

The first four places I looked at wouldn't work—disused factories and workshops sounded good at first, but they were all owned by big companies who'd want forms filled out. The fifth place, an "artist's studio" I found on the internet, turned out to have no roof. The sixth was too small, the seventh was perfect...and the owner was on vacation and couldn't be contacted. By now, the battery indicator on my phone was eaten down to a slender red line, my list was a mass of crossings-out and my throat was raw from talking. I was close to giving up.

I saw the place completely by chance: a mansion all on its own on a hill overlooking the city. Three floors, lots of windows...there were even honest-to-goodness turrets. It reminded me most of all of the Addams Family house. It must have been worth a fortune, once.

A very long time ago.

Now, half the windows were broken and the shutters were drooping or had fallen off entirely. The iron fence around the property was bent and broken in places, the lawn was up to knee height and I thought I could see vegetation growing on the roof.

It was awful...and strangely wonderful. And quite possibly, perfect.

There was a faded realtor sign in the garden. A phone call revealed that, yes, the house had been for sale several times over the last decade, but the owner—a Mrs. Baker—had taken it off the market. The realtor gave me her number just to get rid of me.

Esmeralda Baker turned out to be pushing eighty. Her accent was pure old-money Boston. "Where we should have stayed," she sniffed as she walked me across the overgrown yard. "But my great-grandmother wanted to run off with the stable boy, and *he* in turn decided he was going to join the California gold rush. To everyone's astonishment, he actually struck it rich. He built my great-grandmother this house just to spite her father."

She unlocked the front door and swung it wide. "Of course," she said, "it's seen better days."

My jaw dropped open. I took in the dark wood staircase that

swept up to the second floor, the galleried landing, the once-beautiful black and white tiled floor.

But mostly, I stared at the tree.

It had erupted through the floor and thrust out branches to touch all four walls as it grew. It stretched right to the top of the double-height room. In fact—I leaned forward and craned my head back to look—yep, some branches were actually poking through the roof. That explained the vegetation I'd seen up there.

"How did it—" I asked weakly.

"It's an American Sycamore," she said sternly. "Those things grow *fast*. The floor was torn up by the plumbers to get at some pipes, right down in the foundations, and there was a hole in the roof and...well, at the same time I was running a little short of money so the work ground to a stop, and the house was unoccupied for several years while I was living with my sister. A seed must have blown in. I came back and..." She waved her hand at the tree.

The house was completely unsellable—no one in their right mind would take on such a disaster. "Can I see the rest?" I asked with growing excitement.

The living room had a huge hole in the floor but the kitchen and two of the other reception rooms were in a good state of repair. There was even power and water. I spun around to Mrs. Baker. "I want to make you an offer," I said.

"To *buy?*"

"To rent."

She shook her head.

"Look," I pressed, "you aren't going to sell it. You must know that."

"Renting it's not worth my while," she sniffed.

I was desperate. "*Ten thousand dollars.* For one month." When she hesitated, I said, "Come on, it's sitting here doing nothing. In a month we'll be gone and you'll have ten thousand in the bank for repairs."

She looked at me sternly. "Young lady, I was *not* born yesterday. What are you planning to do here: run a brothel? A gambling den?" But there was a gleam in her eye that hadn't been there before, as if I was bringing back old memories. I wondered what her family had been involved with, back in the day.

"Ten thousand," I said levelly. "We give you back the house as we found it and you don't ask any questions. Anything goes wrong, it's on us and you had no idea. You're just a nice old lady who got duped."

For a while, I thought she wasn't going to go for it. Then she crossed her arms and nodded. "Cash up front."

My smile of relief only lasted a few seconds. I told her I'd be back with the entire amount in an hour, but then I sat in my car staring out at the night. We'd spent all of our money. We couldn't scrape together a thousand dollars to give her, never mind ten.

Which only left one solution.

I pulled out my phone and stared at Sean's number for a long time before finally putting it back in my purse. If I told him, he'd stop me. And this was our only shot.

I took a deep breath and went to see Murray.

45

LOUISE

As I'd thought, Murray moved around. I had to dig out the loan papers, find his number and call him to find out where his latest temporary office was. Yes, he said, he'd see me even at this late hour. In fact, he sounded worryingly pleased to hear from me.

This time, his place was up on the second floor of a mostly-abandoned office building. The scary thing was how much less alien it felt, going to see a loan shark. The last five months had changed me: dealing with criminals was almost normal, now.

In his lobby, the two heavies in suits were waiting as before. This time, though, they gave me a knowing, leering grin, much more obvious than before. Was it because Sean wasn't there? Or was it because they knew what me being back here meant?

Murray was leaning back in his chair, his hands behind his head. His grin only got wider when I told him I needed another ten thousand.

At first, I tried to brazen it out. "Come on," I said. "What's another ten thousand? Add it onto my original loan."

He let me have a few seconds of hope. Then, savoring the word, "No."

I stared at him, getting a sick feeling in the pit of my stomach. I could sense the power in the room shifting.

"You're a bad risk," he told me, leaning forward so that our faces were only a foot apart. I could feel his excitement, almost sexual—he was *thrilled* to see what I'd do next.

I got to my feet. "I'll find someone else."

"You think we don't all talk to each other? You think we don't swap names and numbers? Ten seconds on the phone and you're blacklisted, Louise."

I felt my knees go weak. After the air conditioning failure and then Malone and now the eviction, all in one day, I didn't have any more fight to give. Now *this?!* I could feel the mansion, our last shot at saving the crop, slipping away from me.

"Of course," said Murray as if throwing me a lifebelt, "there's always the other option. The one I offered you before."

I thought of Kayley, growing steadily weaker.

"What is it?" I asked. My voice was a low croak.

Murray mockingly tilted his head to one side. "Sure you don't want to call Sean? He was *so* against you taking that option."

"*What is it?*" I wanted to throw up. But I couldn't walk out of there without the money.

He opened a desk drawer and pulled out a printed contract. It already had my name on—all he had to do was write in the updated amount. My stomach twisted: he'd been *that* sure I'd come back.

"Sign it," he told me, pushing it and a pen across the desk.

With shaking hands, I started to flip through the pages.

"Fucking sign it," he said victoriously. "Or get out."

He knew I had no choice, no matter what it said. A few phrases leapt out at me from the densely-printed text.

...provision of modeling services...

...understand that recordings will be adult in nature...

...including open leg, toys, male/female, gang—

I stopped reading.

She was my sister. What else could I do?

I neatly signed my name, just below where it said that the contract would run for two years.

Murray whipped it out of my hand and threw it into a drawer, then opened up his safe and took out ten thousand: in hundred-dollar bills, it looked like a pathetically small stack, given what I'd just signed away. He seemed to delight in handing it to me, wrapping my fingers around the bills. "Come back here tomorrow," he told me. "I'll take you to meet some people. I think we can set you up with your first performance right away."

I stumbled towards the door on legs that felt waxy. I could feel a tug in my guts—it was as if I was leaving a part of me there in Murray's office, locked away in his desk drawer, and I'd never be whole again.

"Get your hair done," Murray told me as I opened the door. "Nails, too, and make-up."

I paused on the threshold. "What should I wear?" I croaked.

The two heavies in the lobby heard that and laughed. Behind me, Murray laughed too. "Whatever the fuck you want," he told me. "Thirty seconds in, those guys will have you naked anyway."

I tried to stalk through the lobby, to not let their leers and laughter bother me, but whatever pride and confidence I'd built up over the last five months had just been stripped away. I'd gone from *civilian* to *criminal* and now I'd changed again. Now I was *meat*.

Back in my car, I took some deep breaths and forced down the tears that threatened to spill out. Then I drove straight to Mrs. Baker's place and handed over the ten thousand dollars

There. Now it was done, and it couldn't be undone. But I still didn't want Sean to know. We had too much to do and no time to argue. I forced my face into a mask and drove to meet him.

One thing was for sure: after the things Murray would make me do, Sean wouldn't want me anymore. No one would want me. Just as things were beginning to work out between us, I'd wrecked them for good.

46

SEAN

We had less than ten hours before the realtor came around to inspect the house. But it's amazing how fast you can move, given the right motivation.

I hired a truck, backed it up to the garage and we started loading plants. There were two hundred to move and it had to be done carefully, without damaging them. I provided the brute force, lifting and carrying the pots, while Louise knelt in the back of the truck arranging them and packing them in tightly so they didn't move around. I could tell something was bothering her—she'd been almost silent, ever since she'd called me to tell me she'd found a place. But she kept telling me she was fine and I knew better than to push...for now. As soon as we got this done, I needed to find out what the hell was going on.

The tables had to be disassembled and packed, too, and the lights. All of the wiring that controlled them and the maze of pipes Louise had set up to drip-feed water to the plants. The monitoring sensors. The mattress. The horizon started to lighten and we tried to go faster, with me carrying bigger and bigger loads and Louise frantically trying to cram stuff into the truck. By the time we reached the bags of fertilizer in the garage, I was literally throwing them up to her and she was stuffing them into any available space.

We drove to the new place...but, as we arrived, I slowed to a stop in the street outside. *"Here?"* I asked, looking at the broken windows and holes in the roof. "Are you serious?"

"We're growing in it," she told me, repeating what I'd told her five months ago. "Not living in it."

We parked the truck but didn't unload it, yet. There was one more thing we had to do.

Back at the grow house, dawn was creeping quickly across the sky. Inside, I started carefully pouring gasoline in trails from room to room.

"You sure we have to do this?" Louise asked nervously, curling her hair around her finger. "There's no other way?"

"However much we try to clean it up, we'll leave a trace," I told her. "Bits of leaf between the floorboards. Soil ground into the carpets. They'll know we were growing here. Hell, they'll know from the smell. This way, we get rid of everything." I pulled out a box of matches. "Get ready to move," I told her.

"Wait!"

I stopped.

She walked up beside me and held out her hand for the matches. "You've destroyed enough," she said quietly. "It's time for me to take some of this on."

Just when I thought she was done surprising me, she found a new way.

I handed over the matches. She lit one and tossed it. There was a soft little *wumph* as the gasoline caught and then a wall of heat hit us as the flames rushed outward.

We backed outside and hid across the street. We waited until we were sure the house was unsaveable, then called the fire department. Then we started banging on doors, making sure all the neighbors were out. The houses were spaced far enough apart that I was sure the fire wouldn't spread, but we weren't taking any chances.

When the fire service arrived, I told them a story about knocking over a can of gasoline in the garage and a lit cigarette. As I'd expected, once they'd triple-checked that there was no one inside, they didn't risk sending in guys just to save a house that was clearly finished anyway. They damped down the flames from the outside as best they could but, by the time the realtor rolled up to inspect the place, it was a smoking pile of blackened wood.

"I can't believe I just burned down a house," Louise whispered.

"Don't feel too bad. They were going to knock it down and sell the land anyway," I told her.

As soon as we'd answered everyone's questions, we headed over to the mansion. When I saw the interior for the first time, I dropped the fertilizer I was carrying.

"What do you think?" she asked nervously.

"It's very...you," I said slowly. "Especially the tree."

She bit her lip. "Did I screw up?"

I grabbed her, picked her up and pulled her to my chest. After all the stress of the night, I even let myself laugh. "No! It's great." I shook my head, looking around. "Incredible."

She nodded, relieved...but she still seemed too tightly wound, considering what we'd just pulled off. "Louise..."

She immediately hurried out to the truck. "Come on! We've got to get the plants back under the lights."

I sighed and followed her. It took us most of the morning to get all the tables set up in the undamaged rooms and rig up the lights and watering systems. I carried the mattress upstairs—I figured we might as well use it, now we *had* an upstairs—while Louise set up the monitoring sensors. When we were all done, I stood with her in the kitchen and looked at our relocated jungle.

"We did it," she said, letting out a long sigh. But her face didn't show any relief.

And that's when, finally, I figured it out.

"Louise," I said, barely wanting to form the words, "how did you pay for this place?"

She raised huge, scared eyes towards me.

"Oh Jesus," I breathed.

"I didn't have a choice!" she snapped, her fear coming out as anger. But her eyes were filling with tears. "We didn't have any time left and I thought—I thought that if I told you, you'd talk me out of it and then we wouldn't be able to afford a place and then...we'd have to abandon the whole thing and you'd walk away!"

I let out a long, slow breath, trying to control my rage. I took her by the shoulders and pushed her up against the nearest wall. "Haven't you fuckin' worked it out yet? I'm not going to walk away! Not from you!"

She sniffed and nodded and then I was covering her lips with mine, letting her know that I was there for keeps. I tasted salty tears but I kissed them away and went on kissing, wrapping my arms around her waist and holding her tight until she finally relaxed against me.

I pulled her in tighter and kissed her neck, then the top of her head. "No more keeping shit from me," I growled. She nodded...but I knew that it was going to swing both ways: if I wanted her to be honest with me, I was going to be honest with her about my past.

One problem at a time.

I gave her one last squeeze and then pulled her towards my car. "Come on," I told her. "We're going to see Murray."

47

LOUISE

When we arrived, Sean took his hammer and told me to wait in the car. But I crept up the stairs behind him and waited outside Murray's office, ears straining. I had to know what was going on. What if Murray's heavies had guns? This wasn't like smashing up a dealer's operation or a grow house: sleazy as it was, Murray's business was at least partially within the law. He could opt to call the cops.

I heard the heavies get to their feet. "Unless you're here with the redhead, O'Harra, fuck off."

I didn't have to see their leering grins—I could hear it in their voices. "Murray said we could hang around on set. I'm looking forward to seeing her get stuffed. Maybe they'll even need us to help, if they run out of cocks."

Sean's heavy footsteps. Then a choking noise and the sound of something heavy hitting the wall. I peeked around the door frame.

Sean had pinned the two men against the wall, the handle of his sledgehammer across both their throats. Their toes just barely touched the ground. "You ever talk about her like that again," he said, "and I'll knock your fuckin' heads off."

The men gurgled and choked, their faces turning blue. One of them tried to reach under his jacket. Sean kneed him in the groin.

When he finally released them, both of them fell to their knees, holding their throats. Sean snaked his hands under their jackets and my stomach tightened when he pulled out two guns. He tossed them on the floor and then swung the hammer down on both of them, reducing them to twisted lumps of metal and leaving a dent in the floor.

I pulled back behind the door frame so that he didn't see me. The next thing I heard was the crash as he opened Murray's door—with his foot or the hammer, I couldn't see.

"That contract is legal," I heard Murray say. "It's fucking legal, O'Harra. You can smash all you like but she'd better come here, today, ready to meet her new boyfriends, or she owes me ten thousand."

There was a cracking, splintering sound and I guessed that Sean had just brought the hammer down on Murray's desk. "It's not about the fucking contract!" he yelled. There was rage in his voice like I'd never heard. A metallic bang echoed through the building—he must have slammed the hammer into Murray's safe. "It's about her! She's not one of your girls!" A hard thump and the crunch of plaster—I imagined him burying the hammer in the wall, right next to Murray's head. "She's better than that! Better than all of us!"

For once, Murray's voice was shaky. "I want paying," he said. "You can have the contract but you gotta buy it out."

I heard Sean snarl and closed my eyes, waiting for the sound of the hammer hitting bone. That would be it: Murray dead, Sean in jail —I might never see him again.

But the noise that came instead was tiny, the barely-audible thump of something small being tossed down on the floor. A moment later, Sean stormed out of the office. He did a double-take when he found me lurking outside, then pushed something into my hand: my contract.

"Tear it up," he told me, and I did—in long, loud rips that felt like freedom.

"But how did—you don't have any money either!" I said.

He shrugged and kept walking towards the street, laying his hammer over his shoulder. He took out his phone and started dialing.

"What are you doing?" I asked, frowning.

"Calling a cab."

I glanced at the Mustang, confused. Then I realized what he'd done and my face fell. "Oh my God...but that car's the only thing you care about!"

He stopped walking and turned back to me. "No," he said. "It's not." He put his finger under my chin and tilted my head up and then his lips were coming down on mine. Hard and ferocious, forcing my lips apart. I gladly opened for him, molding my body to his. Every press of his lips sent fresh ripples of pleasure through me and I gave myself up to it completely, floating on a river of pure relief. My chest was going fluttery at what he'd just said...what he'd just *done.*

His tongue explored my lips and then dived inside, the kiss turning deeper and hotter. His hands slid through my hair and then clasped my shoulders, holding me in place for a second. But that wasn't enough for him. Before I knew what was happening, his hands had slid down my body and I was being lifted like a doll, one hand on my ass and the other across my back. He growled and kissed me again and again, arms locked around me in an unbreakable hold. I moaned in pleasure—it was like nothing I'd ever experienced, even from him. He'd kissed me plenty of times but I'd never felt so...*kissed.*

And then I realized what it was: he was kissing Murray right out of me.

When he finally released me, he drew in a long breath, still refusing to put me down. "Let's get back to the mansion," he said. "There's something I want to show you."

48

LOUISE

At the mansion, I insisted on checking on the plants before we did anything else. But they seemed to have survived the move just fine: they were shooting up and we were nearly ready for the final phase, where they'd flower. Maybe, just maybe, we could still pull this off.

Sean took me by the hand and led me up the staircase, both of us watching carefully for rotten planks. I hadn't even gone upstairs when I rented the place: I'd only been interested in whether there was room to grow. Now I looked around in wonder at the antique wallpaper and the wood paneling. It was a beautiful place, even if it was in an appalling state. With enough work, it could make a great home for someone.

Then Sean pushed open a set of double doors and I just stopped and stared in amazement.

The master bedroom was missing nearly all of the glass in its windows, but the holes had been sealed with cardboard and the summer weather meant it wasn't too drafty. The roof was intact and even the floor seemed to be solid. But none of that mattered.

What mattered was the bed.

It was a huge four poster built out of dark, varnished wood. There were no drapes but it was easy to imagine them hanging down from the thick cross-beams. And lying ready on the bed springs was the mattress from the grow house.

"I mean, y'know..." Sean sounded embarrassed. "I know there's no sheets or anything. But...I thought you'd like it."

"I *love it!*" I yelled and dived on, bouncing on my back on the mattress. Even without drapes, being on the bed was like being in a separate little room, intimate and magical. It didn't matter that there were cracks in the room's plaster and peeling paint: *instant princess!* And along with all the innocent, little-girl dreams that brought back, a few full-on adult ones swam into my mind. This was the sort of bed you didn't so much *make love* on as *got ravished* on.

Sean joined me on the bed, but even as he reached for me, I jumped up and crossed the room, hungry to explore. There was a huge, silvered mirror hanging on the wall opposite the bed. Like the bed, it must have been too big or too much trouble to move when Mrs. Baker left. And next to it was a free-standing closet taller than me—taller even than Sean. You could have driven a small car through its huge, polished doors. I ran my fingers over the dark wood in wonder and then opened it up, just to see how big it was.

And found the dress.

It was emerald green with a low-cut, almost square neckline and a long, flaring skirt. A dress that was so simple and classic it could have passed for anything from medieval gown to modern day red carpet. I had no idea how old it was—twenty years, fifty, more? I sniffed it, but it didn't smell musty at all. I turned around holding it, to show Sean.

He was kneeling up on the bed and looking at me in a very strange way. "What?" I asked, glancing down at the dress in case there was a killer spider or something crawling up it.

"*Put on the dress,*" he ordered. His voice was actually strained with lust—I could hear it in every silver-edged, panty-melting Irish syllable.

I swallowed and looked at the dress, excited but uncertain.

He tilted his head to one side and gave me a *don't make me come over there* look.

I took the dress and hurried out into the hallway. It felt wrong to change in front of him and spoil the effect. Whoever the dress had been made for, she'd had the same hips as me, but slightly smaller boobs. Fastening up the eyelets on the back of the dress made it lift and squeeze everything together and—well, there was a lot of cleavage on display. Or perhaps that was the idea.

Barefoot—because sneakers didn't feel right—I looked like some princess stealing out of the castle to see her secret lover...or possibly a maid, summoned to the king's bedchambers, I couldn't decide. "Close your eyes," I told Sean as I opened the door.

When I walked in, he was sitting up on the bed with his hand over his eyes. I took a second just to admire him: his soft, glossy black hair, the hard line of his jaw with its rough stubble, those lips that could snarl or grin or kiss the hell out of you, but were never cruel. Those shoulders, solid as rock and smoothly tan. The forearms, dense with muscle and thickly veined, and those hands that looked as if they could crush rocks.

"Open them," I whispered. I was suddenly nervous—did I just look stupid?

All my reservations were blown away with the very first look he gave me. "Sweet Jesus," he croaked. He'd given me the full heat of those Irish eyes before, but this was beyond that, beyond just sex. He was *entranced*. It felt as if he was drinking in every detail, as if I was some priceless piece of art. And there's no feeling like that in the world.

He got off the bed and strode towards me. Without words, he stripped his tank top off over his head and tossed it away. I tried to look up into his eyes but I was suddenly having a hard time tearing my gaze away from that tanned, sculpted chest. He was breathing slow but deep and, when I finally managed to look up, the look in his eyes was almost primal. Sure, I was some piece of art...one he had to have. *Right. Now.*

He came closer and closer, close enough that he could put his hands on my waist. He touched me almost gingerly: not as if he was scared, more as if he knew that, once he touched me, his self-control was going to disappear very, very fast. I'd never seen him so turned on, so *animal*. It would have been scary, if it had been anyone else. But I knew he'd never hurt me or do anything I didn't want him to. And that made it just incredibly hot.

"*You...*" he said, his breathing so harsh now that he almost had trouble getting the words out. "*Look...*" He shook his head as if, in his eyes, words couldn't do me justice. He ran his hands up the dress, following the bodice as it went in and then out, staring at my neckline. Those powerful fingers moved closer, closer....

"Wait—are you thinking about ripping it off me?" I asked.

His thumbs stroked the point where the fabric met the sides of my cleavage as if to say, *Fuck yes*. I started to rapidly melt, but: "Don't rip it," I said quickly. "It's not ours. You can do anything else, but don't rip it."

Out of nowhere, a twist of dark heat darted straight down my body and exploded in my groin. I really liked the way that sounded. So I said it again. And this time, I threw in *to me*. "You can do anything else to me." Another twist of heat, even stronger than before.

Sean tilted his head to one side questioningly. His eyes widened and he mouthed *Louise!* looking mock-shocked. But then his lips twisted into a dark, knowing grin.

I swallowed. My mind was swimming back to those historical romances I used to read, where the heroines wore dresses not so different from this one. I'd started to breathe fast and, every time I panted, my breasts lifted. With the tight dress, low neckline and no bra, there was a lot of...well, *heaving*.

I pressed just a little closer to him. How would those heroines have said it? I looked up into his eyes and gave him the full thing. "You can—You can do what you will with me, but please don't rip my dress you...you...*Irish beast!*"

I wasn't sure *beast* really came off right, without a British accent. But it didn't seem to matter.

With a sudden yell, Sean grabbed me around the waist and threw me—*literally threw me,* in a yelping bundle of kicking legs and flapping skirt—to land with a soft *wumf* on the mattress. By the time I managed to sit up, he was stalking towards me. His eyes were gleaming in a way I'd never seen before.

"Do what I will, Lady Louise? Are you *sure?*" *Oh God,* he was good at this. And he had the accent for it, too, He stripped his jeans off, taking his jockey shorts with them. He was already hard and he ran a hand up and down his shaft, brandishing it like a weapon.

I stared at it, transfixed. Maybe it was the fantasy, but I actually went a little heady, the blood pounding in my ears. Much more of this and I was going to full-on swoon. Between the dress, the four poster bed and his Irish gorgeousness, I really did feel like I was a maiden about to be ravished. He started to lift the dress up my legs, baring them, and I started to struggle—well, thrash around on the bed. I didn't want to actually get free. "Un—Unhand me!" I shrieked.

He pressed my ankles down on the bed with one big hand and continued. At which point I learned, to my delight, that when a big Irishman decides he's going to ravish you, you can struggle as much as you like and you won't put him off his game. I started to buck and wriggle, feeling the heat spike higher and higher inside me with every inch the dress climbed. *God, what's happening to me?*

I began to strain upwards with my ankles but by now he'd used his legs to pin me, leaving both hands free to pull the dress up my legs. My thighs were bared, then my very un-medieval panties. Which turned out not to matter at all because he simply grabbed and, with a twist and pull of his powerful arm, snapped the elastic. I shrieked again as I felt myself bared, and crossed one leg over the other as tightly as I could. I was panting, now, and the heat was thrumming through my whole body, making it sing like an instrument. I'd never felt anything like it before.

Sean stopped pulling the dress up when it reached my navel. Then he leaned down to kiss my lips and—

Suddenly I was twisting my head away, moving one way then the other to avoid him. I was panting, my face glowing. "You beast!" I managed. "How *dare* you!"

A truly evil grin spread across Sean's face. He moved fast, stretching out on top of me. I bucked and writhed under him, but his muscled legs easily pinned mine down. His chest pushed down against my breasts, trapping me against the mattress. I started to push at his shoulders with both hands, but he didn't budge even an inch. The realization that *I really couldn't stop him* made me go melty inside.

Then he grabbed my wrists, methodically capturing one and then the other and finally pinning them down with one strong hand. With his other hand, he grabbed my chin and roughly made me look at him.

And then he kissed me long and deep, forcing my lips open, twisting and pushing and *God* teasing my tongue with his, strong and utterly assured. I panted and thrashed and made a lot of outraged sounds like *mmf!* and finally melted into submission, just like all the princesses in the books. He lifted his lips from me but captured my lower lip for one last slow, languorous suck that made me grind my tightly-closed thighs together. Then he raised himself up so that he could look down at me, still holding my wrists above my head.

He watched my reaction as he shoved one hand roughly into the top of the dress and found my breast, massaging it in slow circles and then lightly pinching my nipple. I arched my back, my lips pressed into a tight line. The pleasure throbbed down from that aching bud in hot, rhythmic pulses made stronger by their edge of pain. I felt my hips begin to circle. I tried to stop them because I wanted to keep playing the haughty, aloof princess, but I couldn't control them.

"Tell me what you want, Lady Louise," Sean growled, and it made me think of my fantasy of him, months before, when I'd imagined him breaking into my apartment. Back then, I'd thought he really *was* like this: I thought he'd take what he wanted by force. The reality was so much better.

I shook my head violently against the mattress.

He leaned close, his breath hot in my ear. "You want it. You want *this."* And I sucked in a breath as I felt the hot length of his cock press against my thighs. I shook my head again, copper hair tossing.

Sean growled and pressed his knee into the dark line where my tightly-closed thighs joined. He started to exert pressure, allowing his weight to bear down on me. But he wasn't willing to wait for my muscles to tire. Oh, no. Suddenly, his hand was gone from my breasts and his fingers were sliding down over my pale belly, down into the tangles of copper curls between my legs, probing between my thighs. I closed them as hard as I could, but even his thick fingers were too slender for me to stop. They slid down and curled...and suddenly, they were stroking at my lips.

"You're wet for me," he told me, relishing the words.

Free to move my head, now, I twisted it to the side, refusing to look at him. But I *was* wet. Soaking.

He brought his thumb into play, drawing gentle but insistent circles on my clit. His fingers started to work at my lips, long, slow strokes up and down their length. I clamped my legs together as hard as I could but I was no match for his strength. He began to grin as both of us felt me moisten and heat. It was impossible to stop myself grinding against him.

He leaned down and kissed the corner of my mouth, then spoke into my ear. "You *do* want it. You want the whole thing up inside you."

Inside me. My whole body was writhing against the mattress, now, my cheek moving in slow circles as I pressed it against the rough cotton. "N—Never!" I panted. "I'll never let some Irish barbarian inside me!"

Sean's grin grew even darker. "Oh. It's like *that?*" He redoubled his efforts and I began to moan. "You don't want the *big, rough* Irishman inside your pristine body?"

"N—No!"

He growled and thrust a thick finger up inside me. With my legs pressed so hard together, it was *tight*...and glorious. I felt my legs easing of their own accord as the pleasure washed over me. "N—No," I said again. But my muscles were turning from iron into gooey honey and his power and weight began to win. His leg slid down between

mine, tan muscle dividing my paleness and I groaned in dismay—
and delight—at his victory.

He inserted his feet between mine and *pushed*. My exhausted legs
opened easily and then his whole body was between them, powerful
hips pinning mine to the bed as he slid down into position. He must
have rolled on the condom while he was rubbing me, because I felt
the hot, thick head of him pushing at my lips almost immediately. I
made a last attempt to close my legs and a shudder of excitement
went through me when I found I really couldn't move them.

Then he was plunging into me and both of us could feel how
slickly hot I was for him. I gave up my act completely and let my body
go limp as he slid smoothly inside me, groaning as he filled me to the
limit. Then, as he began to thrust, I came alive, swirling my hips as I'd
longed to do all along, arching my back and grinding up against him.
He still had my wrists above my head so I couldn't use my hands and
that made it even better—I was free to buck and thrash and writhe
under him, but I still had that feeling of being roughly taken. "God," I
panted. "God, *yes!*"

He sped up, his hips slamming between my widely-spread thighs.
He supported himself on his elbows so that one hand was free to dive
into the top of the dress again, this time forcing it down just enough
that one breast spilled out. He rubbed his thumb across the nipple
until it was achingly hard, then lowered his head and sucked it into
his mouth, lashing it with his tongue until I squealed and kicked my
heels against the bed.

His cock was so perfect inside me: steel-hard and throbbing,
stretching me just the right amount. And it had such power: every
time he drew back I felt panting and empty, desperate for him to
return; every time he slammed into me I was the helpless, trapped
princess again. I went from wanton hussy to blushing virgin a
hundred times a minute, until the room dissolved and I was floating
in a crimson void of raw pleasure.

He fucked me for what felt like hours, slowing down and then
speeding up, taking me towards my peak twice and backing off before
finally allowing me to finish. When I finally came, my legs wrapped

around him and my spit-wet breasts throbbing from his fingers and tongue, it was with a scream that filled the whole house.

And the best part? When my breathing settled and reality oozed back in, and I realized just how kinky we'd gotten and I felt like some sort of freak...he took me into his arms and whispered in my ear that I was his best ever. And suddenly, I didn't feel like a freak at all.

Afterwards, we lay looking up at the ceiling. "Sean?" I said.

"Mmm?"

"We can't burn this place down." I sat up and rolled over to face him, propping myself up on my forearms. "When we move out, we can't burn it down."

I expected him to argue, but he looked around and slowly nodded. "Yeah. I know." Then, when he saw my shocked expression. "What?" His eyes burned right into me. "You think I can't appreciate beautiful things?"

He slid an arm under my body and pulled me close. I snuggled into his chest.

"I like it," he said. "Reminds me of the places my mum and dad used to take me. Used to love those places." He ran his eyes over me, following the curve of my breast and the swell of my hip. Then he smiled a tiny, secret smile. "'Specially the statues."

I blinked, wondering what the hell that was all about. "So we'll find some other way?" I said.

He let out a long sigh and ran his hand through his hair. "Yeah. Christ knows how. But yeah." And then he clutched me around the waist with those big hands of his and hoisted me up in the air, making me yelp, before bringing me down to straddle him, facing his feet. Then he shuffled us down the bed until we were sitting on the end of it. He sat up, his chest pressed against my back, and kissed my neck...and then he nodded towards the mirror.

I looked up into its silvered surface and gasped. We were framed by the dark wood posts of the four poster. The green dress was up around my hips and pushed down below my breasts. My hair was falling down over my naked shoulders. I really did look like a ravished princess.

And behind me, the man who'd done it: massive and tanned, black-haired and with those cobalt-blue eyes gleaming in the dim light. He wrapped his hands around my waist and lifted...

...and lowered me slowly. I drew in my breath as I felt the head of his cock nudge at the lips of my sex. "Ready for more?" he murmured, kissing my shoulder.

I nodded. And we spent the next panting, moaning, shuddering hour watching a princess and an Irish rogue in the mirror.

Eventually, way past noon, when we were both limp and exhausted, he left me in the bed and borrowed my car to go for food. He returned with pepperoni pizza and we devoured it sitting on the bed. I insisted on taking off the dress, not wanting to get grease on it. But as soon as he saw me naked...well, we very nearly didn't get to the pizza at all.

Afterward, we lay there, sated in every possible way. It was only mid-afternoon, but with the cardboard over the windows and the lights off, the room quickly darkened as the sun moved to the other side of the house. "How'd they die?" Sean asked.

I was a little thrown. It wasn't that I minded him asking, it was the shock of him asking anything at all. He'd avoided asking about my past and I'd always assumed it was because he thought it was unfair to ask when he was so closed off himself. *So does this mean...?* "Car crash," I said. "Both at the same time."

He didn't say anything, didn't use words like *sorry* that would have felt inadequate. He just tightened his arms around me, his chest warm against my back, and that was enough. "Sometimes, I think it was better that way," I said. "I mean, I didn't have to watch one of them missing the other. But worse, too. One morning they were there and then...they never came home."

He was silent for a long time, just holding me. I sensed that he was working up to something. Then, "I was born in Ireland. The north." Each word came slowly and with great difficulty, as if it was being dug up from deep underground. "Irish dad but American mum. I've got lots of brothers. We were happy, mostly. Moved around between Ireland and America. And then...something happened."

He stopped, but I could feel his chest straining with the pain. I pressed my body back against him, wondering if that was going to be it. I wanted to tell him how glad I was he'd finally told me something, that it was fine to leave it there for now if he wanted to. I opened my mouth to speak—

"My dad killed my mum," he said.

49

LOUISE

I lay there trying to process. I had no words. Even losing my own parents hadn't in any way prepared me for something like *this*. I wanted to turn around and hug him, but I was worried he might not be able to get the words out, if he had to look me in the face. So I reached back with one hand and stroked his side instead, hoping I could transmit how sorry I was through my touch.

"It's complicated," he said.

I nodded. There was so much pain in his voice, I was tearing up myself.

"My dad isn't the bad guy," he told me.

I nodded again

"My dad used to go off on these jobs, sometimes for months, and he'd leave us at home with mum. Usually in Ireland but one summer, it was in America." He swallowed. "At the end of the summer, he comes back...."

I closed my eyes, knowing what would come next. The lover. The discovery. The enraged husband, a crime of passion. *My dad isn't the bad guy.* But I couldn't have been more wrong.

Sean swallowed. "He came back to find...she'd got mixed up with a cult."

I twisted around and pressed close to him. "*What?*"

"Not a religious one. A...personality cult, I suppose you'd call it. Mixed in with doomsday stuff. A really fucking evil one."

I put my head on his chest. "Go on," I whispered.

"We knew something was wrong. We'd known all summer, we'd seen her changing. Weird people coming to the house. But we were kids—what were we going to do? It was scary...the person she was just disappeared, within a few months. Then my dad got back and we thought, *thank God,* now everything'll be okay. But she wouldn't listen to him, treated him like a stranger. Said he was trying to take *her* children away from her, and she had to do what was best for us."

He stopped for a moment, staring off into the darkness. "She wanted to take us into the cult. They had these...camps, where followers could live. And those places...I didn't know at the time, but I heard things later...they *do things* to people in there. Even to children. Bad shit."

"Jesus," I breathed.

He wrapped his arms around me and pressed me in tight to him, running a hand down my back from shoulder to ass. We were both naked, but it didn't feel sexual—we were way beyond that, now. It felt like he was stroking me for comfort, to reassure himself that there was another person there in the blackness. "So us kids: our mum's telling us she's going to take us all off to paradise, our dad's trying to explain that she's not well—because he still loved her, he loved her through all of this. And our mum's saying he's evil, that he's trying to trick us. This went on for *weeks.*"

I clung to him, rubbing his shoulders and upper arms, letting him know I was there for him. I thought of a young Sean, terrified and confused, and I've never wanted a time machine so much.

"Eventually, my mum realizes she's going to lose—she's not going to get custody, if they split and it goes to court. So she takes Bradan, one of my brothers, and she delivers him—she *fucking delivers him*— to the cult, knowing that he's going to be separated from her, maybe forever. She actually believes she's doing the right thing, she thinks the cult can raise him better than she can herself. That's how strongly they controlled her." He started to speak again, but his voice broke on the first word and he stopped.

He doesn't want to cry I pressed myself as hard as I could against his chest, feeling his lungs fill and empty as he struggled for control. "It's okay," I whispered. "It's okay. I'm here."

"Do you know why Bradan?" he asked, his voice bitter. "Why she took him first, separately?"

I shook my head.

"Because they asked for him. Because they'd questioned her for hours about all her kids. Seen photos. They knew his personality, his talents. They picked him out and ordered her to bring him to them. That's the sort of people they are."

"Oh my God..."

"Then she comes back home to get the rest of us. She's going to take us all with her to one of the camps and then, most likely, the cult would gradually split us up and find...*uses* for all of us. Only that never happens. Because, when she arrives home, my dad's there."

And now I saw it coming towards me like a freight train. I squeezed my eyes closed.

"They have a screaming row, right in front of us. My mum's out of her mind, by this point—she genuinely believes she's saving us, can't believe the cult would ever hurt us. My dad...he's already lost one son, he knows he might never see Bradan again. Now he's about to lose his whole family. He loves her—that never changed—but he can't let her take us.

So they get into a fight, us kids are trying to stop them, half of us are crying. My mum grabs a kitchen knife—" His arms tightened around me. "My dad wrestled with her. He didn't want to do it. If it had been just him, I don't think he would have done it—he would have let her kill him, rather than hurt her. But he knew that if he was gone, there'd be no one to save us kids. They fought and fought...and finally he slammed her down on the floor and she hit her head. And that was it. We all saw it happen."

I clung to him like a child...but in that moment, I wanted it to be the other way around. I wanted to be like a mom to him, to comfort him.

"Afterwards...it was fucking chaos. They hauled my dad off for murder."

I tilted my head up and blinked up at him. "*What?* But...the cult!"

"Turns out the cult had a lot of friends in high places, from local police all the way up to judges. At the trial, they made out that my dad was this violent, drunken Irishman—he'd had one beer, that day —and that my mum had been trying to get us away from him. The cult was barely mentioned. My dad got twenty years: he's still in prison now."

"What about Bradan?"

"We were trying to tell everyone the cult had taken him, but no one believed us. They split us up: I was the youngest so I got put in foster care in the US. Everyone got different treatment and it happened *fast*. We mostly lost touch. I know Aedan went back to Ireland and lived there for a while. Carrick was older so he managed to slip away and go on the run until he was old enough to look after himself...." Sean sighed. "It was a mess. The only one I know about for sure is Kian: he went into the military. He's in Washington, now."

Jesus. I knew what it was like to lose both parents, but at least Kayley and I had had each other.

"*We* were a mess, too," Sean told me. "I mean, some of us sided with my dad, some with my mum, the whole thing just tore us apart. We loved each other but...seeing the others just reminded us. That's why we don't talk."

"What happened to you, in foster care?"

"I ended up with this pretty well-off couple who couldn't have kids of their own. The woman was okay, but the man...he wanted his own kids. Called me a little Irish shit when she wasn't around. Then, when he'd had a bad day, he'd take it out on me. Punching me, hitting me. I was a clumsy kid, worse when I was scared, so I'd break stuff. He hated that." He nodded over his shoulder. "Those scars are cigarette burns. He used to get me to take my shirt off and kneel down facing away from him while he sat in his armchair. I used to think it was so I couldn't see the cigarette coming, to make it worse. But now I think it was because he couldn't look me in the face while he did it. The fuckin' coward. He told me over and over I wasn't good for anything apart from wrecking stuff—that's what I'd done, he said, wrecked his life. You hear that enough times, you start to believe it."

He went quiet for a while, reliving it in his head. "I started building myself up, learned how to fight, so I could fight back. And I did, eventually—he got scared of me and left me alone. I thought I'd won..." He sighed. "But the fucker had messed me up. By then, I thought all I was good for was destroying. Smashing stuff up started to feel good: it let out some anger. At school, I didn't trust anyone and no one wants to be friends with the scary Irish kid who gets into fights all the time and breaks stuff." He shrugged his massive shoulders. "I moved out of their house as soon as I could. Then I just kept scaring people and smashing stuff...only this time, people paid me for it. My foster mum eventually left the bastard. She lives across town."

I hugged him for long minutes before I asked, "What about Bradan?"

"Some of us tried to track him down—I know I did. But the cult's fucking impenetrable unless you're a member. We don't know if he's alive or dead."

"And Kian...you don't want to see him?"

He ran his hands over my back, massaging the muscles, using the feel of me to calm himself. "I *do*, but...Jesus, you don't know what it's like—seeing any of them just makes it all come back."

I nodded sadly. "When did you get the shamrock tattoo?" I asked quietly.

He reached back between his shoulder blades and fingered it. "Just before we got split up, all us brothers got them. We found a guy who wasn't bothered that some of us were kids, as long as he got paid, and we all lined up and had it done, one after the other. It was supposed to be a sign that, one day, we'd get what was left of our family back together."

I closed my eyes, wrapped him tight into my arms and held him there.

50

LOUISE

I got back to the apartment by mid-afternoon. I walked into the kitchen, expecting to find stacks of dishes waiting to be loaded into the washer. But every surface was spotless.

"Good, huh?" Kayley said from behind me. She stifled a yawn. "Stacey helped."

I spun around. And tried not to let my smile falter as I saw how thin she was getting. I'd seen her only the previous morning but now, under the harsh kitchen lights, her cheeks looked hollow. And she looked so *small,* in her clothes, like she'd lost even more weight. Had she looked that ill yesterday?

Or had I just been so focused on the plan that I hadn't noticed?

I grabbed her and pulled her into my chest, wrapping my arms around her and wanting to keep them there forever. Kayley gave an exaggerated *"Ulp!"* and then, after a few seconds, started to wriggle. *"Must...escape...crushing...ribs..."*

I let her go, a little relieved. The old Kayley was still in there. "Thank you for cleaning up," I told her. "But no more. That's my job."

Kayley rolled her eyes. "I'm fourteen," she reminded me. "I can take care of myself."

But you shouldn't have to. Especially not when she was ill.

"Anyway, how'd it go last night?"

That caught me off guard. "Last night?" She'd been dozing in her room when I'd dressed for the jazz club...hadn't she?

"I heard you and Stacey talking. And then I got the details out of her when you were gone." She grinned. "You slept over at his place last night?"

"No!" I swallowed. "It's not like that!"

"Louise, it's okay. I'm glad you're seeing someone." She grinned. "Is he hot? When can I meet him?"

"Never!" My head was spinning. I'd only just wrapped my head around being with Sean. He was still caught up in crime—that was his life. Maybe I could learn to accept that, but I couldn't have a guy like that around Kayley. "Look...things are complicated right now."

She pouted. "Why are you being so mysterious? Why can't you just tell me what's going on?"

I sighed. "Come on," I said. "Let's go thank Stacey for hanging out here all day. Then we can do something fun together."

So we did. I took her out to a fancy ice cream place and we talked about movies and the vacation we'd take when this was all over and who we'd most like to be shipwrecked with. But she left her ice cream half eaten, her appetite worryingly poor.

That night, after I'd tucked her in, I was just about to leave her when she grabbed my wrist. "Can you stay with me?" she asked. "Just for tonight?" Her voice had suddenly lost that teenage, all-knowing, tone.

She hadn't asked for that for years. I sat down on the edge of the bed, wracked with guilt. *I've been away too much.* "Of course," I said, my voice cracking. And I stretched out next to her.

I hated lying to her. We'd always been so close and it felt as if all the secrets had driven a wedge between us. *Just hang on,* I thought as I watched her sleep. *Another month. That's all I need.* Then this whole thing would be over and I could end this double life.

I didn't know that I was about to run out of time.

51

SEAN

September

The next few weeks passed *fast*. There was so much that needed doing at the mansion, just to make sure the floor didn't collapse under us or the roof didn't come down, that I was there all day, every day. Given that, before I met Louise, I'd spent most days sleeping off a sex-and-booze-fueled hangover, it was an adjustment. But, in time, I found I kind of liked seeing mornings.

And it was worth it, to be with Louise. We were together a lot, now, every hour she didn't have to be at her job or looking after her sister. Most of the time, we were working, but I still managed to coax her away from the plants long enough to go up to the big four poster in the bedroom...or I'd push her down on one of the tables and slowly strip her...or I'd just catch her as she walked past and press her up against the wall....

When she was there, it was great. When she wasn't, though...that's when I got to thinking. Like right now, as I hammered down a new floorboard.

In another few weeks, it'll all be over. Louise would bring in a great crop—I didn't doubt that for a second. If I could keep her safe until then, we could sell it to Malone and Kayley could get her treatment.

...and *then* what?

Against all my expectations, it felt good to have opened up to her. It felt *great*. But once we'd sold the crop and she'd gone back to her normal life...would she still want me? What the hell could I offer her? All I was good at was being a scary fucker and smashing stuff up.

I heard a noise from the next room, where the plants were. *Shit.* Probably just a bird—there were enough missing slates on the roof that they got in, sometimes. But I wasn't taking any chances: I kept the claw hammer in my hand. As I crept through the doorway, I drew it back....

No one there. I could see right across the room, between the shifting foliage. I sighed, lowered the hammer and started walking the aisles, looking for the bird. I'd heard *something*....

I was on my third aisle when I heard the rustle. I spun around, lifting up the hammer again...but there was no one.

Not at *that* height.

It wasn't until I glanced down that I saw the intruder, sitting on the floor against a table leg.

"Hi," said Kayley.

52

LOUISE

I'd just finished my shift at the garden store. On the phone, Sean had just said *you need to get over here,* so I didn't understand how bad the situation was until I glimpsed Kayley's bandana between the plants. *Oh shit.*

I skidded to a stop in front of her and Sean. He and I exchanged horrified looks.

"This is for Switzerland, isn't it?" Kayley said. "This is for my treatment."

I looked at Sean and then looked at her. I nodded.

"Are you *INSANE?*" Kayley yelled. "You're growing *drugs!* You...you *asshat,* Louise! This isn't..." She looked at me helplessly. "This isn't *you!*"

"I know," I said softly. "But it was the only way. We had to have the money." I took hold of her arms. "Look, this is just a one-time thing. And it's all over in another few weeks."

Kayley swallowed, turning pale. I could see her working it out in her head. This is what had terrified me all along: not just her finding out I was breaking the law, or being scared for me, but figuring out why I needed to do it. Watching the realization wash over her was the most heartbreaking thing I've ever seen.

"I'm going to die, aren't I?" she whispered. "If this doesn't work, if I don't go to Switzerland...I'm going to die."

Before I could answer, Sean stepped forward. "That's fuckin' *irrelevant*," he said heavily. "Because this *is* going to work." And he said it in *that* voice. The same one he used when he told a trespassing dealer they were leaving town, *now*, or the owner of a poker den that the game was *over*. It sounded like slabs of stone the size of houses, so fucking *sure* that even I was convinced.

Kayley nodded, tears in her eyes. Then she suddenly ran to me and threw her arms around me, pressing her face to my chest. I hugged her tight, nodding silent thanks to Sean over the top of her head.

"You're still an asshat," Kayley said at last, her voice muffled. "You really thought I'd never find out?"

"How *did* you find out?" I asked.

She pushed back from me a little. "I snuck a look at your phone while you were asleep and found this place pinned on Google Maps. So I got a cab over here while you were at work. At first, I thought *he* must live here—the guy you were dating. Then I snuck in a window and saw *this*." She waved at the plants, then walked closer to look at one. "Good plan, telling Stacey you're dating. You totally have her fooled." She chose that moment to glance up and see Sean and my guilty faces. "Oh. Oh *shit!*" She clapped her hand to her mouth. "You two are—"

My face flashed red. I'd been so concerned with her finding out about the grow house, I hadn't thought about that side of it. I exchanged looks with Sean, but there was zero chance of hiding it. And there'd been enough lying already. "Yes," I said at last.

"*Fuck!*" Kayley breathed.

I tried to claw back some shreds of parental authority. "Okay, under the circumstances I'm giving you a free pass up until now. But if one more curse comes out of those lips, I'm suspending your Kindle account."

Kayley gave me a look...but she also looked strangely relieved that things were back to normal. Well, *sort of* normal.

"So you'll be here all the time?" she asked, looking around.

"Most of the day, yes, when I'm not at the garden store. I'll be back at the apartment every night. No more emergencies...I hope."

"But I'll barely see you," Kayley said. "Can't we all just move in here? There's plenty of space."

"*WHAT?*"

"I could help with the plants."

"*NO!*" My chest had clamped tight with fear. "Kayley, you are *never* to come here again, understand? *Ever.*"

"Okay, okay, whatever." She looked around ruefully. "But this place is *awesome!*"

"We need to get you home," I said. "Right now. Come on, I'll drive you."

She sighed but trailed along behind me. The fact she knew—about the growing and about Sean—had my stomach in knots. But, oddly, I felt lighter. It was only now I'd stopped lying that I realized how much it had been tearing me up inside.

We were almost out of the room when Kayley suddenly broke away from me and ran back to Sean. He'd started to turn away and swung back towards her running footsteps just to get a small warm wrecking ball in the chest. He *oofed* and staggered back a step, then looked up at me in wonder as he realized she was hugging him.

"Thank you," said Kayley. "I know she wouldn't have pulled this off on her own."

Sean looked down at her awkwardly, as if he'd never had a kid hug him before. Then it hit me that, in all probability, he hadn't. "That's okay," he said at last.

Kayley finally pushed back and looked up at him. "Don't you dare break her heart," she said hotly.

Sean nodded solemnly, then glanced at me. "I won't."

53

LOUISE

With the secret out and the tension between Sean and I gone, I thought things would get easier. But as we hit the flowering stage, things went from stressy to *insane*. This period was critical: every tiny adjustment in light, water, air and fertilizer now made a huge difference. This was when the plants would shoot up and turn potent...*if* we got it exactly right. It was like sitting a college degree course that has a single final exam right at the end worth 100% of the credits: you could work your ass off the whole time but then blow it all at the end.

I'd get up early, get Kayley up and dressed and set her some schoolwork, make breakfast, rush off to my job, work a shift, drive to the mansion and then work straight through until the evening, rush back to the apartment and cook dinner, then spend a few hours trying to figure out which bill to pay to avoid anything being cut off. Kayley offered to help: "I'm four-freaking-teen," she told me. "I can cook my own dinner." But every day, she was getting weaker. No way was I leaving her to fend for herself, not now.

Dr. Huxler was starting to get worried. When I brought Kayley in for her next blood test, he took me aside. "I don't need to see the test results," he told me. "She needs to be in Switzerland *now.*"

"You said six months," I said.

"Leukemia doesn't stick to a calendar. I held it off for as long as I could—any more chemo would have killed her. Now it's free to progress and it's going faster than I'd hoped." He shook his head. "From this point on, every day counts."

Just another week, I thought. *That's all I need.* But every day, Kayley got paler and weaker. I couldn't leave her...but I couldn't leave the plants, either. I felt like I was tearing myself in half: if I left Kayley on her own, I was the worst mom and sister ever. If I left the plants on their own, I was going to blow it all and Kayley would die. Something had to give, but I couldn't take any more time off work: I'd used up every bit of vacation time and every personal day I had.

"Quit," Sean told me one morning.

"*What?* We need that money!" Sean had been contributing some cash from the jobs he still took from Malone and the other dealers, but it wasn't nearly enough.

He put his hands on my shoulders. "The plants need you. Kayley needs you. This'll give you more time for both. And the money won't make a difference—not now. If for some reason we can't sell the crop, we're fucked anyway."

I slowly nodded. Going all-in made my stomach twist and tighten into a cold, iron knot...but it also made me realize that really I'd been all-in from the start, ever since that first conversation in Dr. Huxler's office. If we pulled this off, I'd just have to find a new job and a way to pay off my debts. If we didn't, if Kayley died...I honestly wouldn't care about any of it, anymore.

So I quit my job and started running the grow house like the laboratory I'd always wanted to work in. For the final week, everything was timed down to the minute. I taped up the doorways with plastic sheeting so that I could control airflow, precisely timed the lighting cycles, brought in exotic mixes of plant nutrients to give them that final boost....I could see it working but I was utterly exhausted. On the fifth day, I fell asleep face-down on a table and didn't even wake when my phone's alarm went off. Sean, who'd been fixing a leak in the plumbing, had to gently shake me awake.

"Shit," I said, looking at the time. "Shit, shit, *shit!*" I scrambled up out of my seat, tripped over the leg of the stool and went sprawling. I got to my feet, waving away Sean's hand, and lumbered towards the door, drunk with fatigue. "I said I'd take Kayley to see a movie. I need to be picking her up *now.*"

Sean stepped in front of me and put a big, solid hand on my chest. "*Stop,*" he commanded. "When did you last sleep?"

I shrugged and *harumphed* and pushed soil-flecked hair out of my face. "I have to go."

"You have to *go upstairs and sleep,*" he told me.

"But—"

"*I'll* take Kayley to see the movie." He pushed me towards the stairs. "No arguments. Go."

Before I could stop him, he'd left. And after a few more seconds of staring after him in disbelief, I reluctantly crawled up the stairs and collapsed on the bed. I slept for fourteen hours and woke to a text from Kayley saying how much she liked Sean and "could they do it again, please?"

My heart swelled. I rolled over and saw Sean stretched out on the bed next to me—he'd crept into bed without waking me, one arm wrapped protectively around me. Kayley liked him and I needed him on a level I'd never known before. It was so, so tempting to imagine some future where we could all be together. But every day, he disappeared for a few hours to work another job for a dealer, smashing up someone's car or house or business, scaring them into submission. I knew now where all the anger came from. I knew that he didn't *want* to be doing that work. But that didn't change the fear I felt every single time he put his hammer in the trunk of his car and drove off. *What if he doesn't come back?* Or what if more of his enemies came looking for revenge, as the Serbians had done? There was no way I could put Kayley at risk by having Sean in our lives, however much I wanted him.

Gradually, my efforts paid off. The plants shot up and the buds grew sticky, creamy and huge. When the time came to harvest, I finally dared to admit that maybe this was going to work. Me being me, I'd been cautious about my estimates all along: I'd planted enough that we could lose at least ten percent, but we'd lost almost none. And judging by the look of the buds, this really was premium stuff.

Sean helped me dry it and cure it, sealing it into carefully-weighed plastic bags. It really was a bumper crop: more like $550,000 worth, although I knew we'd be lucky to get that much out of Malone. For a second, I actually felt aggrieved. Who was he, to set the price? Maybe we could negotiate, threaten to go elsewhere....

What the hell am I doing? I caught myself just in time. When did I start thinking like a criminal, trying to squeeze every last cent out of the crop? *This is not what I do! This is just a one-time thing.* Getting greedy was tempting fate. All we needed was the $500,000 to pay for Kayley's treatment and not a cent more. I felt like I was stepping back from a deep, dark chasm and it took another hour focusing on the mindless task of bagging before I felt fully normal again.

When we bagged the last bag, the crop filled an entire large tabletop: we'd stacked the bags like bricks, making a solid mass of weed three feet high.

Sean whistled and ran his hand down the stack. "We're going to need to rent a van to move it. It's too much to fit in your car."

I slipped my arm around his waist. "I can't believe we've done it. We've done it, right? I mean, this is *it.*"

He squeezed me and nodded. "This is it. And *we* didn't do it. You did. This is all you and your green fingers."

I shook my head and put my arms around his neck, grinning. "No. No way, I'm not letting you even *start* down that road. I couldn't have done it without you." I winced when I thought how many ways I would have messed it up without him: I wouldn't have known about hiding the smell of the plants, I would have fallen prey to some loan shark like Murray, I wouldn't have had any idea how to set up a meeting with someone like Malone. God, I'd been about to grow *in my own apartment!*

Sean shrugged and grunted, but he was smiling. "We should celebrate," he said. "How about—"

My phone rang and he went quiet while I answered. I was still grinning so hard that it took several seconds for what I was hearing to sink in. Then I grabbed Sean's hand and ran for my car.

Kayley had been rushed to the hospital...and she was critical.

54

LOUISE

We crashed through the doors of the hospital and sprinted up to the desk. "Kayley Willowby," I panted to the woman. "Kayley Willowby—where is she?"

"One second." She started tapping at her computer.

"I should have been here," I sobbed to Sean. I'd been too frantic on the drive over to cry, but now the tears were starting to burn my eyes. "I should have been at the apartment with her but I was off—"

Sean grabbed me and pulled me in tight to his chest, stroking my hair. I could feel the tension in his body, too, every muscle knotted under the thin cotton of his tank top.

"Date of birth?" asked the woman behind the desk.

I told it to her between sobs. *Come on. COME ON!*

The woman frowned. "No Kayley Willowby has been admitted."

I clutched at the edge of the desk, close to meltdown. "Are you sure? Are you checking the ER?"

"Louise," said Sean behind me.

My stomach lurched. "Jesus, is she—Have you checked the—" I swallowed. "Would it show up if she was already—"

"*Louise!*" said Sean, and this time he gripped my upper arm so hard it hurt. I turned around. "Call her," he said.

I looked at him as if he was crazy. "She won't be able to answer!" I snapped. "She's *critical!*"

"*Call her.*"

I pulled out my phone and viciously stabbed at the screen, not understanding why I was doing it. One ring. Two rings.

"Yo," said Kayley's voice.

The phone almost slipped from my fingers. "Are you—are you okay?" I spun slowly, looking at the hospital around me. "Where are you?"

"I'm fine," she said, bemused. "I'm at the apartment."

I looked up into Sean's horrified face. I'm guessing I was doing the exact same expression.

We ran for the car and raced back across town, tires screeching and engine howling. We made it back to the mansion less than an hour after we'd left it.

But it was too late.

The table was empty. The entire crop was gone.

55

SEAN

"No," said Louise. The horror of it hadn't sunk in, yet. She was still just staring at the empty table in disbelief.

Me? I was cursing myself. How had I not realized the phone call was fake? I should have got her to call the hospital to confirm or at least stayed at the house to protect the crop. I'd left it exactly when it was most vulnerable: we'd done everything except fucking gift wrap it for them.

"No," said Louise again. The mounting fear in her voice resonated right through me, making my heart ache.

I never would have made that mistake, six months ago. I would have seen it for the obvious ploy it was. Hell, if I'd been asked to steal someone's crop, it's exactly the sort of thing I would have done myself.

I'd gotten soft.

I'd gotten *involved*.

"*No!*" Louise's voice had risen to a wail. "*No!*" She was gripping the edge of the table, staring at the empty surface as if she could wish the crop back into existence if she only wanted it hard enough.

"It's Malone," I told her. "I called him this morning, while we were bagging, to tell him we were ready to make the deal." My voice grew tight. "He must have figured, why pay when he can just take it?"

"But *how?* How did he even know where we were growing?"

I shrugged. "My guess is, he tracked you down and found out where you lived, then had someone follow you here one day."

She didn't reply. She just staggered away from the table, tears in her eyes. I gave her space for a moment—she was too fragile to even touch, right now, a bomb ready to explode.

"It's not just money," she said in a choked voice. "Doesn't he understand that? It's not just money that he can steal, it—it's *life.* It's *Kayley's life!*"

I nodded. The weight of it all was crushing me down, a black granite rock a thousand miles high. "I know," I said. And now I *did* reach for her, but she backed away, shaking her head.

"All that time," she croaked. "This whole six months, we could have been—Jesus, *I've barely seen her! I've barely seen my sister!*"

"I know," I said slowly. I held out my arms. "Come here." I could see she was close to cracking and I needed to get her into my arms before—

"I got it wrong," she whispered. "I got it *all wrong.*"

She ran and I grabbed for her just too late. By the time I caught up with her, she was already roaring off in her car.

56

LOUISE

It had started to rain—one of those chill, torrential downpours that makes your windshield run as if someone's pouring from a bucket on the roof. But my tears were doing just as much to blur things, big wracking sobs jolting their way up from my guts to escape as scalding streams.

I wanted to go back. Right back to Dr. Huxler's office, when he'd said this would be *a very difficult conversation*. I wanted to go back and I wanted to be a fucking adult this time. I wanted to grow up and make the hard choice, accept Kayley's death and *be with her* instead of going on some stupid crusade to try to save her. We could have been together all day, every day. I could have gotten a loan from Murray and used it to take her on vacation instead of wasting it on fucking fertilizer and grow lights. She could have *lived* these last six months, instead of just surviving.

But I'd been too fucking selfish. I'd wanted a whole lifetime with her and so I'd squandered her last six months.

I pulled up outside our apartment building and ran all the way up to our floor, too desperate to wait for the elevator. I crashed in through the door and headed straight for Kayley who was—

Oh Jesus. She was sitting there doing the schoolwork I set her. All that work. I'd made her life a misery because I was *so* determined that she'd get well and go back to school. I grabbed her and hauled her out of her chair, hugging her to me. Then the tears really started, floods of them, my shaking body jolting hers along with me.

At first, she just grabbed uncertainly at my upper arms, trying to comfort me. Then her muffled voice piped up, "Is it Sean? Did the two of you have a fight?"

My heart tore in two. Everything that was going on and she was worried about *me*. It killed me to shake my head, but I slowly did it.

Her hands gripped me harder. Then harder still. I felt the realization go through her in a cold wave. She didn't want to say it, didn't want to ask the question. Her tears started, mingling with mine, and we hugged each other tighter and tighter until, finally, she pushed back from me and stared up with red eyes. "We're not going to Switzerland, are we?" she asked.

My voice was so raw, so tight with guilt, that I barely sounded like myself. "No."

She didn't say anything. She just mashed herself into me as hard as she possibly could, scrunching her eyes shut and trying to find comfort in my warmth, in the bigger, stronger body that was meant to protect her.

I'm sorry, I thought. *I'm so, so sorry.*

And then I let her go, turned and walked out of the apartment.

I knew what I had to do.

Downstairs, I walked straight past my car and towards the street. I'd failed as a sister and as a stand-in mother. There was only one thing I could do now, one way I could make things right. I had life insurance—not nearly enough for Switzerland, but it would ensure Kayley had the best possible care for her last few weeks.

All I had to do was make it look like an accident.

With the rain pounding down, it wasn't difficult. Big semi-trucks thundered right past our apartment and, in the wet, they wouldn't be able to stop. I'd run across the street at the last minute, pretend to trip...it would all be over in a heartbeat.

The next truck approached. I took a deep breath in.

Headlights turned the street into a shining silver strip. Visibility
was down to maybe fifty feet. He'd barely have time to see me, never
mind stop.

I exhaled. Inhaled...

And ran. *Don't look. Don't look.* Headlights blazed across my vision
from the left. The asphalt was slick with rain. I barely had to twist my
foot and then I was sprawling, hands scraping on the street, knee
going numb as it banged down hard. I rolled onto my side, rain filling
my mouth, headlights turning my vision pure white. An airhorn
blared—

Something huge and solid grappled me under the arms and
dragged me out of the way. We sprawled together on the sidewalk as
the truck roared past and I looked up, blinking rain and tears, into
Sean's face.

"You stupid bloody mare!" he spat through the rain coursing
down his face. And then he pulled me to him and hugged me like he
meant to never let me go again.

"It's over," I sobbed into his ear. "It's over. I screwed it all up."

He pushed me back to arm's length so he could glare at me. "You
need to learn some stuff. You came to me because I was a criminal—
right?" When I didn't answer, he shook me. "*Right?*"

"Yes!"

"Yeah, because you don't know a fuckin' thing about it. You
know what we do when someone steals our stuff? *We go and get it
back.*"

"*How?*" I asked. "It's Malone! He's got an army!"

"That's why I can't do this without you." He swept my sodden hair
back from my temples and then sank his fingers into it, his skin
warming where the rain had chilled me. "I need that big fucking
brain of yours. I need us to be a team. I need *you* because I'm in
fuckin' love with you. I did it all for you!"

My sobbing stopped but the tears kept coming, welling up and
making my vision swim. "I—I'm in love with you, too," I croaked,
knowing the truth of it the moment I said it. "But I can't—Sean, once
this is over, I can't have all this in my life." I imagined people like the

Serbians, coming to our apartment in the dead of night. "I can't have it in Kayley's life."

He gripped my shoulders. "We sort this out and save Kayley," he said, "and I'll go fuckin' straight. I'll leave all this shit behind, if that's what it takes to be with you."

I gaped up at him. "Wh—*What?* But that's *who you are!* You said you didn't know anything else!"

He lifted his head just a fraction, challenging me. "Thought you said I could learn?"

I felt my jaw drop open and then I was grabbing hold of him and pressing my soaked body against his, sobbing with relief and fragile hope into his chest.

57

LOUISE

Sean took me back to my apartment so I could comfort Kayley. When I thought of how I'd broken down in front of her, my stomach knotted. I was supposed to be her mom, unshakeable and stoic. "I'm sorry," I told her. "Sorry you had to see me—"

She punched me surprisingly hard in the chest. "You idiot," she said. "Whoever said you weren't allowed to *cry?*" And she hugged me, the warmth of her body chasing away some of the rain's chill.

When she let me go, she scrunched up her forehead and said, "So now you two have to go and fix things?"

Sean and I looked at each other. "Yeah," I said. "We have to come up with a plan."

Kayley nodded firmly. "Then sit down," she said. "I'll get you towels and coffee."

I started to gently push her into a chair. "No. I can do that."

"Damnit, Louise, *let me help!* I get why you won't let me be involved. But I can make a freaking cup of coffee for you while you think! Why do you never, ever, let me do *anything?*"

I stood there opening and closing my mouth for a few seconds, then looked at Sean. He was no help—he just exchanged a look with Kayley and then nodded at me firmly.

I sat down. "I guess...I just wanted you to be able to be a kid," I said in a small voice.

"Well...thanks. Really. But I think you need all the help you can get today. Okay?" And she stomped off into the kitchen.

"God..." I said, stunned.

"She reminds me of someone," rumbled Sean. "Now let's sort this out."

I sighed and shook my head. "Even if, by some miracle, we *can* get the drugs back off Malone, what the hell do we do with them? No one's going to want to touch them once they've been stolen from him. *And* he'll be after us."

Sean put his hand on mine. "One thing at a time," he said. "First, we need to find out where our drugs are."

"How do we do *that?*"

Sean thought about it while we toweled ourselves dry and changed clothes, then sipped the coffee Kayley brought us. "Malone'll want to split up the crop and sell it. He's probably already called the bigger dealers. I could ask them."

"Why would they tell you?"

Sean looked at me seriously. "Because I'm going to be fuckin' persuasive." That same look came into his eyes, the one that scared the ever-living-*fuck* out of people. The one that had scared the hell out of me, when I first met him. But now, knowing that cold rage was fueled by me, by the need to get justice for me...was it wrong that it made a little flash of heat go through me?

I stood up and headed towards the door. "Okay. Let's go."

Sean blocked my path. "Where are *you* going? *I'm* going to talk to him. I'll call you."

"No way. You're not sidelining me now. We're in this together."

"This'll be dangerous. I'm not having you hurt."

"I'll stay close," I told him. "I'll do what I'm told—"

"*That,* I fuckin' doubt."

"—but I'm not staying here." I stared him down, even though it meant looking up.

He sighed and rubbed a hand over his face. "Alright," he said at last. "Let's go break stuff."

58

LOUISE

I gazed at the house, astonished. "I knew dealers had money," I mumbled. "But...."

The place was *huge*. Seven or eight bedrooms, a pool, and there were three cars outside: a big old Lincoln town car, a Porsche and an SUV.

"This whole business is soaked in money," Sean told me. "And Lennie's only a dealer. Think how much Malone makes. But the money falls off *fast* after the top few rungs." He opened the trunk of my car and took out his sledge hammer.

I looked up at the iron gates. The place wasn't just big, it was tasteless. Everything was fake: reproduction stone columns that were vaguely Roman mixed with lion statues straight out of Japan. It was as if Lennie had browsed a catalog and stabbed his finger at anything he thought represented wealth. But none of that made the gates any less solid. "How do we get in?" I asked.

Sean raised the hammer. "We knock," he said. "Stay behind me."

And he swung the hammer at the center of the gates as hard as he could. They probably would have stood up to a car trying to ram through them...but they couldn't cope with all that energy concentrated in exactly the right place. The lock shattered and the gates creaked inward. Sean was marching forward before they were fully open and I scuttled after him.

An alarm started to sound. The first guy, a blond heavy in a suit, ran out to meet us as we got to the front door. Sean swung the hammer low, catching him in the ankles with the shaft and knocking him face-first to the ground, then giving him a good whack on the back of the head with the handle to keep him there.

As we reached the hallway, two more guards appeared. Sean swung the hammer's handle up, catching one of them under the chin, then punched the other one right in the face. They dropped to the floor almost at the same time, landing in one crumpled heap.

A shot rang out, and a chip of wood flew from the door frame a foot away from Sean. I screamed.

Lennie, a thin guy with long, greasy dark hair, was standing in the living room, a handgun gripped in his shaking hands. "Stay there!" he yelled.

Sean marched forward.

"I've got a fucking gun!" yelled Lennie, going pale.

"I've got a fuckin' hammer," said Sean. And swung it right at the gun. There was a crack of breaking bones, a scream and the gun clattered against the far wall. Then Sean pushed Lennie into a reclining armchair and tipped it all the way back, until he could rest a booted foot next to Lennie's head to keep the chair in place. "Where're our fuckin' drugs?" he roared.

Lennie shrank back in the chair...but didn't speak.

I came closer and looked around. Like the outside of the house, the inside was all about showing off. There were exotic plants in pots, but all of them were sickly and dying because Lennie didn't have any idea how to look after them properly. There were vases and statues from around the world, but I had a feeling he'd never been to any of those places. There was even a glossy black grand piano in the corner, but there was no music on the music stand. "Answer him," I said, trying to make my voice hard.

"I'm not telling you shit," said Lennie.

Sean nodded as if he'd expected this. He stepped away from the chair and looked around, rubbing his stubble—*what should I break first?*

Then he seemed to decide: *all of it.*

The vases were first. He shattered them two at a time, sending shards flying across the room. The bigger ones smashed where they were. The smaller ones flew across the room like baseballs, staying almost in one piece until they hit the far wall. Lennie winced at each crash, but didn't weaken.

Next were the statues. They lost heads, then legs, then crumbled completely under the heavy iron head of the sledge hammer. Then, finally, Sean stepped up to the piano.

"Shit." said Lennie suddenly. "Wait! That costs more than my fucking car!"

Sean brought the hammer back. "Where are the drugs?"

"Where are the drugs?" I repeated.

"Malone'll kill me if I talk!" yelled Lennie.

Sean brought the hammer down in the exact center of the piano and it crumpled into splinters of wood and ivory with a discordant crash. Then he stepped up onto the chair again, his boot next to Lennie's head, and placed the cold iron head of the sledge hammer on the man's forehead. "Talk," he said warningly.

"You two are *fucking nuts,*" Lennie blustered. "You think you're going to get them back from *Malone?* You got a private army?"

"No harm in telling us, then," said Sean.

Lennie looked around at the devastation, looked up at Sean's face, and gulped. But his mouth stayed shut. This could take hours. And we might not have hours. Once Malone split the drugs up and sold them, we were screwed. Kayley was going to die because this asshole was too scared, too proud, too arrogant to tell us what we needed to know.

I was suddenly tired of being the good girl. Malone didn't play by the rules. Well, neither would I.

"Give me the hammer," I said.

Sean and Lennie both turned to look at me. "What?" asked Sean.

"*Give me. The hammer.*" The blood was pounding in my ears.

He slowly handed it over. I nearly staggered under the weight. *Jesus, how does he swing this thing?* Lennie laughed.

"Duct tape his legs apart," I said. I'd started to pant, fear and adrenaline sloshing together through my veins.

Sean gave me a long, steady look...then nodded. He pulled the duct tape from his pocket and grabbed one of Lennie's legs.

"Wait..." said Lennie slowly.

Sean shook his head. "You had your chance with me," he told him. And wrapped duct tape behind Lennie's knee, pulled it to the arm of the armchair and secured it there. He did the same with the other knee, so that Lennie was sitting with his legs wide apart.

I stepped in front of Lennie and heaved the sledge hammer back over my head, like Sean did. For the first time, I really understood the power of it. My heart was thumping like I'd never known it. "Lennie," I said warningly. "Where are our drugs?" I focused on the crotch of his suit pants.

Lennie started to pant with fear. "You wouldn't," he said, struggling against the duct tape. "You're the brains. You're a fucking science nerd."

"You'd be surprised what I'm capable of when someone threatens my family," I said coldly. I shifted my weight from foot to foot, preparing to swing. "I'll count to three."

Lennie shook his head.

"One."

Lennie's breathing hitched.

"Two."

His eyes were locked on mine, now, trying to reassure himself that I was just some scared civilian. He tried to find that person I used to be. But he couldn't. Because she'd stepped out for a minute.

"Thr—"

"They're at the jazz club! Malone's auctioning them off tonight!" The words came out so fast, it was like he was being sick. "He wants everyone there at ten. I'm going—everyone's going. That's all I know!"

I stepped back a step and let the hammer slide from my fingers. Sean caught it before it hit the ground. Then I watched as he duct-taped Lennie's arms, wrists and head to the chair so he couldn't move, then finally stuck tape over his mouth so he couldn't yell for help. He dragged the three heavies into the room and I helped him duct-tape them, as well. I was still nervous and shaky, amazed at what I'd nearly done.

"You weren't faking, were you?" Sean muttered to me as we duct-taped one guy's wrists.

I slowly shook my head.

Sean stared at me in amazement...then grinned. "Good for you."

We finished taping and looked at the four bound men, three of them unconscious and one of them glaring at us in rage. "So we know where they are," I said. "What the hell do we do now?"

Sean turned to me. "I've got a plan," he said. He reached out and stroked my head. "But I need your big brain to make it work. And it means getting nasty. You ready to get nasty?"

I thought of Kayley.

"You're goddamn right I am," I told him.

59

LOUISE

We stopped off at some abandoned buildings Sean knew. When we found one that still had glass in the windows, Sean swung his hammer and sent it crashing down in lethal, razor-sharp shards. Then he picked carefully through them, looking for the right shape. "This'll work," he told me at last, holding one up. I nodded silently and watched as he wound duct tape around one end to make a safe handle.

Then I took him somewhere *I* knew, a small patch of woodland where my Mom used to take me when we first moved to California. We tramped along the well-worn paths for over an hour before I finally saw what I wanted and crouched down. "This is it," I said.

He crouched down behind me, his big body dwarfing mine. "You sure you're ready to do this?" he asked, looking at it over my shoulder.

I thought of Kayley again and nodded.

We held hands as we walked down the street towards Malone's jazz club. I hoped that the guys watching us didn't see that my knees were shaking, that I was only barely able to keep going even with Sean's hand to cling to.

There were a *lot* of guys. Guys lounging in doorways, guys sitting in their parked cars, one or two even up on the rooftops. Malone had gathered all of the city's major dealers together and they'd all brought their own security. We were up against an army.

"What if they just shoot us?" I whispered.

"They're going to be too fucking curious," he told me.

The club was closed that evening—Malone had given the whole place over to his meeting. When we neared the door of the club, the security guys weren't even bothering to hide their guns. One of them held up his hand for us to stop while another called someone on the radio—presumably Malone himself. After several seconds, we were waved forward...and made to pass one by one through the metal detector. Sean had left his hammer at the mansion, since he didn't want to lose it. When the detector didn't beep, the guards led us inside.

A table had been brought in at one end of the huge room and stacked up on it was our crop, the plastic-wrapped packets gleaming in the spotlights. Malone—off his couch for once—was leaning against it, scowling. Men with guns surrounded the other three sides of the table. The rest of the room was full of dealers: respectable-looking guys in suits, weasley-looking guys in bright shirts and leather jackets, a few who looked Italian and one or two who could have been Russian. Everyone wanted a piece of the crop.

Malone was holding up a packet. "You've all tried a sample," he announced in that deep bass rumble. "This is premium shit and it commands a premium price. We'll start with ten packs." He hefted them. "What am I bid?"

Immediately, the dealers began to yell. "Three grand!"

"Thirty-five hundred!"

"Four!"

"Five!"

I gritted my teeth. Despite my fear, the rage was building inside me, clouds of roiling black smoke shot through with red fire. At these prices, Malone could have easily afforded to pay us *six* hundred thousand dollars and still made hundreds of thousands of dollars for himself. We really had made the quality crop we'd promised...and we weren't going to see a cent of the money. Not unless we could pull off our miracle.

After a while, Malone called a break, told the dealers to have a beer and a smoke from the sample packet he'd opened and swaggered over to us. "What the fuck are you doing here?" he asked. "If you're gonna appeal to my better nature...I ain't fucking got one."

Sean stepped forward. "Talking's not my thing," he told Malone. "This is."

And he ran at Malone, shoulder-charging him backwards into the table. The table crumpled under the combined weight of the drugs and the two muscled men, its legs collapsing and the packets avalanching onto the floor. Sean only got in one good punch before he was hauled off Malone, but it was a good, meaty crack to Malone's jaw that looked like it had all of his anger behind it.

The guards hauled Sean upright...but, as soon as he was on his feet, he grabbed both men and cracked their skulls together. Then he was free and diving at another group of guards, punching one and head-butting the other. He opened his mouth and screamed like a Viking berserker, wild and terrifying, his eyes wide and every muscle hard as iron.

A space cleared around him. Malone's guards were taken by surprise—no one had thought that Sean would be crazy enough to go on the attack, when he was unarmed and so obviously outnumbered. And no one wanted to be the one to go toe-to-toe with *The Irish*. That gave Sean an advantage and he made the most of it, grabbing guards and throwing them, smashing them down on tables and causing as much chaos as possible.

Most of the dealers backed the hell off—this wasn't their fight. A few tried to grab the fallen packets of weed.

Sean was like a tornado in a confined space, hurling chairs and tables at his opponents. At one point, he hurled a chair directly at the bottles behind the bar, bringing them down in an alcohol-soaked rain of glass. The guards pulled out guns...but put them away again at a gesture from Malone. "Alive!" their leader spat, touching his lip and finding blood there. "I want the fuck to suffer!"

Sean screamed a battle cry and tackled two more guards, bearing them down to the floor and unleashing a flurry of punches. But by now, Malone's guards had shaken off their surprise and were surrounding him. In seconds, Sean would be overwhelmed.

But with everyone watching the crazy Irishman, no one was watching me. I started to sidle closer to Malone.

Sean had a man on each arm, now, and one trying to grapple his legs, but he was still managing to move, twisting those broad shoulders to hurl off his captors, kicking away the man on his legs. As soon as he escaped one pair of hands, though, two more grabbed him. Eventually, he was pinned: six men had his arms and legs and another had his arm across his throat.

That was my cue to step right up to the distracted Malone and slash the piece of glass right across his chest.

60

LOUISE

At first, there was no blood, just a jagged tear across his shirt. I actually thought I'd missed.

Then, as hands grabbed my arms from behind and the shard of glass fell to the floor, the blood welled up in a scarlet arc, soaking through Malone's white shirt. It went right across the curve of one big pec and into the other.

"What the *fuck?*" Malone pawed at himself. "*Jesus,* I'm bleeding!"

I heard the metallic click of a gun being cocked and cold steel pressed against my temple. I closed my eyes.

"Wait!" snapped Malone. "Bitch does that to me, she's going to die slow." Strong fingers caught my jaw and pushed on my cheeks, popping my mouth open like a goldfish's. I opened my eyes and Malone was right in my face, sneering at me. "That the best you got?" He drew back his hand and slapped me hard across the face. My head snapped to the side and the room spun for a second, pain blazing across my cheek. I saw Sean, held tightly by a small army of heavies, growl and try to lurch forward to protect me.

Malone grabbed my jaw again. "If you're going to knife someone," he told me, "you gotta *stab* that motherfucker." He looked down at his chest. "Slashing away like that don't do *shit*. Hell, I might not even need stitches."

I saw one of the guards frown as he heard Malone slur, but everyone was too scared of him to point it out.

"You gotta go deep," he told me. "That's what we're going to do to you, bitch. Go *deep*. You understand me? And we'll make that Irish fuck watch." He grinned, but there was something not quite right about his eyes. He kept blinking. And he kept swallowing, as if—

"Mouth getting dry?" I asked.

Malone swallowed again, forcing his throat to work. He frowned at me.

"Am I getting blurry?" I asked.

For the first time, he looked scared. "What did—" He pressed his lips together and then opened them again, trying to make them work properly. "What did you do to me?"

"It's belladonna," I told him. "Deadly nightshade. I'd say you've got a minute before the convulsions start. Maybe less. Next will be your heart."

A ripple ran through the crowd. A gun pressed against my forehead.

"Wait! WAIT!" snapped Malone. He was breaking out in a sweat, now, little salty beads gleaming across his dark skin. "How do I fix it?"

"We'll get you to hospital," said one of the heavies. "Come on, let's get you in the car."

Sean's voice broke out, loud and clear and full of authority. "Nearest hospital's five minutes away. We checked. He's got half that."

There was silence for a second.

"Bullshit," said one of the heavies.

"*Really?*" asked Sean. He nodded towards the crop. "You want to bet against *her* when it comes to plants?"

I wanted to hug him. There was silence again as Malone and his men debated it. Meanwhile, the dealers were looking at each other, unsure of what to do.

The indecision ended when Malone's body gave a jerk, as if he'd been touched by a live wire. It was enough to send him staggering backwards into one of his heavies...and then they found themselves supporting his weight because his legs had started to fail. "Bitch," he croaked. "*Fix it!*"

"This is how it works," I said. "There's an antidote: here, in the club. We walk out of here with our drugs. As soon as we're gone, we'll call you with where the antidote is."

The guard pointing a gun at my head slowly lowered it and I breathed a silent sigh of relief.

Then Malone shakily pulled out a gun and pointed it right at Sean. "You tell me where the antidote is right now," he croaked, "or I'll kill your boyfriend." He glared at me, waiting for me to break. I was only some stupid civilian, after all, the good little girl who'd wandered into the big boys' club.

I closed my eyes for a second. Opened them...and glared right back at him. I wasn't *good* anymore. I'd had *enough.*

We glared at each other for several long seconds. I saw Malone's finger tighten on the trigger...and then he broke and lowered the gun. "Let them go," he said, his voice a dry rasp.

The hands holding my arms let go and I pulled away. Across the room, Sean was doing the same.

"You got a van?" Sean asked the nearest heavy. He nodded. "Good. Load up every packet. Every fuckin' packet"—he turned to the dealers—"including the ones you took off the floor. We find *one* missing, no phone call."

"Do it," Malone growled. "All of them."

His men formed a human chain, moving the packets of weed from the pile on the floor to the door and outside. The dealers who'd swiped packets for themselves in the confusion hastily put them back. No one wanted to be responsible for Malone's death. Even the packet Malone had cut open to give samples from was loaded up.

Walking down the line of Malone's men to the van was one of the scariest experiences of my life. Every one of them was armed. Every one of them wanted to kill us. If they sensed weakness for a second, they'd pounce.

Sean took my hand and, immediately, I felt better. *Most of this shit is just attitude,* I remembered. And forced myself to walk with my head high and my back straight. The doors to the van were open for us, the keys inside. We climbed in.

"You're dead," said one of Malone's guards, just before he slammed the door. "We'll find you, even if it takes a year."

I tried to look unafraid, however much I wanted to throw up. We pulled away, Sean behind the wheel. "You okay?" he asked immediately.

I nodded weakly. "Did we do it?" I looked behind me, into the back of the van. "Tell me we did it."

"We did it," he reassured me. "Now hang on."

He put his foot down and the buildings started to flash past. He switched between roaring down main streets and cutting down side alleys, until we were sure we weren't being followed. Then I made the call. Malone answered on the first ring.

"The antidote is the Physostigmine you use to treat your glaucoma," I told him. "It'll counteract the Belladonna. You probably want to chug the whole bottle." I waited, every muscle screaming with tension, listening to the plastic cap unscrewing and the gulping as he drank. I was terrified that it wouldn't work. However much I hated the guy, I wasn't a murderess.

After long minutes, he spoke. "I'm going to find you," he whispered. "I'm going to find you, bitch, and when I do...."

I took a deep breath and tried one last attempt at reason. "Look, we have our drugs back. You're going to be fine. No one got killed. We can just walk away from this and never see each other again."

Sean was glancing across at me, his expression halfway between pity and adoration at my naivety. I didn't expect it to work either, but a little part of me held out hope. That was crushed in seconds. "I'm putting the word out," Malone said. "*Everyone* is going to be looking for you, all over the city, all over the *state,* I will *fucking find you—*"

I ended the call, my stomach twisting.

We had the crop back, but no one to sell it to. No other dealers would dare touch it, not once they heard it had been stolen from

Malone. Even if we *could* find a buyer, Malone would hunt us for the rest of our lives.

Our problems had only just begun.

61

LOUISE

We didn't dare go back to the mansion: Malone knew that place. For the same reason, I'd asked Stacey to take Kayley to her apartment.

We headed for the docks, where we could disappear among all the other vans and trucks. Then we prowled around for somewhere to put the van where it would be out of sight. Eventually, we found some long-abandoned garages, the windows broken and the white paint nearly invisible behind a coating of graffiti. "But the door's chained shut," I said.

Sean climbed out, wrapped the chain around his fists and heaved, the muscles of his back standing out in the moonlight. There was a sudden *crack* and *clang* as the chain broke and snapped against the metal door like a whip. He hauled the door open so that we could back the van in.

We didn't dare leave the van, so we wound up climbing up on a dumpster and then onto the flat roof of the garage. We sat on the edge with our legs hanging down, looking out over the black water of the harbor and the reflections of the lit-up cranes. Sean put his arm around my shoulders and, for the first time since we left the jazz club, we *stopped.*

It hit me, then, how much had changed. Six months before, I wouldn't have even run a red light at an empty intersection. Now I was on the run from a drug dealer whose life I'd threatened, sitting on the roof of a graffiti-covered derelict building at midnight. Beneath me was a van containing half a million dollars in weed and beside me was the scariest, most badass man I'd ever met.

And then that badass turned my head to face him and kissed me, long and deep, and I felt my body relax. Just having him close made things seem better. That was the biggest change of all. For the first time since my parents died, I didn't feel like Kayley and I were on our own.

We sat there in silence while both of us had a very long think. But however evil and devious I got, I couldn't come up with a way to turn the van full of marijuana into cash, not without going through dealers.

The worst part was, *it had worked.* We'd pulled it off. The van was loaded with a bumper crop of high-grade weed that was easily worth the money we needed—probably more. After all the months of effort, we'd done exactly what we'd set out to do...only to be defeated by a problem further down the chain—Malone's greed—that was nothing to do with us. It was human nature that had got in the way. The science—the *process*—had worked just fine.

And then I had a revelation. Something Stacey had said to me. All along, I'd been thinking about the crop—that was the product of all my hard work - that was what I'd created. But maybe I'd created something else, as well.

"We need to stop thinking like criminals," I said. "And start thinking of this like a business."

Sean frowned. "The whole fuckin' drugs game is a business. Supply and demand, distribution...it *is* a business."

"Not completely. There's still a few things real businesses do that these people don't." I thought again. "We need to contact a dealer."

He sighed and rubbed my shoulders. "We can't. No one below Malone's level is big enough to handle this sort of volume. No one *at* Malone's level is going to side against him. They don't want a war."

"That's why we have to go *up*. Above Malone."

"Who's above Malone. Wait, the *cartels?* The *Mexicans?*" He shook his head. "Louise, that's all backwards. The Mexicans import weed *to* the US, they don't need to buy more of it."

"No," I said. "But I think I've got something else that will interest them."

And I laid out my plan.

62

SEAN

I t was crazy...but maybe exactly the sort of crazy we needed. And the sort of thing I'd never have dreamed up: I was too mired in the way things had always been done in the drugs game. Only an outsider like her—with that big brain of hers—could have made the leap and come up with it.

"It might work," I said slowly. "But do you realize who we're getting into bed with, here? Malone's an evil son-of-a-bitch but *the cartel?* They won't waste time on speeches and intimidation. When someone gets in their way, they don't use someone like me to scare them: they just kill them."

Her eyes were big with fear...but then she lifted her jaw and looked resolute. "We'd better hope they like my offer, then."

I looked at her for a long moment and then shook my head. I didn't want her anywhere near those cartel bastards...but I couldn't kill our only chance of saving Kayley, either. "Jesus," I muttered eventually. "Okay. Alright. I'll make some calls."

The temperature was dropping so I stood up, moved behind her and sat down again, my legs either side of hers and my chest pressed to her back to keep her warm. She snuggled into me and the smell and feel of her copper hair as the wind whipped it across my shoulders made my whole body ache for her. The last six months had put us both through the emotional grinder: all I wanted to do was drag Louise into a deep, warm nest and hibernate with her for about a year. The dreams I'd had of her were coming back to me: the two of us happy in some idyllic life somewhere, rolling around in a meadow.

One more time. One more desperate play and then either we'd be dead...or free.

I pulled out my phone. Six degrees of separation: in the drugs game, everyone knows someone up and down the chain. Put enough links together and you can talk to anyone. The problem is getting them to trust you.

After an hour of pleading, threatening and promising, I finally got to talk to a guy called Francisco, who was the number two guy to Isabella Gallego, queen of the Gallego cartel. I laid it out for him: what we had, the ridiculously low price we were asking. "Two hundred and fifty thousand," I told him, "and it's yours."

"What went wrong?" he asked. He sounded smart, and older than us. I imagined him with a gray-flecked beard. "Why aren't you selling it locally?"

I closed my eyes and told him everything—even why we needed the money. Francisco went quiet for a long time and then said that he had to make some calls.

An hour later, he called back. "We'll do it," he said. "But the deal has to be done in Texas. We're passing through there tomorrow night. Eight p.m."

"You want us to get the weed to *Texas?*"

"Don't be late." He gave me an address, then hung up.

"Did you really just say Texas?" asked Louise.

If they catch you with weed, you're in trouble.

If they catch you with a *lot* of weed, you're in big trouble.

If they catch you with a van full of weed, driving across state borders, you go to jail. Go *directly* to jail, do not collect two hundred dollars, do not ever think about seeing sunlight again. This was the most dangerous thing we'd done so far. I'd chosen the grow house location to be pretty much off the police radar. Even the mansion had been well away from prying eyes. But out on the highway we'd be an easy target.

We couldn't use the van: Malone's people would be looking for it. But we had virtually no cash left. So we went to the cheapest car dealership I knew, woke up the owner and bought the one vehicle with storage space that he had.

An ice cream truck. So old that I didn't even recognize half the ice creams on the menu.

"It runs," said Louise hopefully, revving the engine. "And it only has to get us there: one journey. Hell, it doesn't even have to get us *back.*"

I nodded, unconvinced. One little problem, one cop pulling us over and we were screwed. I double-checked all the lights and replaced a couple of bulbs that were broken. Then we loaded all of the weed into the truck's empty freezers. Even with the plastic wrapping and the freezers shut, the smell of it still hung around in the air—there was just so much of it, in such a confined space, that there was no way we could cover it up.

By now, it was midnight. We had twenty hours to get to Texas and Google said the drive would take eighteen. It was going to be a virtually non-stop road trip.

I slid behind the wheel. "I'll take the first stretch. You get some sleep."

Louise climbed up into the passenger seat and started to get herself comfortable. Just before she settled down for the night, she leaned across and slipped her arms around my neck to kiss me. Immediately, the touch of her bare skin on mine made every little hair stand on end. Every muscle grew hard and tense, ready to grab her and pull her into my lap.

So I did. Just in case it was the last chance we had. I hauled her across the cab, making her yelp in surprise, until she was sitting on top of me, my cock instantly hard and straining at the feel of her.

Then I kissed her hard, parting her lips with my tongue, closing my eyes, and drowning in her sweet, feminine softness. I imagined we were in some place with no more risks, no more danger, where no one could touch us ever again. And she responded, relaxing into me, leaning back on my arm so I could tilt her head back and kiss her even deeper. Her full breasts thrust out towards me and I ran a hand up under her top, gently squeezing one, feeling the warm skin and the hardening bud of her nipple stroke my palm.

She broke the kiss—just. Our lips stayed so close that each syllable stroked them together. "Did you really mean it?" she asked. "About going straight?"

I drew back just enough that I could look into her eyes. "I'll find a church and become a bloody preacher, if you want me to."

She pressed herself hard against me, then slid off my lap and onto her own seat. "Then let's do this."

I put the van into gear and we drove off into the night.

63

LOUISE

Y ou may think you know what tension feels like. You're wrong.

Tension is driving down a highway with half a million dollars worth of drugs in the back, waiting for a cop to pull you over. *Tension* is driving knowing that one little mistake—a single dangerous overtake, drifting a mile over the speed limit—could result in the red and blue lights and then the death of someone you love. *Tension* is doing all this in a truck with scratchy, lumpy seats, a gear shift that feels like stirring a lead rod in a barrel of broken parts and the steering from an ocean liner.

For six hours straight.

Sean had driven for the first six hours. He would have kept going for longer but, when he roused me at a gas station to see if I wanted to use the bathroom, I looked at his drooping eyelids and insisted I take a shift. As morning broke, the cops came out in force. They were looking for easy tickets to make their quotas, but the traffic was light, so pickings were thin. That made us a prime target.

I'd never realized how much I zoned out on a long drive until I couldn't do it anymore. Even when I was just sitting in my lane, cruising along, I was constantly checking the mirrors for approaching cops, checking my speed, checking I wasn't doing anything else wrong. When a cop overtook us, I'd sit there bolt upright, arms so stiff on the wheel that my muscles screamed, eyes straight ahead. They'd get closer and closer and closer, right up alongside us...then they'd pass by and I'd breathe again. I was soaked with sweat by the end of the first hour.

Now it was nearly noon and I was a wreck. My hands throbbed from gripping the wheel so tightly; my thighs burned from the awkward pedal position, made for someone with longer legs than me; my arms, shoulders and back were on fire from the constant stress.

And it wasn't just the drive itself. My mind kept going back to what we were attempting here. A deal with the cartel, people who made Malone, with all his heavies and his jazz club, look like a spoiled child. I'd seen the news stories. If they weren't happy with the deal I offered them, they'd simply shoot us. And my plan pretty much guaranteed that they *wouldn't* be happy. And even *if* we could somehow cut a deal with them, we still had Malone to deal with. Wherever we ran, he'd hunt us down—

An ear-splitting *whoop!* from behind me. *Whoop! Wh-wh-wh-whoop!*

I checked the rear view mirror and saw the cop car, six feet behind me, lights flashing. The officer behind the wheel jerked his thumb for me to pull over.

Fuck.

64

LOUISE

S ean came awake fast, but there was nothing we could do except glance helplessly at one another. I slowed and pulled over at the side of the highway. The cop car's siren cut out and it was suddenly very quiet: just the soft roar of passing cars and the desert wind whipping across the hood.

It *stank* of weed. The cop was going to smell it as soon as he got close.

"Open the windows," Sean said quickly. "Open all the windows!"

I wound mine down—the truck was too old to have electric windows—and he did the same on his side. The wind blew through the car and lifted away some of the smell but, every time the wind died, it came back.

I heard a door slam. In my side mirror, I saw the cop climb out of his car and amble towards us. I looked across at Sean and he was grinding his teeth, hands twitching as if looking for something to hit, something to smash. But for once, violence wasn't going to help us. Fighting the cops was out, as was running—we'd just wind up with every cop in the state on our tails.

All we could do was sit there and accept it. It was over.

The cop strolled up to my window. *God, he's going to get a promotion for this,* I thought, imagining his face when he found the crop. *Cop of the year, probably.*

I tensed as the cop leaned against the door and took off his sunglasses. "You know why I pulled you over, ma'am?" His voice had a deep Texas twang, homely and warm. At any other time, it would have been comforting.

"No," I said gingerly.

"You were drifting out of your lane," he said almost sadly. "Maybe drifting off a l'il bit? White line fever?"

My heart sank. *That?!* All my tension and care and it came down to *that*? I'd been worrying so hard about the cartel, I'd lost concentration for a few vital seconds. At the same time, I felt a tiny spark of hope. If that was all it was, maybe there was a slim possibility we could get out of this. The wind was blowing steadily through the truck, carrying the scent of weed away from the cop. *Please keep blowing. Please keep blowing.* "Um. I *am* kind of tired. Early start this morning. Forgot to have my coffee." I smiled my most ingratiating smile. "I'm really sorry. I'll pull over and take a rest at the next gas station."

The cop tilted his head to one side. "Where are you folks from?"

I could still feel the wind against my cheek. I tried to do the same puppy-dog eyes that Kayley did to me when she was in trouble. "LA, sir,"

"Well, now don't they have coffee in LA?" the cop shook his head. "You get yourself off the road at the next gas station and don't get back on it until you've had a bellyful of joe—you hear me?"

The wind died a little, then came back stronger, tickling my hair against my neck. I willed it to keep going, thinking of hurricanes and tornadoes, gusts strong enough to lift you off your feet. "Yessir. I will. I promise."

The cop sighed, straightened up and turned to walk away. "You drive careful, y'hear?"

The wind died. And then gave one solitary gust—just a tiny little breath—in the wrong direction.

The cop took a single step away. And sniffed.

He could have a cold. He could be wearing so much cheap cologne it drowns out the smell. He could have been doing lines of coke for years and lost his sense of smell.

Just a little bit of luck. Please!

The cop put his hands on the roof and leaned right in through the window. He took a big lungful of air, his chest swelling.

"That there is weed," he said, his voice hardening. "Ma'am, step out of the vehicle."

65

LOUISE

I had to put one hand on the top of the door and the other on my seatback in order to climb down. My legs were shaking so hard I couldn't stand up on my own. I automatically faced the truck and put my palms on the window sill where someone had once served ice cream. *I drifted out of my lane.* It kept going through my head. *I drifted out of my lane one lousy time and now I'm going to jail and Kayley's going to die.* And Sean: his life was over, too. He might not have been happy before, smashing stuff and playing guitar on the rooftop, but at least he'd been free.

A single tear fell from my eyes and landed in the dust beneath me. I didn't want to cry and tried to take a slow, calming breath. But...we were in Texas. Did that mean we'd be put in jail in Texas? There was no one who could post bail for us.

I wasn't going to see Kayley again, before she died.

My shoulders shook and then I was off: choking sobs that burned and ached in my chest. With my head down, the tears couldn't run down my cheeks properly: they hung from my eyelashes and then dropped to the dust, making dark little splodges.

"Aw, for cryin' out loud..." said the cop behind me. "There ain't no need to cry about it." There was a rasping sound, like sandpaper.

When I looked at his shadow on the ground, I saw that he'd taken off his hat and was scratching at the stubble on the back of his neck. "What the hell did you think was gonna happen, driving through my state like this?"

I nodded, gulping. It had been a stupid plan.

He sighed. "Well...it should be a DUI. But...level with me: how stoned are you?"

I blinked through my tears. *Stoned?* He thought I was *stoned?* I swallowed, still sniffing and blinking back tears, and thought fast. "N—Not at all, sir," I croaked. "It was last night, before we set out. We smoked a joint in the back of the truck: that's why it smells in there. I swear, I'm fine. I really was just tired."

"Turn around."

I turned to face him.

He studied my face. "Really?"

"Yessir."

He stared at my tear-red eyes for another few seconds and then said, "Walk that white line for me. One foot in front of the other."

I looked down and put my sneakers on the line. Then I walked along it, willing my legs not to shake. When I dared to look round, he was staring at me. "Just tired, huh?" he said thoughtfully.

"Yes sir! I was stupid. And smoking the joint was stupid. I swear I'll never do it again."

He sighed. "You said you smoked it in the truck. If I go in there and search it, am I gonna find any drugs?"

Six months ago, I hadn't been able to lie at all. Even now, it took every last shred of ability I possessed...but I kept my voice level. "No sir. We left all that stuff in LA. This is a fresh start for us." I stared into his eyes, *begging,* and that part I didn't have to fake.

"Fresh start, huh?"

I nodded. "We're going to sell ice cream at fairs and...and rodeos and things. That's what the truck's for. We're going to do it up, paint it and everything. Vintage. Traditional."

The cop stepped closer. "You seem like a sweet girl," he said. "So this one time, I'm going to let this go. But you promise me you'll behave." He nodded to the truck and lowered his voice. "I've seen your boyfriend, all muscles and attitude. He probably persuaded you to smoke that joint, didn't he? Guys like that ain't nothin' but trouble."

I nodded solemnly. "I'll be careful."

"And stay away from the drugs!"

"That's absolutely my intention, sir."

He gave one last long-suffering sigh. "You drive careful." And then he was ambling back to his car.

I went around to the passenger side and climbed in, motioning Sean to move over. "You drive," I said weakly. "I can't—I can't even...."

I collapsed into the passenger seat as the cop pulled away and drove off into the distance. I let my head tip back against the headrest and just melted into the seat, nothing but a floppy bag of twitching nerves.

"What the fuck happened?" asked Sean as started the truck.

"Karma," I whispered, closing my eyes. "That was every speed limit I've ever stuck to, every empty intersection I've ever waited at. It finally paid off."

66

LOUISE

T he meet was at an old, abandoned airfield way out in the boonies. We got there with only twenty minutes to spare and pulled up alongside the runway, the ice cream truck sitting incongruously next to a couple of rusted aircraft carcasses. Even in September at nearly eight in the evening, the Texas sun was hot, bleaching the tufts of grass that had grown up through the cracks in the concrete and gleaming off the broken panes of glass in what had once been the tiny passenger terminal.

The door to the control tower had long since been broken open, so we climbed up to the top and stood looking out over the airfield. Some local teens must have discovered the place, because there were empty beer cans and graffiti all over the inside. "You think we can pull this off?" I asked, nudging a can with my foot.

Sean wrapped his arms around me from behind. "Just remember," he said. "It's all about attitude."

The sun glinted off a speck in the distance, a speck that slowly grew bigger and bigger in the clear blue sky. Then, with a roar of engines that shook the tower, the private jet was throttling back and sweeping in to land right in front of us. Sean led the way down the stairs.

The first three people out of the plane were men in suits, all carrying machine guns. The fourth was an older guy in slacks and a shirt. He removed his big, gold-rimmed sunglasses as he approached us. "Sean? And Louise?"

They'd demanded our full names on the phone. With the cartel, you didn't fuck around with false ones. We nodded.

"I am Francisco." He sounded cautious, but not unkind. "These men will search you." It wasn't a request.

Two of the men stepped up to us while the third kept his gun pointed right at us. Hands swept up my legs and over my ass, up my sides and across my back. Having a man do it should have felt uncomfortable—awkward, at least. But the men were as clinically professional as doctors, far from Malone's heavies or Murray's leering thugs. It made it even scarier: I suspected they'd be just as clinical if they were ordered to drag our bodies into shallow graves.

The men stepped back and nodded that we were clean. "The weed is in the truck?" asked Francisco. Sean nodded. Francisco spoke in rapid-fire Spanish to two of the men, and they hurried off to the ice cream truck. "We'll try some samples," he told us as an afterthought. Again, not a request.

We spent an agonizing ten minutes standing there while the packets of weed were unloaded, counted and stacked up on the runway. Packets were selected at random to be sliced open and tested. Francisco sniffed the weed, rubbed it between his fingers and finally smoked joints of it, just one slow inhalation of each sample before he crushed the joint underfoot. It was impossible to read his expression. At last, he pulled out his cell phone and made a call. Just one word: *Sí.* Then he crossed his arms and just stared at us as if waiting for something.

"So?" Sean asked at last. "Are we making a deal?"

"Not with me," said Francisco. "With her."

Behind him, a woman emerged from the plane. Her long, coal-black hair blew in the wind, as did the long, gauzy layers of her exquisite white dress. Everything about her was coolly elegant and *off-the-scale* confident. One of those people who've held so much power for so long that they've become accustomed to it, like a president. The men with guns stepped back respectfully as she approached.

I'd seen her in photos, but only grainy black and white ones shot with a long lens. This was Isabella Gallego. The head of the entire Gallego cartel.

It was very difficult to gauge her age. She could have been anywhere between mid-thirties and mid-fifties. Her skin was soft and barely lined, her hair still completely black—natural or dyed, I wasn't sure. She was *incredibly* beautiful.

She looked both of us up and down, speaking to Francisco without turning to him. "So it's good?" she asked in heavily-accented English.

"It's really good," said Francisco. "Smooth. Strong."

"And consistent?" asked Isabella.

"Very."

Isabella drew in a long, slow breath. "Okay," she said. "Two hundred and fifty thousand, as agreed."

I took a deep breath and glanced at Sean. He nodded at me. *You can do this.*

"No," I said.

Isabella slowly took off her sunglasses. Her eyes were a beautiful deep brown, but they were utterly without warmth. "Excuse me?"

"I have a counter-offer," I told her.

"That isn't how this works. We agreed a price."

I looked nervously at Sean. "We said two-fifty on the phone to get you here. But the weed is worth six hundred thousand. You know that. We know that."

Isabella stared at me...and then laughed out loud. "In *Texas,* maybe. But we're not from Texas. We'll sell it to our dealers for seven hundred thousand...maybe eight. If we pay you six, it's barely worth the trouble." She shook her head. "Two-fifty. Take it."

I wanted to take it. I was terrified. But two hundred and fifty thousand wouldn't pay for Kayley's treatment. I shook my head again.

There was a tiny noise, barely audible, from off to my left. The men with guns, readying themselves in case they were told to fire. Isabella was looking at me pityingly, urging me to do the smart thing. I felt myself weakening. *This is not me. This is not my life.* I was a freaking botany geek, for God's sake! I just wanted to run and let someone else deal with this.

And then Sean put his hand on my back. Just a gentle touch, but I could feel the whole strength of him throbbing through me, letting me know he was there, that he was beside me in every possible way, forever. My legs stopped shaking.

"Six hundred thousand," Sean and I said together.

Isabella shook her head. "You are wasting my time," she said. And turned to walk away. I saw her nod towards the men with guns and there were three clean, crisp metallic clicks as the guns were cocked.

It was time for my Hail Mary pass.

"Six hundred thousand for the weed," I said, "...and something better."

Isabella took another few steps towards the plane and, for one horrible moment, I thought she was going to ignore me. But then she lifted her hand. No bullets came, so I assumed she'd put the gunmen on hold. "What?" she asked, irritably.

"Me."

Isabella slowly turned around. "Explain. But do it in the next thirty seconds."

"I increased the THC content of that crop *at least* thirty percent above normal. I did it through a combination of custom fertilizer mixes, lighting cycles and precise watering. It's complex, but replicable. Maybe the crop isn't worth $600,000 to you, but *the value is in the process.*" I offered up a silent prayer of thanks to Stacey. "I can teach your farmers the same method. How much money could you make, if you can grow stronger weed? *Millions. Tens* of millions, over the next decade. And I don't even want a percentage: all I'm asking for is $350,000. A one-time fee. Plus another $250,000 for the crop itself, which you already agree it's worth." I was ready for her to haggle me down to $500,000, which was the amount we actually needed.

Isabella studied us for a long moment. "Risky way to make an offer," she said at last, nodding towards the gunmen.

"If we'd just told you on the phone, would you have taken it?" asked Sean. "We had to promise you cheap weed so you'd come here and sample it, see how good it is."

Isabella stared at him. "I don't appreciate being tricked, Mr. O'Harra." She turned to Francisco. "Do you believe she can do it?"

Francisco tilted his head to one side. "I believe it's worth three-fifty to find out."

Isabella sighed. "I'd need you in Mexico," she told me. "You'd have to visit our farms, teach them individually. It would mean several trips."

I nodded quickly. "Anything. Sure."

Sean stepped forward. "Me too. I don't leave her side."

Isabella sighed again. "Yes, yes, you can bring him."

"And I want a month, before I start," I told her. "One month. Then you can have me for as long as you need me."

Isabella pressed her lips together in a tight line and nodded at Sean. "This one said on the phone that you needed the money to save your sister. That she's sick. Is that true? Or was that another trick?"

I looked right into her eyes. "That's true," I said.

She stared at me for a long time, searching my face for any hint of a lie. I stared right back at her. And at last, after the longest time, I saw the briefest flicker in those ice-cold eyes. "Family," she said, "is very important."

Then she slipped her sunglasses back on and she was back to brutal efficiency. "Transfer the money," she told Francisco. "Load the drugs," she ordered the men. They scurried to do her bidding. A measured nod of farewell to us...and she was gone, her heels clicking across the runway to the plane.

Francisco pulled out his phone and muttered into it in Spanish. After a few minutes, he scrawled something down on a piece of paper and then passed it to me, pointing to each line in turn. "The name of the bank in Switzerland," he said, "your account number and your password. Six hundred thousand dollars is in there now. Call them and they'll transfer it anywhere you want."

Six hundred thousand dollars. It hit me that Isabella hadn't haggled. We had a hundred thousand dollars more than we needed. I took the piece of paper and folded it *very, very* carefully into my jeans pocket.

By now, the men had loaded the drugs into the plane. We watched as Francisco boarded and the steps were pulled up. Moments later, the plane taxied and roared off down the runway, then climbed towards the sun.

I turned to Sean. "Is that...*it?* Did we do it?"

He nodded slowly, then pulled me close. He gazed down into my eyes, dumbstruck.

"What?" I asked, worried.

"Just...you," he said, brushing a lock of hair from my cheek. "You're amazing, you know that?" And he kissed me.

67

SEAN

The truck was empty but it still stank of weed and we decided we'd probably used up our quota of luck and then some. So we played it safe, taking the truck to a scrapyard and then buying a couple of cheap plane tickets to LA. For the first time in a long while, money wasn't an issue.

What was still an issue was Malone. And I needed to deal with that on my terms. Louise had solved one half of our problem with brainpower. Now it was time for what I did best: brute force and intimidation.

Fortunately, Malone was predictable. Every Sunday, he ate lunch at a fancy restaurant downtown. He was driven there and back in a huge, glossy black BMW that I suspected was tricked out with bulletproof glass. But that was fine: I wasn't going to use bullets.

I'd picked out a spot: the exit of the restaurant's parking lot. As the car cruised towards the exit, I could see Malone in the back, taking up most of the rear seat. A guard was with him, a second guard in the passenger seat up front, and then there was the driver. All three guards, and possibly Malone, too, would be armed.

As Malone's driver paused to wait for a gap in the traffic, I stepped out from behind a wall...and, with all my strength, swung the sledge hammer down into the center of the car's hood.

The whole car sank on its suspension a few inches and an airbag went off inside. The hood caved in and the engine died instantly as it took the full force of the blow.

It took the men in the car a few seconds to react. Their first instinct was to open the doors, but the restaurant entrance was narrow: a concrete wall blocked the doors on the driver's side. And just as they started to open the other set of doors, I slammed the hammer into the pillar between front door and rear door, caving it inward enough that the doors couldn't open. Another airbag went off and the men inside shied away from the doors, coughing and choking on the smoke the airbag released.

"Shoot him!" I heard Malone yell. Two of the guards drew their guns.

"Good plan," I snapped. I nodded behind the car. There'd been a line of cars waiting to leave the restaurant behind Malone's car, but now their owners were panicking and screaming and clutching their cell phones to their ears as they called the cops. "The cops arrive and I'm lying here dead...and you're sitting there holding the murder weapon."

The guards hesitated, looking at one another. They were starting to realize that I'd turned their safe, secure car into a prison...potentially, a tomb.

I jumped up onto the hood of the car and swung the sledge hammer again, aiming for the very front of the roof. It bent down and the windshield shattered. Another swing did the same at the back. The men huddled together in the center of the car as the space inside got smaller and smaller. When I jumped down behind the car and looked through the hole where the rear window had been. Malone was twisting around to glare at me...but there was panic in his eyes. He wasn't sure whether I was going to just keep going and flatten the whole car like a pancake, with them inside it.

I leaned close to him. "Here's what's going to happen, if you touch one fucking hair on Louise's head," I growled. "I will come and I will *fuck. Your. Shit. Up.* Every business you've got an interest in. Every house you own. That boat you keep in the harbor. Every one of them: destroyed. And then I'll find *you* and do the same to you. I'll smash you bone by bone, you fucker, and I won't put you out of your misery for a good long while." I indicated the car. "I can get to you. Remember that."

He scowled at me...but he was scared. For years, he and people like him had thought he could control me: I was a dangerous attack dog, but they held the leash. Now I'd slipped my collar and that terrified him.

There's nothing scarier than a man with a big hammer.

I knew it had worked. I could see it in his eyes. We weren't going to have any more problems from him. But he couldn't back down completely. "You're finished in this business," he spat. "No one's going to hire you again, not after *this!*"

"Fine by me," I said mildly. "I quit." I tossed the sledge hammer onto the roof of the car, making him flinch...and I walked away.

68

LOUISE

W e were nearly too late. While we'd been away, Kayley's condition had worsened and Stacey had rushed her to hospital. I ran up the stairs and burst into Dr. Huxler's office just as he was telling Stacey something about *keeping her comfortable right up unto the end.*

"Louise!" He looked up, startled. "Sit down. We should talk. It's...time."

"You're goddamn right it is," I panted. "I got the money. We're going to Switzerland."

When I pulled out my phone to organize everything, though, I started to panic. It hit me that I hadn't considered all the things that could go wrong: what if it took days of paperwork to organize the treatment? What if the clinic in Switzerland didn't have space for weeks? Everything we'd been through might be for nothing.

Fortunately, I'd completely underestimated the yawning chasm between the world of the super rich and the rest of us.

When I dialed the clinic, the phone was answered on the first ring —despite it being the early hours of the morning—by the most efficient woman I'd ever met. The conversation went like this:

Hello. My name is Stephanie. Please let me know if you would prefer me to speak in French or German. How may I help?

Um...hello. I need to arrange treatment for my sister at your clinic. I'm in Los Angeles. I gave her a brief history of Kayley's leukemia.

We will require a fee of five hundred thousand Swiss Francs, payable in advance. She gave me some bank transfer numbers and I scribbled them down. *Would you like me to arrange flights for you?*

Flights? Um...yes. Yes please. You mean today?!

(The rattle of a keyboard) Can you be at LAX by 3 p.m.?

The entire conversation took less than four minutes. I called the magic number Isabella had given me and asked them, in a disbelieving tone, to transfer the money to the clinic. Moments later, Stephanie called back to say she'd received the money and gave us our flight numbers. I sat back in my seat, stunned.

Sean, Kayley, and I barely had time to pack our bags. I was about to call a cab to the airport when my phone rang to tell me that our limo had arrived. I winced, thinking of our rapidly-diminishing funds. Then winced again when we got to the airport and were told that we were flying first class. Of course the clinic's clients would be the sort of people who would *always* fly first class. But when I saw Kayley's face as she sank into her huge leather armchair and cued up a whole list of movies to watch, it was difficult to stress about it too much.

When we landed, there was another limo to whisk us from the airport to the clinic. The place was nothing like the huge, bustling hospital in America. It was neat, compact, and, like Stephanie, very, very efficient. Kayley was examined and tested within an hour of our plane landing. Two hours, and she'd started her first round of treatment.

While we waited, I checked my email and started going through the information Stephanie had sent me. Since Dr. Huxler had last heard about the clinic and its $500,000 treatment, the exchange rate had plummeted. 500,000 Swiss Francs wasn't half a million, anymore: we'd saved almost fifty thousand dollars. Plus we'd sold the weed for

$100,000 more than I'd originally intended. We had about $150,000 left in the account.

Stephanie wanted to check us into the same super-luxury hotel all of their visitors used, but this time I managed to reign her in. "We have very simple tastes," I told her. She rattled away at her keyboard for a few seconds and checked us into a modest but comfortable place instead, frowning in confusion as she did it.

By the time they said we could see Kayley, she was sleeping. I sat down by her bedside, reached out, and touched her cheek. It was the first time I'd been able to stop and think for days and it all hit me at once: this was it, everything we'd been building towards. Either this would work, or....

Sean sat down beside me, wrapped his arms around my waist, and lifted me onto his knee, the warmth of his chest pressed against my back. We didn't speak. We just sat there in the dimly-lit room, watching Kayley sleep, and hoped.

69

LOUISE

Her eyes. That's where I saw it first. On the eighth day of treatment, the gleam came back to them, the one that had disappeared even before I'd taken her for those fateful first tests. It was like she was becoming *her* again.

She was still pitifully weak, of course. She'd have to regain all the weight she'd lost in the last few months and her body would take a long time to get back to full strength. But that gleam in her eyes was the tipping point. I told Sean and he pulled me close, wrapping me up in his arms.

On the tenth day, the doctors started to agree. The test results were good enough to be cautiously optimistic, they said. What reassured me wasn't the numbers but the sight of her chowing down on a breakfast of croissants and hot chocolate.

On the twelfth day, she started to quiz Sean on his history, his tattoos, and his intentions. Sean flushed and looked at me, lost for words. That's when I knew she was back.

On the fourteenth day, the doctors said the words we'd been waiting to hear: *reversal of disease* and remission. I pulled Kayley into an enormous hug and, for once, she let me hang onto her good and long. But then she pushed me gently back.

"What?" I asked. "What's wrong?"

Then I saw she was waving Sean forward. He glanced at me to check whether it was okay, and I nodded. Then all three of us were hugging, that huge strong body of his like a warm rock face that both of us could hang from.

EPILOGUE

One Month Later
Sean

"O'Harra! *Irish!*"

I'd been so focused on knocking down the wall, that I hadn't heard my boss's call. "Hmm?"

"End of the day. Get out of here."

Already? I looked around. Yep, the construction site was clearing out and the boss and I were the last ones there. I got like that, sometimes, when I was wrapped up in my work. Nothing else existed. Now, though, I was starting to become aware of the pleasant ache in my shoulders from swinging the hammer.

Maybe Louise could rub oil into them, tonight. She was really good at that. And then afterwards, while we had the oil handy....

"What are you grinning at?" muttered my boss. "Go on, go home already!" But he was smiling. I'd survived my first week and people seemed happy with me—every site needed a big guy who could haul stuff around or move a heavy beam into place. But what I was really good at was smashing stuff. They just had to point me at a wall and, a few minutes later: no more wall.

There were plenty of people on the site to learn from, too, and I was learning as fast as I could. A little roofing here, a bit of plumbing there. It would take years to get good, but I was enjoying it.

I rode the metro home. Working a regular job was taking some getting used to. Getting up every morning, commuting.... Even seeing numbers on a payslip instead of cash pressed into my hand was weird.

But the upside was huge.

As I walked up the hill towards the mansion, I could see bright, warm light shining out from every window. The cardboard was gone, now, replaced by glass, and the holes in the roof were fixed. The tree was still there, though cut down to size a little. Louise wouldn't hear of moving it, so we had the only house in the world with a tree growing through it.

Yeah, we bought the mansion. Mrs. Baker didn't want much for it, we had cash in the bank and living there—even with only half the rooms habitable—made more sense than paying two sets of rent. I was using what I learned on the construction site to do it up. It might take a year or more but, when I'd finished, we'd have a place we could sell for much more than we paid for it. Or maybe we'd just carry on living there. That sounded pretty good, too.

Moving in with Louise and Kayley had been another huge life change. But when Louise and I were lying there at night in the four poster bed, the moonlight making her copper hair gleam on the pillow, and Kayley was asleep in the next room, it felt like...home. The sort of home I hadn't known in a very long time. And that was worth changing for.

Louise

I'd gone back to college to complete my final year. I even managed to score a job with the campus groundsman, helping him look after the gardens. Between that and Sean's construction job, we were doing okay.

I'd already taken two trips to Mexico, touring farms and explaining my system with the help of diagrams, charts and a very patient interpreter. It seemed to be working: I'd seen Isabella on one occasion and she'd seemed happy (or as happy as that coolly unreadable face ever got). She'd even mentioned something about a permanent job...but I'd told her no. Doing what I'd done to save Kayley...I could live with that. Doing it for profit would be different. I was going to get my degree and then go back to my original plan of getting ajob with a research company. I was back to being the good girl.

That didn't mean I hadn't changed, though. You can't go through something like that and not be changed a little. I still waited at red lights, but now I only apologized when something was actually my fault. I waited patiently in line, but I'd tell you where to get off if you tried to cut in front of me. I had *attitude,* now. Just a little bit.

Living in the mansion was crazy, ridiculous, and idyllic. One of those decisions I'd have been far too sensible to make on my own, but could stretch to with Sean by my side. The best part was the garden, something we'd barely explored while we'd been growing there. There was enough space to grow anything I wanted, and I'd already started with some fruit trees and flowers. We'd even paid a visit to the old grow house, in the dead of night, dug up the rose Sean had planted and moved it here. Like its owner, it seemed to be settling in fine. And Kayley *loved* the mansion, especially her huge bedroom...although she now wanted a four poster bed of her own. Sean had promised to make her one.

I heard the door bang downstairs as Sean arrived home and ran down the stairs two at a time to meet him. I launched myself into the air when I was still four steps from the bottom, hurling myself into his arms and trusting him to catch me. Which he did—magnificently. I wound my arms and legs around him as he tilted my head back and kissed me, deep and sensual and unhurried at first...then with slowly gathering pace. I ground my groin a little harder against his abs. He could never control himself, once we started kissing, and neither could I.

I didn't want to break the kiss but I had a surprise planned. Coming up for air, I panted, "Can you go back out again? Just quickly? We need milk." The refrigerator was actually full, but I needed the excuse.

He gave just a hint of a tired sigh, but then his expression softened. "Kiss me again," he ordered, "and then I will." I gladly complied, running my hands up and down his back and then over his ass for good measure.

When he eventually put me down, he asked, "Can I take your car?"

"Sure," I told him, trying not to grin. "It's in the garage."

He strolled outside to get it and I followed behind him, wanting to see but trying not to look suspicious. I managed to contain myself until he hauled open the garage door.

Inside, parked in front of my car, was his Mustang.

"Took a while to track it down," I said, slipping my arm around his waist. "It had been bought and sold a few times since Murray had it. But I got there in the end. We had *just* enough money."

Sean ran his hand over the gleaming paintwork. "Thank you," he said at last. His voice sounded just a little bit choked up.

"Want to take me for a drive?" I asked.

We climbed in and I passed him the key. He started up the engine and gave a little satisfied sigh as it roared into life. Then he put his hand on the gearstick and, just like that first time he'd taken me out in it, his palm was suddenly very close to my knee. He glanced up and we locked eyes.

"Let's drive somewhere deserted," he growled.

I swallowed and nodded, that familiar heat blossoming inside me. He might have gone straight, but he hadn't lost any of that bad boy dark charm.

"You realize," I said as we drove out of the garage, "that in a couple of years, Kayley's going to want to borrow this thing?"

"Over my dead body."

That evening, we were out in the garden. It was just warm enough to be comfortable, though I'd put on a long skirt so my legs didn't get cold. We were right in the middle of the rear lawn: I'd mowed it short at the front, but at the back I'd left the grass long and sowed some wildflowers. With bees buzzing around, it was practically a meadow.

Kayley was doggedly chasing a butterfly, trying to get it to land on her finger. Her hair had slowly started to grow back and we were already debating what sort of cut to go for, once it got long enough to style.

Sean suddenly grabbed me around the waist and picked me up, making me yelp in surprise, bare feet kicking in the air. Then he tumbled us backwards to the ground, hauling me onto his lap so that I was sitting astride him. I blinked into the setting sun and felt him run his hand through my hair, making it catch the light. "God, you're beautiful," he muttered.

I leaned forward until I was lying full length on top of him, my head on his chest. "I didn't think this was possible," I murmured. "Being this happy. I mean, even before it all started, back before I met you. When it was just Kayley and me...I didn't think we'd ever be a family again."

Sean gave a low *mmm* that vibrated against my cheek. I raised my head and looked down at him because I knew that *mmm*. "What? What's on your mind?"

He gazed at me for a long time, running his fingers through my hair. "Family," he said at last.

"You thinking it's time to track down your brothers?" I asked cautiously.

He shrugged those massive shoulders. "I dunno. It's been a long time. The whole thing's a mess...but...."

I waited.

"...but yeah. Maybe it's time."

I nodded and pressed my cheek to his chest again. "Then go do it. Take a weekend, take a week. We'll be here when you get back."

"*Hmm,*" he said, the vibration buzzing through me. "I'll think about it." Then a big hand landed on my ass. "Right now, though, I want—" he muttered pure filth into my ear until I flushed and squirmed. And then he kissed me.

Kayley glanced over and rolled her eyes. "I'm going inside to watch a movie," she said. But she was smiling.

As she disappeared into the house, Sean rolled us over so that he was on top. I giggled, loving the feeling of the soft grass under my head, and looked up at him, grinning.

Then I saw the look in his eyes. "*Here?*" I asked incredulously. Sure, we were partially hidden by the long grass, but...what if someone saw? *We should be sensible. We should go inside.*

Sean gazed down at me and those cobalt-blue eyes blaze, half-closed in lust. I felt the dark heat start to build inside.. and, suddenly, I was closing my eyes and parting my lips for his kiss. I moaned as his lips met mine.

I was back to being a good girl. But I could still be bad when I wanted to.

The End

Thank you for reading!

Five of my books feature the O'Harra brothers. The order you read the first four in isn't too important because they're all standalones, but you should read *Brothers* last.

The story of Aedan, the bad boy Irish boxer, is told in *Punching and Kissing*.

Sean's story you've just read.

The story of Kian, the bodyguard who winds up protecting – and falling for – the President's daughter, is told in *Saving Liberty*.

The story of Carrick, a biker who makes a vow to a woman who saves his life by the side of the road, then returns a decade later to keep his word, is told in *Outlaw's Promise*.

Finally, *Brothers* brings all four O'Harra brothers – and their women – together to search for their missing brother.

Printed in Great Britain
by Amazon

37073975R00199